CONAN
THE PEOPLE OF THE
BLACK CIRCLE

"Yasmina screamed her loathing and horror."

CONAN
THE
PEOPLE
OF THE
BLACK CIRCLE

ROBERT E. HOWARD
edited by Karl Edward Wagner

The Authorized Edition

Published by
Berkley Publishing Corporation
•
Distributed by
G.P. Putnam's Sons, New York

SBN: 399-12147-1

Library of Congress Catalogue Number: 78-20392

PRINTED IN THE UNITED STATES OF AMERICA

"Strike, I command you! Strike!"

Contents

"He heard Yasmina scream."

Foreword

THE GENRE OF epic fantasy is as old as the human race. In an age before there was paper or pen or written language, skin-clad savages grouped about their fires, told and sang of the heroes and villains of the race's dawn; scratched and painted scenes of hunters and prey, gods and devils, on the walls of cave and cliff. The tradition persisted when man learned to reproduce his language with cuts and impressions on clay tablets: the Epic of Gilgamesh has been traced to sources at least as early as 2000 B.C. Such antiquity makes the *Iliad* and the *Odyssey* of Homer seem comparatively recent, and the *Aeneid* of Vergil no more than yesterday's best-seller. Indeed, the history of every race and culture has its legends and mythologies, preserved as formal literature or no more than oral tradition. The settings will vary, the names and pantheons are different, but the grandeur of the epic remains the same. These are tales of men and gods, of warriors and monsters, of savage battles and duels, of kingdoms and unexplored lands, of heroism and villainy, of love and hate, of triumph and tragedy, that transcend the age of their creation.

It is a tradition that survived the fall of the classical world, transmuted by new cultures and through new ages, in legends of Arthur or Beowulf or Roland, in

1

epics as the Nibelungenlied or the Eddas. With the Renaissance came the transition to the printed page: Sir Thomas Malory's *Le Morte D'Arthur*, first printed by William Caxton in 1485; Ariosto's *Orlando Furioso*, published in 1516. A century later Cervantes would parody the popular chivalric romances in *Don Quixote*. Picaresque novels with their dashing rogues gave way to the brooding hero-villains of the gothic novels in the late eighteenth century.

The epic tradition continued into the nineteenth century through the pens of authors such as Sir Walter Scott, H. Rider Haggard, Edwin Lester Arnold, George Griffith, S. R. Crockett, and William Morris. Moving into the present century, the popular lost race novels offered readers an escape from the modern world, while new works of epic fantasy appeared from such noted writers as Lord Dunsany, A. Merritt, E. R. Eddison, James Branch Cabell, Arthur D. Howden Smith, and John Myers Myers. Many of these novels would first appear in the pages of popular magazines, as serials in such pulps as *Blue Book, Argosy, All-Story, Cavalier,* or *Adventure*. And in 1923 a new pulp appeared on the stands, presenting a new string of authors, and specializing in fantasy fiction. The pulp was *Weird Tales*, and one of its new authors was Robert E. Howard.

Born in Peaster, Texas in January, 1906, Robert Ervin Howard lived most of his life in small Texas towns, growing up in Cross Plains where he spent his adult years. Loner and introvert, Howard was largely self-educated, reading omnivorously as a boy from the meager libraries of rural Texas. In a letter he tells of breaking into schoolhouses during the long summer recess to gain access to whatever books their tiny bookcases might hold: "In my passionate quest for reading material, nothing could have halted me but a bullet through the head."

While he hated school, Howard did graduate from Brownwood High School in spring of 1923. Aside from some business courses that he took on occasion from the academy at Howard Payne College in Brownwood, he had no further formal education. He could not afford college, nor was he certain he wanted to attend after his deep hatred of school: "But what I hated was the confinement—the clock-like regularity of everything; the regulation of my speech and actions; most of all the idea that someone considered himself or herself in authority over me, with the right to question my actions and interfere with my thoughts."

Early in his life Howard decided he wanted to be a writer; he was nine when he wrote his first story and fifteen when he set out to write professionally: "I took up writing simply because it seemed to promise an easier mode of work, more money, and more freedom than any job I'd tried. I wouldn't write otherwise."

While the freedom may have been there, the easier work and more money were not. Howard's first professional sale—"Spear and Fang" to *Weird Tales*, written when he was eighteen—was not until 1925 and brought him $16.00. It was, after all, a beginning, but there was a long hard road ahead. Sales were few and efforts to break into markets other than *Weird Tales* were unsuccessful. Total sales from 1925 through 1928 amounted to a whopping $297.50—all but $20.00 of that coming from *Weird Tales*. That's a little under $75 a year—tough going even in pre-Depression rural Texas—and Howard supplemented his income through a variety of jobs, none of which was long to last.

In 1929 his career turned the corner; Howard finally

managed to crash some other pulp markets, while his work had become a regular feature in *Weird Tales*. Sales from 1929 totalled $772.50. Still no fortune, but Howard's star was definitely on the rise. He had solved the riddle of "splashing the field" (selling to multiple-category fiction markets), the *sine qua non* of a professional writer, and he had introduced the first of the series characters who would bring him acclaim in his lifetime and far greater fame after his death. 1928 saw the debut of Solomon Kane, 1929 the first appearance of King Kull, 1930 that of Bran Mak Morn, 1931 that of Turlogh Dubh O'Brien, and 1932 marked the first publication of Conan.

Conan, a barbarian adventurer from savage Cimmeria in the mythical Hyborian Age, quickly became Howard's most popular character—among those in *Weird Tales* and including his characters who appeared in the nonfantasy pulps, during Howard's lifetime and after his death. Indeed, with the exception of Seabury Quinn's occult detective, Jules de Grandin, Conan was the most popular character ever to appear in *Weird Tales'* thirty-two-year existence. It was a popularity that survived Howard's death and the disappearance of the pulps. Arkham House's monumental Howard anthology, *Skull-Face and Others*, put five of the Conan stories into hardcover in 1946 (with the editor, August Derleth, commenting acidly that a collection of the entire Conan tales "would almost have to be printed on blood-colored paper"). In the early 1950's Gnome Press did bring out a collection of the Conan stories in several hardcover volumes, but lacking one Conan tale and presenting edited versions of three others. Then in the 1960's Lancer Books published the Conan tales in a series of paperbacks (subsequently reprinted by Sphere Books in Britain), in which the Conan stories were presented with editorial emendations and mixed with numerous pastiches by other writers. The 1970's saw the transition of Conan to comic book form by the Marvel Comics Group, introducing their version of Conan to a new generation of fans. Ironically, even as the comics brought unprecedented popularity to Conan, contractual difficulties resulted in the disappearance of Howard's barbarian hero from the paperback stands.

This, then, marks the return of Conan in a low-priced paperback edition. However, there is more in store here for the reader than that. This edition marks the first time that the Conan stories have been reprinted in a popular edition without editorial emendations.

Prior reprintings of these stories were slightly revised and edited, mainly in the area of usage of commas, spelling variants, and apparent inconsistencies. In an effort to fill in portions of Conan's saga not chronicled by Howard, there have been numerous posthumous collaborations in the form of completed fragments, revisions of non-Conan stories, and straight pastiches. It is this editor's feeling that the Conan stories should be presented exactly as Howard wrote them, and that examples of pastiche writing have no place in a collection of the original author's own stories. Pastiche-Conan is not the same Conan as portrayed by Robert E. Howard—and I say this as one who has written Howard pastiches.

In order to present Conan as first published, I have prepared the manuscript for this edition from photocopies of the stories from the actual pages of *Weird Tales*. Unless specifically noted, there has been no alteration of the original text from the *Weird Tales* appearance, except to correct obvious typographical errors (e.g., *liks* for *like*), and to standardize the dropping of lines to indicate transition as opposed to the frequent column breaks used for the double-column pages of the pulps.

This edition contains no emendations, no completed fragments, no revisions, no collaborations, no pastiches. This is Conan exactly as Robert E. Howard presented Conan; Conan as you would have discovered Conan in the issue of *Weird Tales* you had just purchased. For the reader familiar only with the Marvel-Comics Conan or the pastiche-Conan, there may well be a jolt.

Robert E. Howard wrote only twenty-one tales of Conan. Of these, seventeen appeared in *Weird Tales* between December 1932 and October 1936. Four others were discovered as completed manuscripts among Howard's papers, and were not published until long after his suicide in 1936. While these were finished stories, *Weird Tales* was Howard's only market for the Conan series, and rejection by editor Farnsworth Wright meant back to the salvage heap. While there is a loose chronology to the series in terms of Conan's career, the stories appeared in *Weird Tales* in no particular order. The first Conan tale to appear, "The Phoenix on the Sword" (*Weird Tales*, December 1932) is one of the last tales in terms of Conan's lifetime.

In a few words, after a childhood and early youth fighting in wars in the barbaric kingdoms of the North, Conan left Cimmeria in his late teens to wander about the civilized kingdoms of the world. He wandered throughout the world of the Hyborian Age, as thief, pirate, mercenary, leader of men, adventurer. He was about forty when he seized the throne of Aquilonia, and in his midforties when he makes his final appearance in "The Hour of the Dragon."

Although there is no strict chronology to the series, the tales can be assigned a certain sort of order based on the stages of Conan's career and allusions to earlier episodes. Early in 1936 two Conan fans, P. Schuyler Miller and

6

John D. Clark, drew up an outline of Conan's career, based on the published tales, and submitted it to Howard for his approval. Howard replied in a letter, dated March 10, 1936, that their outline "pretty closely" followed his own visualization, but that: "In writing these yarns I've always felt less as creating them than as if I were simply chronicling his adventures as he told them to me. That's why they skip about so much, without following a regular order. The average adventurer, telling tales of a wild life at random, seldom follows any ordered plan, but narrates episodes widely separated by space and years, as they occur to him."

This is of no great consequence, for the stories are entirely self-standing. Only rarely does a character other than Conan appear in more than one story. Conan's predicament at the opening of a given story seldom has any relation to his situation at the conclusion of any other; and, while Conan often rides away with the gold and/or the girl at the end of one adventure, as a rule each new adventure finds Conan without either.

Due to present contractual problems, we are not able to publish all twenty-one of Howard's Conan tales at this time. Because of this, instead of presenting the stories in the chronology of Conan's career, this edition will instead offer the stories in the order in which they were published in *Weird Tales*. It is hoped that the former order of presentation can be achieved once contractual matters are settled.

But now...It is summer of 1934. You have just spent two-bits for the August issue of *Weird Tales*. Margaret Brundage has done the cover again—a rather unlikely Conan wrapped up in a huge green serpent, a semi-draped blonde watching the struggle. You open to the first story: "The Devil in Iron..."

7

CONAN
THE PEOPLE OF THE
BLACK CIRCLE

ASGARD

CIMMERIA

NEMEDI

BELVERUS

numalia

PICTISH WILDERNESS

MARCH CRIAN

Cimberian

TAUBAN

black river

POSTHURA RIVER

SHALE R.

aquilonia

TARANTIA

SHAMAR

THORRIAS R.

poltain

ALIMANE

TYBOR R.

ophir

OCEAN

ZING ARA

ARGOS

lands of

MESSANTIA

asgalun

RIVER STY

Baracha Isles

khemi

luxur

✦ Isle of the
Black Ones

sukhmet

WESTERN

xuthal

xuchotl

kush

legend

land:
highlands
lowlands
sea:
coastal shelf
depths
scale of miles

0   100   200   400   600

the hyborian world

steppes

BRYTHUNIA

ZAMORA

inthia

arenjun

shadizar

zhurah

koth

khorala

turan

akif

VILAYET SEA

Isle of
Iron Statues

em

DESERT

khawarism

zamboula

Aghrapur

Kapur

Mayer

ZAPOROSKA R.

stygia

keshan

alkmeenon

keshia

punt

zembabwei

IRANISTAN

arfar

black kingdoms

to khitai

to vendhya

The Devil in Iron

THE FISHERMAN LOOSENED his knife in its scabbard. The gesture was instinctive, for what he feared was nothing a knife could slay, not even the saw-edged crescent blade of the Yuetshi that could disembowel a man with an upward stroke. Neither man nor beast threatened him in the solitude which brooded over the castellated isle of Xapur.

He had climbed the cliffs, passed through the jungle that bordered them, and now stood surrounded by evidences of a vanished state. Broken columns glimmered among the trees, the straggling lines of crumbling walls meandered off into the shadows, and under his feet were broad paves, cracked and bowed by roots growing beneath.

The fisherman was typical of his race, that strange people whose origin is lost in the gray dawn of the past, and who have dwelt in their rude fishing-huts along the southern shore of the Sea of Vilayet since time immemorial. He was broadly built, with long apish arms and a mighty chest, but with lean loins and thin bandy legs. His face was broad, his forehead low and retreating, his hair thick and tangled. A belt for a knife and a rag for a loin-cloth were all he wore in the way of clothing.

That he was where he was proved that he was less dully incurious than most of his people. Men seldom visited Xapur. It was uninhabited, all but forgotten, merely one among the myriad isles which dotted the great inland sea. Men called it Xapur, the Fortified, because of its ruins, remnants of some prehistoric

13

kingdom, lost and forgotten before the conquering Hyborians had ridden southward. None knew who reared those stones, though dim legends lingered among the Yuetshi which half intelligibly suggested a connection of immeasurable antiquity between the fishers and the unknown island kingdom.

But it had been a thousand years since any Yuetshi had understood the import of these tales; they repeated them now as a meaningless formula, a gibberish framed to their lips by custom. No Yuetshi had come to Xapur for a century. The adjacent coast of the mainland was uninhabited, a reedy marsh given over to the grim beasts that haunted it. The fisher's village lay some distance to the south, on the mainland. A storm had blown his frail fishing-craft far from his accustomed haunts, and wrecked it in a night of flaring lightning and roaring waters on the towering cliffs of the isle. Now in the dawn the sky shone blue and clear, the rising sun made jewels of the dripping leaves. He had climbed the cliffs to which he had clung through the night because, in the midst of the storm, he had seen an appalling lance of lightning fork out of the black heavens, and the concussion of its stroke, which had shaken the whole island, had been accompanied by a cataclysmic crash that he doubted could have resulted from a riven tree.

A dull curiosity had caused him to investigate; and now he had found what he sought and an animal-like uneasiness possessed him, a sense of lurking peril.

Among the trees reared a broken dome-like structure, built of gigantic blocks of the peculiar iron-like green stone found only on the islands of Vilayet. It seemed incredible that human hands could have shaped and placed them, and certainly it was beyond human power to have overthrown the structure they formed. But the thunderbolt had splintered the ton-heavy blocks like so much glass, reduced others to green dust, and ripped away the whole arch of the dome.

The fisherman climbed over the debris and peered in, and what he saw brought a grunt from him. Within the ruined dome, surrounded by stone-dust and bits of broken masonry, lay a man on a golden block. He was clad in a sort of skirt and a shagreen girdle. His black hair, which fell in a square mane to his massive shoulders, was confined about his temples by a narrow gold band. On his bare, muscular breast lay a curious dagger with a jeweled pommel, shagreen-bound hilt, and a broad crescent blade. It was much like the knife the fisherman wore at his hip, but it lacked the serrated edge, and was made with infinitely greater skill.

The fisherman lusted for the weapon. The man, of course, was dead; had been dead for many centuries. This dome was his tomb. The fisherman did not wonder by what art the ancients had preserved the body in such a vivid likeness of life, which kept the muscular limbs full and unshrunken, the dark flesh vital. The dull brain of the Yuetshi had room only for his desire for the knife with its delicate waving lines along the dully gleaming blade.

Scrambling down into the dome, he lifted the weapon from the man's breast. And as he did so, a strange and terrible thing came to pass. The muscular dark hands knotted convulsively, the lids flared open, revealing great dark magnetic eyes whose stare struck the startled fisherman like a physical blow. He recoiled, dropping the jeweled dagger in his perturbation. The man on the dais heaved up to a sitting position, and the fisherman gaped at the full extent of his size, thus revealed. His narrowed eyes held the Yuetshi and in those slitted orbs he read neither friendliness nor gratitude; he saw only a fire as alien and hostile as that which burns in the eyes of a tiger.

Suddenly the man rose and towered above him, menace in his every aspect. There was no room in the fisherman's dull brain for fear, at least for such fear as might grip a man who has just seen the fundamental laws of nature defied. As the great hands fell to his shoulders, he drew his saw-edged knife and struck upward with the same motion. The blade splintered against the stranger's corded belly as against a steel column, and then the fisherman's thick neck broke like a rotten twig in the giant hands.

2

JEHUNGIR AGHA, lord of Khawarizm and keeper of the
coastal border, scanned once more the ornate
parchment scroll with its peacock seal, and laughed
shortly and sardonically.

"Well?" bluntly demanded his counsellor Ghaznavi.

Jehungir shrugged his shoulders. He was a handsome man, with the merciless pride of birth and
accomplishment.

"The king grows short of patience," said he. "In his
own hand he complains bitterly of what he calls my
failure to guard the frontier. By Tarim, if I can not deal
a blow to these robbers of the steppes, Khawarizm may
own a new lord."

Ghaznavi tugged his gray-shot beard in meditation.
Yezdigerd, king of Turan, was the mightiest monarch
in the world. In his palace in the great port city of
Aghrapur was heaped the plunder of empires. His
fleets of purple-sailed war galleys had made Vilayet an
Hyrkanian lake. The dark-skinned people of Zamora
paid him tribute, as did the eastern provinces of Koth.
The Shemites bowed to his rule as far west as Shushan.
His armies ravaged the borders of Stygia in the south
and the snowy lands of the Hyperboreans in the north.
His riders bore torch and sword westward into
Brythunia and Ophir and Corinthia, even to the
borders of Nemedia. His gilt-helmeted swordsmen had
trampled hosts under their horses' hoofs, and walled
cities went up in flames at his command. In the glutted
slave markets of Aghrapur, Sultanapur, Khawarizm,
Shahpur, and Khorusun, women were sold for three
small silver coins—blond Brythunians, tawny Sty-
gians, dark-haired Zamorians, ebon Kushites, olive-

17

skinned Shemites.

Yet, while his swift horsemen overthrew armies far from his frontiers, at his very borders an audacious foe plucked his beard with a red-dripping and smoke-stained hand.

On the broad steppes between the Sea of Vilayet and the borders of the easternmost Hyborian kingdoms, a new race had sprung up in the past half-century, formed originally of fleeing criminals, broken men, escaped slaves, and deserting soldiers. They were men of many crimes and countries, some born on the steppes, some fleeing from the kingdoms in the west. They were called *kozak*, which means wastrel.

Dwelling on the wild, open steppes, owning no law but their own peculiar code, they had become a people capable even of defying the Grand Monarch. Ceaselessly they raided the Turanian frontier, retiring in the steppes when defeated; with the pirates of Vilayet, men of much the same breed, they harried the coast, preying off the merchant ships which plied between the Hyrkanian ports.

"How am I to crush these wolves?" demanded Jehungir. "If I follow them into the steppes, I run the risk either of being cut off and destroyed, or having them elude me entirely and burn the city in my absence. Of late they have been more daring than ever."

"That is because of the new chief who has risen among them," answered Ghaznavi. "You know whom I mean."

"Aye!" replied Jehungir feelingly. "It is that devil Conan; he is even wilder than the *kozaks*, yet he is crafty as a mountain lion."

"It is more through wild animal instinct than through intelligence," answered Ghaznavi. "The other *kozaks* are at least descendants of civilized men. He is a

18

barbarian. But to dispose of him would be to deal them a crippling blow."

"But how?" demanded Jehungir. "He has repeatedly cut his way out of spots that seemed certain death for him. And, instinct or cunning, he has avoided or escaped every trap set for him."

"For every beast and for every man there is a trap he will not escape," quoth Ghaznavi. "When we have parleyed with the *kozaks* for the ransom of captives, I have observed this man Conan. He has a keen relish for women and strong drink. Have your captive Octavia fetched here."

Jehungir clapped his hands, and an impassive Kushite eunuch, an image of shining ebony in silken pantaloons, bowed before him and went to do his bidding. Presently he returned, leading by the wrist a tall handsome girl, whose yellow hair, clear eyes and fair skin identified her as a pure-blooded member of her race. Her scanty silk tunic, girded at the waist, displayed the marvelous contours of her magnificent figure. Her fine eyes flashed with resentment and her red lips were sulky, but submission had been taught her during her captivity. She stood with hanging head before her master until he motioned her to a seat on the divan beside him. Then he looked inquiringly at Ghaznavi.

"We must lure Conan away from the *kozaks*," said the counsellor abruptly. "Their war camp is at present pitched somewhere on the lower reaches of the Zaporoska River—which, as you well know, is a wilderness of reeds, a swampy jungle in which our last expedition was cut to pieces by those masterless devils."

"I am not likely to forget that," said Jehungir wryly.

"There is an uninhabited island near the mainland,"

said Ghaznavi, "known as Xapur, the Fortified, because of some ancient ruins upon it. There is a peculiarity about it which makes it perfect for our purpose. It has no shore-line, but rises sheer out of the sea in cliffs a hundred and fifty feet tall. Not even an ape could negotiate them. The only place where a man can go up or down is a narrow path on the western side that has the appearance of a worn stair, carved into the solid rock of the cliffs.

"If we could trap Conan on that island, alone, we could hunt him down at our leisure, with bows, as men hunt a lion."

"As well wish for the moon," said Jehungir impatiently. "Shall we send him a messenger, bidding him climb the cliffs and await our coming?"

"In effect, yes!" Seeing Jehungir's look of amazement, Ghaznavi continued: "We will ask for a parley with the *kozaks* in regard to prisoners, at the edge of the steppes by Fort Ghori. As usual, we will go with a force and encamp outside the castle. They will come, with an equal force, and the parley will go forward with the usual distrust and suspicion. But this time we will take with us, as if by casual chance, your beautiful captive." Octavia changed color and listened with intensified interest as the counsellor nodded toward her. "She will use all her wiles to attract Conan's attention. That should not be difficult. To that wild reaver she should appear a dazzling vision of loveliness. Her vitality and substantial figure should appeal to him more vividly than would one of the doll-like beauties of your seraglio."

Octavia sprang up, her white fists clenched, her eyes blazing and her figure quivering with outraged anger.

"You would force me to play the trollop with this barbarian?" she exclaimed. "I will not! I am no market-

20

block slut to smirk and ogle at a steppes-robber. I am the daughter of a Nemedian lord—"

"You were of the Nemedian nobility before my riders carried you off," returned Jehungir cynically. "Now you are merely a slave who will do as she is bid."

"I will not!" she raged.

"On the contrary," rejoined Jehungir with studied cruelty, "you will. I like Ghaznavi's plan. Continue, prince among counsellors."

"Conan will probably wish to buy her. You will refuse to sell her, of course, or to exchange her for Hyrkanian prisoners. He may then try to steal her, or take her by force—though I do not think even he would break the parley-truce. Anyway, we must be prepared for whatever he might attempt.

"Then, shortly after the parley, before he has time to forget all about her, we will send a messenger to him, under a flag of truce, accusing him of stealing the girl, and demanding her return. He may kill the messenger, but at least he will think that she has escaped.

"Then we will send a spy—a Yuetshi fisherman will do—to the *kozak* camp, who will tell Conan that Octavia is hiding on Xapur. If I know my man, he will go straight to that place."

"But we do not know that he will go alone," Jehungir argued.

"Does a man take a band of warriors with him, when going to a rendezvous with a woman he desires?" retorted Ghaznavi. "The chances are all that he *will* go alone. But we will take care of the other alternative. We will not await him on the island, where we might be trapped ourselves, but among the reeds of a marshy point which juts out to within a thousand yards of Xapur. If he brings a large force, we'll beat a retreat and think up another plot. If he comes alone or with a small

21

party, we will have him. Depend upon it, he will come, remembering your charming slave's smiles and meaning glances."

"I will never descend to such shame!" Octavia was wild with fury and humiliation. "I will die first!"

"You will not die, my rebellious beauty," said Jehungir, "but you will be subjected to a very painful and humiliating experience."

He clapped his hands, and Octavia paled. This time it was not the Kushite who entered, but a Shemite, a heavily muscled man of medium height with a short, curled, blue-black beard.

"Here is work for you, Gilzan," said Jehungir. "Take this fool, and play with her awhile. Yet be careful not to spoil her beauty."

With an inarticulate grunt the Shemite seized Octavia's wrist, and at the grasp of his iron fingers, all the defiance went out of her. With a piteous cry she tore away and threw herself on her knees before her implacable master, sobbing incoherently for mercy.

Jehungir dismissed the disappointed torturer with a gesture, and said to Ghaznavi: "If your plan succeeds, I will fill your lap with gold."

3

IN THE DARKNESS before dawn an unaccustomed sound disturbed the solitude that slumbered over the reedy marshes and the misty waters of the coast. It was not a drowsy water-fowl nor a waking beast. It was a human who struggled through the thick reeds, which were taller than a man's head.

It was a woman, had there been anyone to see, tall, and yellow-haired, her splendid limbs molded by her draggled tunic. Octavia had escaped in good earnest, every outraged fiber of her still tingling from her experience in a captivity that had become unendurable.

Jehungir's mastery of her had been bad enough; but with deliberate fiendishness Jehungir had given her to a nobleman whose name was a byword for degeneracy even in Khawarizm.

Octavia's resilient flesh crawled and quivered at her memories. Desperation had nerved her climb from Jelal Khan's castle on a rope made of strips from torn tapestries, and chance had led her to a picketed horse. She had ridden all night, and dawn found her with a foundered steed on the swampy shores of the sea. Quivering with the abhorrence of being dragged back to the revolting destiny planned for her by Jelal Khan, she plunged into the morass, seeking a hiding-place from the pursuit she expected. When the reeds grew thinner around her and the water rose about her thighs, she saw the dim loom of an island ahead of her. A broad span of water lay between, but she did not hesitate. She waded out until the low waves were lapping about her waist; then she struck out strongly, swimming with a vigor that promised unusual endurance.

As she neared the island, she saw that it rose sheer

from the water in castle-like cliffs. She reached them at last, but found neither ledge to stand on below the water, nor to cling to above. She swam on, following the curve of the cliffs, the strain of her long flight beginning to weight her limbs. Her hands fluttered along the sheer stone, and suddenly they found a depression. With a sobbing gasp of relief, she pulled herself out of the water and clung there, a dripping white goddess in the dim starlight.

She had come upon what seemed to be steps carved in the cliff. Up them she went, flattening herself against the stone as she caught the faint clack of muffled oars. She strained her eyes and thought she made out a vague bulk moving toward the reedy point she had just quitted. But it was too far away for her to be sure, in the darkness, and presently the faint sound ceased, and she continued her climb. If it were her pursuers, she knew of no better course than to hide on the island. She knew that most of the islands off that marshy coast were uninhabited. This might be a pirate's lair, but even pirates would be preferable to the beast she had escaped.

A vagrant thought crossed her mind as she climbed, in which she mentally compared her former master with the *kozak* chief with whom—by compulsion—she had shamelessly flirted in the pavilions of the camp by Fort Ghori, where the Hyrkanian lords had parleyed with the warriors of the steppes. His burning gaze had frightened and humiliated her, but his cleanly elemental fierceness set him above Jelal Khan, a monster such as only an overly opulent civilization can produce.

She scrambled up over the cliff edge and looked timidly at the dense shadows which confronted her. The trees grew close to the cliffs, presenting a solid

24

mass of blackness. Something whirred above her head and she cowered, even though realizing it was only a bat.

She did not like the looks of those ebony shadows, but she set her teeth and went toward them, trying not to think of snakes. Her bare feet made no sound in the spongy loam under the trees. Once among them, the darkness closed frighteningly about her. She had not taken a dozen steps when she was no longer able to look back and see the cliffs and the sea beyond. A few steps more and she became hopelessly confused and lost her sense of direction. Through the tangled branches not even a star peered. She groped and floundered on, blindly, and then came to a sudden halt.

Somewhere ahead there began the rhythmical booming of a drum. It was not such a sound as she would have expected to hear in the time and place. Then she forgot it as she was aware of a presence near her. She could not see, but she knew that something was standing beside her in the darkness.

With a stifled cry she shrank back, and as she did so, something that even in her panic she recognized as a human arm curved about her waist. She screamed and threw all her supple young strength into a wild lunge for freedom, but her captor caught her up like a child, crushing her frantic resistance with ease. The silence with which her frenzied pleas and protests were received added to her terror as she felt herself being carried through the darkness toward the distant drum which still pulsed and muttered.

4

As the first tinge of dawn reddened the sea, a small boat with a solitary occupant approached the cliffs. The man in the boat was a picturesque figure. A crimson scarf was knotted about his head; his wide silk breeches, of flaming hue, were upheld by a broad sash which likewise supported a simitar in a shagreen scabbard. His gilt-worked leather boots suggested the horseman rather than the seaman, but he handled his boat with skill. Through his widely open white silk shirt showed his broad muscular breast, burned brown by the sun.

The muscles of his heavy bronzed arms rippled as he pulled the oars with an almost feline ease of motion. A fierce vitality that was evident in each feature and motion set him apart from common men; yet his expression was neither savage nor somber, though the smoldering blue eyes hinted at ferocity easily wakened. This was Conan, who had wandered into the armed camps of the *kozaks* with no other possessions than his wits and his sword, and who had carved his way to leadership among them.

He paddled to the carven stair as one familiar with his environs, and moored the boat to a projection of the rock. Then he went up the worn steps without hesitation. He was keenly alert, not because he consciously suspected hidden danger, but because alertness was a part of him, whetted by the wild existence he followed.

What Ghaznavi had considered animal intuition or some sixth sense was merely the razor-edged faculties and savage wit of the barbarian. Conan had no instinct to tell him that men were watching him from a covert among the reeds of the mainland.

As he climbed the cliff, one of these men breathed deeply and stealthily lifted a bow. Jehungir caught his wrist and hissed an oath into his ear. "Fool! Will you betray us? Don't you realize he is out of range? Let him get upon the island. He will go looking for the girl. We will stay here awhile. He *may* have sensed our presence or guessed our plot. He may have warriors hidden somewhere. We will wait. In an hour, if nothing suspicious occurs, we'll row up to the foot of the stair and wait him there. If he does not return in a reasonable time, some of us will go upon the island and hunt him down. But I do not wish to do that if it can be helped. Some of us are sure to die if we have to go into the bush after him. I had rather catch him descending the stair, where we can feather him with arrows from a safe distance."

Meanwhile the unsuspecting *kozak* had plunged into the forest. He went silently in his soft leather boots, his gaze sifting every shadow in eagerness to catch sight of the splendid tawny-haired beauty of whom he had dreamed ever since he had seen her in the pavilion of Jehungir Agha by Fort Ghori. He would have desired her even if she had displayed repugnance toward him. But her cryptic smiles and glances had fired his blood, and with all the lawless violence which was his heritage he desired that white-skinned golden-haired woman of civilization.

He had been on Xapur before. Less than a month ago he had held a secret conclave here with a pirate crew. He knew that he was approaching a point where he could see the mysterious ruins which gave the island its name, and he wondered if he would find the girl hiding among them. Even with the thought he stopped as though struck dead.

Ahead of him, among the trees, rose something that

27

his reason told him was not possible. *It was a great dark green wall, with towers rearing beyond the battlements.*

Conan stood paralyzed in the disruption of the faculties which demoralizes anyone who is confronted by an impossible negation of sanity. He doubted neither his sight nor his reason, but something was monstrously out of joint. Less than a month ago only broken ruins had showed among the trees. What human hands could rear such a mammoth pile as now met his eyes, in the few weeks which had elapsed? Besides, the buccaneers who roamed Vilayet ceaselessly would have learned of any work going on on such stupendous scale, and would have informed the *kozaks.*

There was no explaining this thing, but it was so. He was on Xapur and that fantastic heap of towering masonry was on Xapur, and all was madness and paradox; yet it was all true.

He wheeled to race back through the jungle, down the carven stair and across the blue waters to the distant camp at the mouth of the Zaporoska. In that moment of unreasoning panic even the thought of halting so near the inland sea was repugnant. He would leave it behind him, would quit the armed camps and the steppes, and put a thousand miles between him and the blue mysterious East where the most basic laws of nature could be set at naught, by what diabolism he could not guess.

For an instant the future fate of kingdoms that hinged on this gay-clad barbarian hung in the balance. It was a small thing that tipped the scales—merely a shred of silk hanging on a bush that caught his uneasy glance. He leaned to it, his nostrils expanding, his nerves quivering to a subtle stimulant. On that bit of torn cloth, so faint that it was less with his physical faculties than by some obscure instinctive sense that he recognized it, lingered the tantalizing perfume that he connected with the sweet firm flesh of the woman he had seen in Jehungir's pavilion. The fisherman had not lied, then; she *was* here! Then in the soil he saw a single track of a bare foot, long and slender, but a man's not a woman's, and sunk deeper than was natural. The conclusion was obvious; the man who made that track was carrying a burden, and what should it be but the girl the *kozak* was seeking?

He stood silently facing the dark towers that loomed through the trees, his eyes slits of blue bale-fire. Desire for the yellow-haired woman vied with a sullen primordial rage at whoever had taken her. His human passion fought down his ultra-human fears, and dropping into the stalking crouch of a hunting panther, he glided toward the walls, taking advantage of the dense foliage to escape detection from the battlements.

As he approached he saw that the walls were composed of the same green stone that had formed the ruins, and he was haunted by a vague sense of familiarity. It was as if he looked upon something he had never before seen, but had dreamed of, or pictured mentally. At last he recognized the sensation. The walls and towers followed the plan of the ruins. It was as if the crumbling lines had grown back into the structures they originally were.

No sound disturbed the morning quiet as Conan stole to the foot of the wall which rose sheer from the luxuriant growth. On the southern reaches of the inland sea the vegetation was almost tropical. He saw no one on the battlements, heard no sounds within. He saw a massive gate a short distance to his left, and had no reason to suppose that it was not locked and

29

guarded. But he believed that the woman he sought was somewhere beyond that wall, and the course he took was characteristically reckless.

Above him vine-festooned branches reached out toward the battlements. He went up a great tree like a cat, and reaching a point above the parapet, he gripped a thick limb with both hands, swung back and forth at arm's length until he had gained momentum, and then let go and catapulted through the air, landing cat-like on the battlements. Crouching there he stared down into the streets of a city.

The circumference of the wall was not great, but the number of green stone buildings it contained was surprizing. They were three or four stories in height, mainly flat-roofed, reflecting a fine architectural style. The streets converged like the spokes of a wheel into an octagon-shaped court in the center of the town which gave upon a lofty edifice, which, with its domes and towers, dominated the whole city. He saw no one moving in the streets or looking out of the windows, though the sun was already coming up. The silence that reigned there might have been that of a dead and deserted city. A narrow stone stair ascended the wall near him; down this he went.

Houses shouldered so closely to the wall that half-way down the stair he found himself within arm's length of a window, and halted to peer in. There were no bars, and the silk curtains were caught back with satin cords. He looked into a chamber whose walls were hidden by dark velvet tapestries. The floor was covered with thick rugs, and there were benches of polished ebony, and an ivory dais heaped with furs.

He was about to continue his descent, when he heard the sound of someone approaching in the street below. Before the unknown person could round a corner and

30

see him on the stair, he stepped quickly across the intervening space and dropped lightly into the room, drawing his simitar. He stood for an instant statue-like; then as nothing happened he was moving across the rugs toward an arched doorway when a hanging was drawn aside, revealing a cushioned alcove from which a slender, dark-haired girl regarded him with languid eyes.

Conan glared at her tensely, expecting her momentarily to start screaming. But she merely smothered a yawn with a dainty hand, rose from the alcove and leaned negligently against the hanging which she held with one hand.

She was undoubtedly a member of a white race, though her skin was very dark. Her square-cut hair was black as midnight, her only garment a wisp of silk about her supple hips.

Presently she spoke, but the tongue was unfamiliar to him, and he shook his head. She yawned again, stretched lithely, and without any show of fear or surprise, shifted to a language he did understand, a dialect of Yuetshi which sounded strangely archaic.

"Are you looking for someone?" she asked, as indifferently as if the invasion of her chamber by an armed stranger were the most common thing imaginable.

"Who are you?" he demanded.

"I am Yateli," she answered languidly. "I must have feasted late last night, I am so sleepy now. Who are you?"

"I am Conan, a *hetman* among the *kozaks*," he answered, watching her narrowly. He believed her attitude to be a pose, and expected her to try to escape from the chamber or rouse the house. But, though a velvet rope that might be a signal cord hung near her,

31

she did not reach for it.

"Conan," she repeated drowsily. "You are not a Dagonian. I suppose you are a mercenary. Have you cut the heads off many Yuetshi?"

"I do not war on water rats!" he snorted.

"But they are very terrible," she murmured. "I remember when they were our slaves. But they revolted and burned and slew. Only the magic of Khosatral Khel has kept them from the walls—" She paused, a puzzled look struggling with the sleepiness of her expression. "I forgot," she muttered. "They *did* climb the walls, last night. There was shouting and fire, and people calling in vain on Khosatral." She shook her head as if to clear it. "But that can not be," she murmured, "because I am alive, and I thought I was dead. Oh, to the devil with it!"

She came across the chamber, and taking Conan's hand, drew him to the dais. He yielded in bewilderment and uncertainty. The girl smiled at him like a sleepy child; her long silky lashes drooped over dusky, clouded eyes. She ran her fingers through his thick black locks as if to assure herself of his reality.

"It was a dream," she yawned. "Perhaps it's all a dream. I feel like a dream now. I don't care. I can't remember something—I have forgotten—there is something I can not understand, but I grow so sleepy when I try to think. Anyway, it doesn't matter."

"What do you mean?" he asked uneasily. "You said they climbed the walls last night? Who?"

"The Yuetshi. I thought so, anyway. A cloud of smoke hid everything, but a naked, blood-stained devil caught me by the throat and drove his knife into my breast. Oh, it hurt! But it was a dream, because see, there is no scar." She idly inspected her smooth bosom, and then sank upon Conan's lap and passed her supple arms around his massive neck. "I can not remember," she murmured, nestling her dark head against his mighty breast. "Everything is dim and misty. It does not matter. You are no dream. You are strong. Let us live while we can. Love me!"

He cradled the girl's glossy head in the bend of his heavy arm and kissed her full red lips with unfeigned relish.

"You are strong," she repeated, her voice waning. "Love me—love—" The sleepy murmur faded away; the dusky eyes closed, the long lashes drooping over the sensuous cheeks; the supple body relaxed in Conan's arms.

He scowled down at her. She seemed to partake of the illusion that haunted this whole city, but the firm resilience of her limbs under his questing fingers convinced him that he had a living human girl in his arms, and not the shadow of a dream. No less disturbed, he hastily laid her on the furs upon the dais. Her sleep was too deep to be natural. He decided that she must be an addict of some drug, perhaps like the black lotus of Xuthal.

Then he found something else to make him wonder. Among the furs on the dais was a gorgeous spotted skin, whose predominant hue was golden. It was not a clever copy, but the skin of an actual beast. And that beast, Conan knew, had been extinct for at least a thousand years; it was the great golden leopard which figures so prominently in Hyborian legendry, and which the ancient artists delighted to portray in pigments and marble.

Shaking his head in bewilderment, Conan passed through the archway into a winding corridor. Silence hung over the house, but outside he heard a sound which his keen ears recognized as something ascending the stair on the wall from which he had entered the building. An instant later he was startled to hear something land with a soft but weighty thud on the floor of the chamber he had just quitted. Turning quickly away, he hurried along the twisting hallway until something on the floor before him brought him to a halt.

It was a human figure, which lay half in the hall and half in an opening that obviously was normally concealed by a door which was a duplicate of the panels of the wall. It was a man, dark and lean, clad only in a silk loin-cloth, with a shaven head and cruel features, and he lay as if death had struck him just as he was emerging from the panel. Conan bent above him, seeking the cause of his death, and discovered him to be merely sunk in the same deep sleep as the girl in the chamber.

But why should he select such a place for his slumbers? While meditating on the matter, Conan was galvanized by a sound behind him. Something was moving up the corridor in his direction. A quick glance down it showed that it ended in a great door which might be locked. Conan jerked the supine body out of the panel-entrance and stepped through, pulling the panel shut after him. A click told him it was locked in place. Standing in utter darkness, he heard a shuffling tread halt just outside the door, and a faint chill trickled along his spine. That was no human step, nor that of any beast he had ever encountered.

There was an instant of silence, then a faint creak of wood and metal. Putting out his hand he felt the door straining and bending inward, as if a great weight were being steadily borne against it from the outside. As he reached for his sword, this ceased and he heard a strange slobbering mouthing that prickled the short

34

hairs on his scalp. Simitar in hand he began backing away, and his heels felt steps, down which he nearly tumbled. He was in a narrow staircase leading downward.

He groped his way down in the blackness, feeling for, but not finding, some other opening in the walls. Just as he decided that he was no longer in the house, but deep in the earth under it, the steps ceased in a level tunnel.

5

ALONG THE BLACK silent tunnel Conan groped, momentarily dreading a fall into some unseen pit; but at last his feet struck steps again, and he went up them until he came to a door on which his fumbling fingers found a metal catch. He came out into a dim and lofty room of enormous proportions. Fantastic columns marched around the mottled walls, upholding a ceiling, which, at once translucent and dusky, seemed like a cloudy midnight sky, giving an illusion of impossible height. If any light filtered in from the outside it was curiously altered.

In a brooding twilight Conan moved across the bare green floor. The great room was circular, pierced on one side by the great bronze valves of a giant door. Opposite this, on a dais against the wall, up to which led broad curving steps, there stood a throne of copper, and when Conan saw what was coiled on this throne, he retreated hastily, lifting his simitar.

Then, as the thing did not move, he scanned it more closely, and presently mounted the glass steps and stared down at it. It was a gigantic snake, apparently carved of some jade-like substance. Each scale stood out as distinctly as in real life, and the iridescent colors were vividly reproduced. The great wedge-shaped head was half submerged in the folds of its trunk; so neither the eyes nor jaws were visible. Recognition stirred in his mind. This snake was evidently meant to represent one of those grim monsters of the marsh which in past ages had haunted the reedy edges of Vilayet's southern shores. But, like the golden leopard, they had been extinct for hundreds of years. Conan had seen rude images of them, in miniature, among the idol-huts of the Yuetshi, and there was a description of them in the

Book of Skelos, which drew on prehistoric sources.

Conan admired the scaly torso, thick as his thigh and obviously of great length, and he reached out and laid a curious hand on the thing. And as he did so, his heart nearly stopped. An icy chill congealed the blood in his veins and lifted the short hair on his scalp. Under his hand there was not the smooth, brittle surface of glass or metal or stone, but the yielding, fibrous mass of a *living* thing. He felt cold, sluggish life flowing under his fingers.

His hand jerked back in instinctive repulsion. Sword shaking in his grasp, horror and revulsion and fear almost choking him, he backed away and down the glass steps with painful care, glaring in awful fascination at the grisly thing that slumbered on the copper throne. It did not move.

He reached the bronze door and tried it, with his heart in his teeth, sweating with fear that he should find himself locked in with that slimy horror. But the valves yielded to his touch, and he glided through and closed them behind him.

He found himself in a wide hallway with lofty tapestried walls, where the light was the same twilight gloom. It made distant objects indistinct and that made him uneasy, rousing thoughts of serpents gliding unseen through the dimness. A door at the other end seemed miles away in the illusive light. Nearer at hand the tapestry hung in such a way as to suggest an opening behind it, and lifting it cautiously he discovered a narrow stair leading up.

While he hesitated he heard in the great room he had just left, the same shuffling tread he had heard outside the locked panel. Had he been followed through the tunnel? He went up the stair hastily, dropping the tapestry in place behind him.

Emerging presently into a twisting corridor, he took the first doorway he came to. He had a twofold purpose in his apparently aimless prowling: to escape from the building and its mysteries, and to find the Nemedian girl who, he felt, was imprisoned somewhere in this palace, temple, or whatever it was. He believed it was the great domed edifice in the center of the city, and it was likely that here dwelt the ruler of the town, to whom a captive woman would doubtless be brought.

He found himself in a chamber, not another corridor, and was about to retrace his steps, when he heard a voice which came from behind one of the walls. There was no door in that wall, but he leaned close and heard distinctly. And an icy chill crawled slowly along his spine. The tongue was Nemedian, but the voice was not human. There was a terrifying resonance about it, like a bell tolling at midnight.

"There was no life in the Abyss, save that which was incorporated in me," it tolled. "Nor was there light, nor motion, nor any sound. Only the urge behind and beyond life guided and impelled me on my upward journey, blind, insensate, inexorable. Through ages upon ages, and the changeless strata of darkness I climbed—"

Ensorcelled by that belling resonance, Conan crouched forgetful of all else, until its hypnotic power caused a strange replacement of faculties and perception, and sound created the illusion of sight. Conan was no longer aware of the voice, save as far-off rhythmical waves of sound. Transported beyond his age and his own individuality, he was seeing the transmutation of the being men called Khosatral Khel which crawled up from Night and the Abyss ages ago to clothe itself in the substance of the material universe.

But human flesh was too frail, too paltry to hold the

38

terrific essence that was Khosatral Khel. So he stood up in the shape and aspect of a man, but his flesh was not flesh, nor the bone, bone, nor blood, blood. He became a blasphemy against all nature, for he caused to live and think and act a basic substance that before had never known the pulse and stir of animate being.

He stalked through the world like a god, for no earthly weapon could harm him, and to him a century was like an hour. In his wanderings he came upon a primitive people inhabiting the island of Dagonia, and it pleased him to give this race culture and civilization, and by his aid they built the city of Dagon and they abode there and worshipped him. Strange and grisly were his servants, called from the dark corners of the planet where grim survivals of forgotten ages yet lurked. His house in Dagon was connected with every other house by tunnels through which his shaven-headed priests bore victims for the sacrifice.

But after many ages a fierce and brutish people appeared on the shores of the sea. They called themselves Yuetshi, and after a fierce battle were defeated and enslaved, and for nearly a generation they died on the altars of Khosatral.

His sorcery kept them in bonds. Then their priest, a strange gaunt man of unknown race, plunged into the wilderness, and when he returned he bore a knife that was of no earthly substance. It was forged of a meteor which flashed through the sky like a flaming arrow and fell in a far valley. The slaves rose. Their saw-edged crescents cut down the men of Dagon like sheep, and against that unearthly knife the magic of Khosatral was impotent. While carnage and slaughter bellowed through the red smoke that choked the streets, the grimmest act of that grim drama was played in the cryptic dome behind the great daised chamber with its copper throne and its walls mottled like the skin of serpents.

From that dome the Yuetshi priest emerged alone. He had not slain his foe, because he wished to hold the threat of his loosing over the heads of his own rebellious subjects. He had left Khosatral lying upon the golden dais with the mystic knife across his breast for a spell to hold him senseless and inanimate until doomsday.

But the ages passed and the priest died, the towers of deserted Dagon crumbled, the tales became dim, and the Yuetshi were reduced by plagues and famines and war to scattered remnants, dwelling in squalor along the seashore.

Only the cryptic dome resisted the rot of time, until a chance thunderbolt and the curiosity of a fisherman lifted from the breast of the god the magic knife and broke the spell. Khosatral Khel rose and lived and waxed mighty once more. It pleased him to restore the city as it was in the days before its fall. By his necromancy he lifted the towers from the dust of forgotten millenniums, and the folk which had been dust for ages moved in life again.

But folk who have tasted of death are only partly alive. In the dark corners of their souls and minds death still lurks unconquered. By night the people of Dagon moved and loved, hated and feasted, and remembered the fall of Dagon and their own slaughter only as a dim dream; they moved in an enchanted mist of illusion, feeling the strangeness of their existence but not inquiring the reasons therefor. With the coming of day they sank into deep sleep, to be roused again only by the coming of night, which is akin to death.

All this rolled in a terrible panorama before Conan's consciousness as he crouched beside the tapestried wall. His reason staggered. All certainty and sanity were swept away, leaving a shadowy universe through which stole hooded figures of grisly potentialities. Through the belling of the voice which was like a tolling of triumph over the ordered laws of a sane planet, a human sound anchored Conan's mind from its flight through spheres of madness. It was the hysterical sobbing of a woman.

Involuntarily he sprang up.

6

JEHUNGIR AGHA waited with growing impatience in his boat among the reeds. More than an hour passed, and Conan had not reappeared. Doubtless he was still searching the island for the girl he thought to be hidden there. But another surmise occurred to the Agha. Suppose the *hetman* had left his warriors near by, and that they should grow suspicious and come to investigate his long absence? Jehungir spoke to the oarsmen, and the long boat slid from among the reeds and glided toward the carven stairs.

Leaving half a dozen men in the boat, he took the rest, ten mighty archers of Khawarizm, in spired helmets and tiger-skin cloaks. Like hunters invading the retreat of the lion, they stole forward under the trees, arrows on string. Silence reigned over the forest except when a great green thing that might have been a parrot swirled over their heads with a low thunder of broad wings, and then sped off through the trees. With a sudden gesture Jehungir halted his party, and they stared incredulously at the towers that showed through the verdure in the distance.

"Tarim!" muttered Jehungir. "The pirates have rebuilt the ruins! Doubtless Conan is there. We must investigate this. A fortified town this close to the mainland!—Come!"

With renewed caution they glided through the trees. The game had altered; from pursuers and hunters they had become spies.

And as they crept through the tangled growth, the man they sought was in peril more deadly than their filigreed arrows.

Conan realized with a crawling of his skin that

beyond the wall the belling voice had ceased. He stood motionless as a statue, his gaze fixed on a curtained door through which he knew that a culminating horror would presently appear.

It was dim and misty in the chamber, and Conan's hair began to lift on his scalp as he looked. He saw a head and a pair of gigantic shoulders grow out of the twilight gloom. There was no sound of footsteps, but the great dusky form grew more distinct until Conan recognized the figure of a man. He was clad in sandals, a skirt and a broad shagreen girdle. His square-cut mane was confined by a circlet of gold. Conan stared at the sweep of the monstrous shoulders, the breadth of swelling breast, the bands and ridges and clusters of muscles on torso and limbs. The face was without weakness and without mercy. The eyes were balls of dark fire. And Conan knew that this was Khosatral Khel, the ancient from the Abyss, the god of Dagonia.

No word was spoken. No word was necessary. Khosatral spread his great arms, and Conan, crouching beneath them, slashed at the giant's belly. Then he bounded back, eyes blazing with surprise. The keen edge had rung on the mighty body as on an anvil, rebounding without cutting. Then Khosatral came upon him in an irresistible surge.

There was a fleeting concussion, a fierce writhing and intertwining of limbs and bodies, and then Conan sprang clear, every thew quivering from the violence of his efforts; blood started where the grazing fingers had torn the skin. In that instant of contact he had experienced the ultimate madness of blasphemed nature; no human flesh had bruised his, but *metal* animated and sentient; it was a body of living iron which opposed his.

Khosatral loomed above the warrior in the gloom.

43

Once let those great fingers lock and they would not loosen until the human body hung limp in their grasp. In that twilit chamber it was as if a man fought with a dream-monster in a nightmare.

Flinging down his useless sword, Conan caught up a heavy bench and hurled it with all his power. It was such a missile as few men could even lift. On Khosatral's mighty breast it smashed into shreds and splinters. It did not even shake the giant on his braced legs. His face lost something of its human aspect, a nimbus of fire played about his awesome head, and like a moving tower he came on.

With a desperate wrench Conan ripped a whole section of tapestry from the wall and whirling it, with a muscular effort greater than that required for throwing the bench, he flung it over the giant's head. For an instant Khosatral floundered, smothered and blinded by the clinging stuff that resisted his strength as wood or steel could not have done, and in that instant Conan caught up his simitar and shot out into the corridor. Without checking his speed he hurled himself through the door of the adjoining chamber, slammed the door and shot the bolt.

Then as he wheeled he stopped short, all the blood in him seeming to surge to his head. Crouching on a heap of silk cushions, golden hair streaming over her naked shoulders, eyes blank with terror, was the woman for whom he had dared so much. He almost forgot the horror at his heels until a splintering crash behind him brought him to his senses. He caught up the girl and sprang for the opposite door. She was too helpless with fright either to resist or to aid him. A faint whimper was the only sound of which she seemed capable.

Conan wasted no time trying the door. A shattering stroke of his simitar hewed the lock asunder, and as he
44

sprang through to the stair that loomed beyond it, he saw the head and shoulders of Khosatral crash through the other door. The colossus was splintering the massive panels as if they were of cardboard.

Conan raced up the stair, carrying the big girl over one shoulder as easily as if she had been a child. Where he was going he had no idea, but the stair ended at the door of a round, domed chamber. Khosatral was coming up the stair behind them, silently as a wind of death, and as swiftly.

The chamber's walls were of solid steel, and so was the door. Conan shut it and dropped in place the great bars with which it was furnished. The thought struck him that this was Khosatral's chamber, where he locked himself in to sleep securely from the monsters he had loosed from the Pits to do his bidding.

Hardly were the bolts in place when the great door shook and trembled to the giant's assault. Conan shrugged his shoulders. This was the end of the trail. There was no other door in the chamber, nor any window. Air, and the strange misty light, evidently came from interstices in the dome. He tested the nicked edge of his simitar, quite cool now that he was at bay. He had done his volcanic best to escape; when the giant came crashing through that door he would explode in another savage onslaught with his useless sword, not because he expected it to do any good, but because it was his nature to die fighting. For the moment there was no course of action to take, and his calmness was not forced or feigned.

The gaze he turned on his fair companion was as admiring and intense as if he had a hundred years to live. He had dumped her unceremoniously on the floor when he turned to close the door, and she had risen to her knees, mechanically arranging her streaming locks and her scanty garment. Conan's fierce eyes glowed with approval as they devoured her thick golden hair, her clear wide eyes, her milky skin, sleek with exuberant health, the firm swell of her breasts, the contours of her splendid hips.

A low cry escaped her as the door shook and a bolt gave way with a groan.

Conan did not look around. He knew the door would hold a little while longer.

"They told me you had escaped," he said. "A Yuetshi fisher told me you were hiding here. What is your name?"

"Octavia," she gasped mechanically. Then words came in a rush. She caught at him with desperate fingers. "Oh Mitra! what nightmare is this? The people—the dark-skinned people—one of them caught me in the forest and brought me here. They carried me to—to that—that *thing*. He told me—he said—am I mad? Is this a dream?"

He glanced at the door which bulged inward as if from the impact of a battering-ram.

"No," he said; "it's no dream. That hinge is giving way. Strange that a devil has to break down a door like a common man; but after all, his strength itself is a diabolism."

"Can you not kill him?" she panted. "You are strong."

Conan was too honest to lie to her. "If a mortal man could kill him, he'd be dead now," he answered. "I nicked my blade on his belly."

Her eyes dulled. "Then you must die, and I must— oh Mitra!" she screamed in sudden frenzy, and Conan caught her hands, fearing that she would harm herself. "He told me what he was going to do to me!" she panted. "Kill me! Kill me with your sword before he bursts the door!"

Conan looked at her, and shook his head.

"I'll do what I can," he said. "That won't be much, but it'll give you a chance to get past him down the stair. Then run for the cliffs. I have a boat tied at the foot of the steps. If you can get out of the palace you may escape him yet. The people of this city are all asleep."

She dropped her head in her hands. Conan took up his simitar and moved over to stand before the echoing door. One watching him would not have realized that he was waiting for a death he regarded as inevitable. His eyes smoldered more vividly; his muscular hand knotted harder on his hilt; that was all.

The hinges had given under the giant's terrible assault and the door rocked crazily, held only by the bolts. And these solid steel bars were buckling, bending, bulging out of their sockets. Conan watched in an almost impersonal fascination, envying the monster his inhuman strength.

Then without warning the bombardment ceased. In the stillness Conan heard other noises on the landing outside—the beat of wings, and a muttering voice that was like the whining of wind through midnight branches. Then presently there was silence, but there was a new *feel* in the air. Only the whetted instincts of barbarism could have sensed it, but Conan knew, without seeing or hearing him leave, that the master of Dagon no longer stood outside the door.

He glared through a crack that had been started in the steel of the portal. The landing was empty. He drew the warped bolts and cautiously pulled aside the sagging door. Khosatral was not on the stair, but far below he heard the clang of a metal door. He did not know whether the giant was plotting new deviltries or had been summoned away by that muttering voice, but he wasted no time in conjectures.

He called to Octavia, and the new note in his voice brought her up to her feet and to his side almost without her conscious volition.

"What is it?" she gasped.

"Don't stop to talk!" He caught her wrist. "Come on!" The chance for action had transformed him; his eyes blazed, his voice crackled. "The knife!" he muttered, while almost dragging the girl down the stair in his fierce haste. "The magic Yuetshi blade! He left it in the dome! I—" his voice died suddenly as a clear mental picture sprang up before him. The dome adjoined the great room where stood the copper throne—sweat started out on his body. The only way to that dome was through that room with its copper throne and the foul thing that slumbered in it.

But he did not hesitate. Swiftly they descended the stair, crossed the chamber, descended the next stair, and came into the great dim hall with its mysterious hangings. They had seen no sign of the colossus. Halting before the great bronze-valved door, Conan caught Octavia by her shoulders and shook her in his intensity.

"Listen!" he snapped. "I'm going into that room and fasten the door. Stand here and listen; if Khosatral comes, call to me. If you hear me cry out for you to go, run as though the devil were on your heels—which he probably will be. Make for that door at the other end of the hall, because I'll be past helping you. I'm going for the Yuetshi knife!"

Before she could voice the protest her lips were framing, he had slid through the valves and shut them behind him. He lowered the bolt cautiously, not noticing that it could be worked from the outside. In the dim twilight his gaze sought that grim copper throne; yes, the scaly brute was still there, filling the throne with its loathsome coils. He saw a door behind the throne and knew that it led into the dome. But to reach it he must mount the dais, a few feet from the throne itself.

A wind blowing across the green floor would have made more noise than Conan's slinking feet. Eyes glued on the sleeping reptile he reached the dais and mounted the glass steps. The snake had not moved. He was reaching for the door....

The bolt on the bronze portal clanged and Conan stifled an awful oath as he saw Octavia come into the room. She stared about, uncertain in the deeper gloom, and he stood frozen, not daring to shout a warning. Then she saw his shadowy figure and ran toward the dais, crying: "I want to go with you! I'm afraid to stay alone—*oh* !" She threw up her hands with a terrible scream as for the first time she saw the occupant of the throne. The wedge-shaped head had lifted from its coils and thrust out toward her on a yard of shining neck.

Then with a smooth flowing motion it began to ooze from the throne, coil by coil, its ugly head bobbing in the direction of the paralyzed girl.

Conan cleared the space between him and the throne with a desperate bound, his simitar swinging with all his power. And with such blinding speed did the serpent move that it whipped about and met him in full midair, lapping his limbs and body with half a dozen coils. His half-checked stroke fell futilely as he crashed down on the dais, gashing the scaly trunk but not severing it.

Then he was writhing on the glass steps with fold after slimy fold knotting about him, twisting, crushing, killing him. His right arm was still free, but he could get no purchase to strike a killing blow, and he knew one blow must suffice. With a groaning convulsion of muscular expansion that bulged his veins almost to bursting on his temples and tied his muscles in quivering, tortured knots, he heaved up on his feet, lifting almost the full weight of that forty-foot devil.

An instant he reeled on wide-braced legs, feeling his ribs caving in on his vitals and his sight growing dark, while his simitar gleamed above his head. Then it fell, shearing through the scales and flesh and vertebrae. And where there had been one huge writhing cable, now there were horribly two, lashing and flopping in the death throes. Conan staggered away from their blind strokes. He was sick and dizzy, and blood oozed from his nose. Groping in a dark mist he clutched Octavia and shook her until she gasped for breath.

"Next time I tell you to stay somewhere," he gasped, "you stay!"

He was too dizzy even to know whether she replied. Taking her wrist like a truant schoolgirl, he led her around the hideous stumps that still looped and knotted on the floor. Somewhere, in the distance, he thought he heard men yelling, but his ears were still roaring so that he could not be sure.

The door gave to his efforts. If Khosatral had placed the snake there to guard the thing he feared, evidently he considered it ample precaution. Conan half expected some other monstrosity to leap at him with the opening of the door, but in the dimmer light he saw only the vague sweep of the arch above, a dully gleaming block of gold, and a half-moon glimmer on the stone.

With a gasp of gratification he scooped it up, and did not linger for further exploration. He turned and fled across the room and down the great hall toward the distant door that he felt led to the outer air. He was correct. A few minutes later he emerged into the silent streets, half carrying, half guiding his companion. There was no one to be seen, but beyond the western wall there sounded cries and moaning wails that made Octavia tremble. He led her to the southwestern wall, and without difficulty found a stone stair that mounted the rampart. He had appropriated a thick tapestry rope in the great hall, and now, having reached the parapet, he looped the soft strong cord about the girl's hips and lowered her to the earth. Then, making one end fast to a merlon, he slid down after her. There was but one way of escape from the island—the stair on the western cliffs. In that direction he hurried, swinging wide around the spot from which had come the cries and the sound of terrible blows.

Octavia sensed that grim peril lurked in those leafy fastnesses. Her breath came pantingly and she pressed close to her protector. But the forest was silent now, and they saw no shape of menace until they emerged from the trees and glimpsed a figure standing on the edge of the cliffs.

Jehungir Agha had escaped the doom that had overtaken his warriors when an iron giant sallied suddenly from the gate and battered and crushed them into bits of shredded flesh and splintered bone. When he saw the swords of his archers break on that man-like juggernaut, he had known it was no human foe they faced, and he had fled, hiding in the deep woods until the sounds of slaughter ceased. Then he crept back to the stair, but his boatmen were not waiting for him.

They had heard the screams, and presently, waiting nervously, had seen, on the cliff above them, a blood-smeared monster waving gigantic arms in awful triumph. They had waited for no more. When Jehungir came upon the cliffs they were just vanishing among the reeds beyond ear-shot. Khosatral was gone—had either returned to the city or was prowling the forest in search of the man who had escaped him outside the walls.

Jehungir was just preparing to descend the stairs and depart in Conan's boat, when the saw the *hetman* and the girl emerge from the trees. The experience which had congealed his blood and almost blasted his reason had not altered Jehungir's intentions toward the *kozak* chief. The sight of the man he had come to kill filled him with gratification. He was astonished to see the girl he had given to Jelal Khan, but he wasted no time on her. Lifting his bow he drew the shaft to its head and loosed. Conan crouched and the arrow splintered on a tree, and Conan laughed.

"Dog!" he taunted. "You can't hit me! I was not born to die on Hyrkanian steel! Try again, pig of Turan!"

Jehungir did not try again. That was his last arrow. He drew his simitar and advanced, confident in his spired helmet and close-meshed mail. Conan met him half-way in a blinding whirl of swords. The curved blades ground together, sprang apart, circled in glittering arcs that blurred the sight which tried to follow them. Octavia, watching, did not see the stroke, but she heard its chopping impact, and saw Jehungir fall, blood spurting from his side where the Cimmerian's steel had sundered his mail and bitten to his spine.

But Octavia's scream was not caused by the death of her former master. With a crash of bending boughs Khosatral Khel was upon them. The girl could not flee; a moaning cry escaped her as her knees gave way and pitched her grovelling to the sward.

Conan, stooping above the body of the Agha, made no move to escape. Shifting his reddened simitar to his left hand, he drew the great half-blade of the Yuetshi. Khosatral Khel was towering above him, his arms lifted like mauls, but as the blade caught the sheen of the sun, the giant gave back suddenly.

But Conan's blood was up. He rushed in, slashing with the crescent blade. And it did not splinter. Under its edge the dusky metal of Khosatral's body gave way like common flesh beneath a cleaver. From the deep gash flowed a strange ichor, and Khosatral cried out like the dirging of a great bell. His terrible arms flailed down, but Conan, quicker than the archers who had died beneath those awful flails, avoided their strokes and struck again and yet again. Khosatral reeled and tottered; his cries were awful to hear, as if metal were given a tongue of pain, as if iron shrieked and bellowed under torment.

Then wheeling away he staggered into the forest; he reeled in his gait, crashed through bushes and caromed off trees. Yet though Conan followed him with the speed of hot passion, the walls and towers of Dagon loomed through the trees before the man came within dagger-reach of the giant.

Then Khosatral turned again, flailing the air with desperate blows, but Conan, fired to berserk fury, was not to be denied. As a panther strikes down a bull moose at bay, so he plunged under the bludgeoning arms and drove the crescent blade to the hilt under the spot where a human's heart would be.

Khosatral reeled and fell. In the shape of a man he reeled, but it was not the shape of a man that struck the loam. Where there had been the likeness of a human face, there was no face at all, and the metal limbs melted and changed.... Conan, who had not shrunk from Khosatral living, recoiled blenching from Khosatral dead, for he had witnessed an awful

53

transmutation; in his dying throes Khosatral Khel had become again the *thing* that had crawled up from the Abyss millenniums gone. Gagging with intolerable repugnance, Conan turned to flee the sight; and he was suddenly aware that the pinnacles of Dagon no longer glimmered through the trees. They had faded like smoke—the battlements, the crenellated towers, the great bronze gates, the velvets, the gold, the ivory, and the dark-haired women, and the men with their shaven skulls. With the passing of the inhuman intellect which had given them rebirth, they had faded back into the dust which they had been for ages uncounted. Only the stumps of broken columns rose above crumbling walls and broken paves and shattered dome. Conan again looked upon the ruins of Xapur as he remembered them.

The wild *hetman* stood like a statue for a space, dimly grasping something of the cosmic tragedy of the fitful ephemera called mankind and the hooded shapes of darkness which prey upon it. Then as he heard his voice called in accents of fear, he started, as one awaking from a dream, glanced again at the thing on the ground, shuddered and turned away toward the cliffs and the girl that waited there.

She was peering fearfully under the trees, and she greeted him with a half-stifled cry of relief. He had shaken off the dim monstrous visions which had momentarily haunted him, and was his exuberant self again.

"Where is *he?*" she shuddered.

"Gone back to hell whence he crawled," he replied cheerfully. "Why didn't you climb the stair and make your escape in my boat?"

"I wouldn't desert—" she began, then changed her mind, and amended rather sulkily, "I have nowhere to go. The Hyrkanians would enslave me again, and the pirates would—"

"What of the *kozaks?*" he suggested.

"Are they better than the pirates?" she asked scornfully. Conan's admiration increased to see how well she had recovered her poise after having endured such frantic terror. Her arrogance amused him.

"You seemed to think so in the camp by Ghori," he answered. "You were free enough with your smiles then."

Her red lip curled in disdain. "Do you think I was enamored of you? Do you dream that I would have shamed myself before an ale-guzzling, meat-gorging barbarian unless I had to? My master—whose body lies there—forced me to do as I did."

"Oh!" Conan seemed rather crestfallen. Then he laughed with undiminished zest. "No matter. You belong to me now. Give me a kiss."

"You dare ask—" she began angrily, when she felt herself snatched off her feet and crushed to the *hetman's* muscular breast. She fought him fiercely, with all the supple strength of her magnificent youth, but he only laughed exuberantly, drunk with the possession of this splendid creature writhing in his arms.

He crushed her struggles easily, drinking the nectar of her lips with all the unrestrained passion that was his, until the arms that strained against him melted and twined convulsively about his massive neck. Then he laughed down into the clear eyes, and said: "Why should not a chief of the Free People be preferable to a city-bred dog of Turan?"

She shook back her tawny locks, still tingling in every nerve from the fire of his kisses. She did not loosen her arms from his neck. "Do you deem yourself

55

an Agha's equal?" she challenged.

He laughed and strode with her in his arms toward the stair. "You shall judge," he boasted. "I'll burn Khawarizm for a torch to light your way to my tent."

The People of the
Black Circle

1. Death Strikes a King

THE KING OF Vendhya was dying. Through the hot,
stifling night the temple gongs boomed and the conchs
roared. Their clamor was a faint echo in the gold-
domed chamber where Bunda Chand struggled on the
velvet-cushioned dais. Beads of sweat glistened on his
dark skin; his fingers twisted the gold-worked fabric
beneath him. He was young; no spear had touched him,
no poison lurked in his wine. But his veins stood out
like blue cords on his temples, and his eyes dilated with
the nearness of death. Trembling slave-girls knelt at the
foot of the dais, and leaning down to him, watching
him with passionate intensity, was his sister, the Devi
Yasmina. With her was the *wazam,* a noble grown old
in the royal court.

She threw up her head in a gusty gesture of wrath
and despair as the thunder of the distant drums reached
her ears.

"The priests and their clamor!" she exclaimed.
"They are no wiser than the leeches who are helpless!
Nay, he dies and none can say why. He is dying now—
and I stand here helpless, who would burn the whole
city and spill the blood of thousands to save him."

"Not a man of Ayodhya but would die in his place, if
it might be, Devi," answered the *wazam.* "This
poison—"

"I tell you it is not poison!" she cried. "Since his birth he has been guarded so closely that the cleverest poisoners of the East could not reach him. Five skulls bleaching on the Tower of the Kites can testify to attempts which were made—and which failed. As you well know, there are ten men and ten women whose sole duty is to taste his food and wine, and fifty armed warriors guard his chamber as they guard it now. No, it is not poison; it is sorcery—black, ghastly magic—"

She ceased as the king spoke; his livid lips did not move, and there was no recognition in his glassy eyes. But his voice rose in an eery call, indistinct and far away, as if he called to her from beyond vast, wind-blown gulfs.

"Yasmina! Yasmina! My sister, where are you? I can not find you. All is darkness, and the roaring of great winds!"

"Brother!" cried Yasmina, catching his limp hand in a convulsive grasp. "I am here! Do you not know me—"

Her voice died at the utter vacancy of his face. A low confused moaning waned from his mouth. The slave-girls at the foot of the dais whimpered with fear, and Yasmina beat her breast in her anguish.

In another part of the city a man stood in a latticed balcony overlooking a long street in which torches tossed luridly, smokily revealing upturned dark faces and the whites of gleaming eyes. A long-drawn wailing rose from the multitude.

The man shrugged his broad shoulders and turned back into the arabesqued chamber. He was a tall man, compactly built, and richly clad.

"The king is not yet dead, but the dirge is sounded," he said to another man who sat cross-legged on a mat in

58

a corner. This man was clad in a brown camel-hair robe and sandals, and a green turban was on his head. His expression was tranquil, his gaze impersonal.

"The people know he will never see another dawn," this man answered.

The first speaker favored him with a long, searching stare.

"What I can not understand," he said, "is why I have had to wait so long for your masters to strike. If they have slain the king now, why could they not have slain him months ago?"

"Even the arts you call sorcery are governed by cosmic laws," answered the man in the green turban. "The stars direct these actions, as in other affairs. Not even my masters can alter the stars. Not until the heavens were in the proper order could they perform this necromancy." With a long, stained finger-nail he mapped the constellations on the marble-tiled floor. "The slant of the moon presaged evil for the king of Vendhya; the stars are in turmoil, the Serpent in the House of the Elephant. During such juxtaposition, the invisible guardians are removed from the spirit of Bhunda Chand. A path is opened in the unseen realms, and once a point of contact was established, mighty powers were put in play along that path."

"Point of contact?" inquired the other. "Do you mean that lock of Bhunda Chand's hair?"

"Yes. All discarded portions of the human body still remain part of it, attached to it by intangible connections. The priests of Asura have a dim inkling of this truth, and so all nail-trimmings, hair and other waste products of the persons of the royal family are carefully reduced to ashes and the ashes hidden. But at the urgent entreaty of the princess of Khosala, who loved Bhunda Chand vainly, he gave her a lock of his long black hair as a token of remembrance. When my masters decided upon his doom, the lock, in its golden, jewel-crusted case, was stolen from under her pillow while she slept, and another substituted, so like the first that she never knew the difference. Then the genuine lock travelled by camel-caravan up the long, long road to Peshkhauri, thence up the Zhaibar Pass, until it reached the hands of those for whom it was intended."

"Only a lock of hair," murmured the nobleman.

"By which a soul is drawn from its body and across gulfs of echoing space," returned the man on the mat.

The nobleman studied him curiously.

"I do not know if you are a man or a demon, Khemsa," he said at last. "Few of us are what we seem. I, whom the Kshatriyas know as Kerim Shah, a prince from Iranistan, am no greater a masquerader than most men. They are all traitors in one way or another, and half of them know not whom they serve. There at least I have no doubts; for I serve King Yezdigerd of Turan."

"And I the Black Seers of Yimsha," said Khemsa; "and my masters are greater than yours, for they have accomplished by their arts what Yezdigerd could not with a hundred thousand swords."

Outside, the moan of the tortured thousands shuddered up to the stars which crusted the sweating Vendhyan night, and the conchs bellowed like oxen in pain.

In the gardens of the palace the torches glinted on polished helmets and curved swords and gold-chased corselets. All the noble-born fighting-men of Ayodhya were gathered in the great palace or about it, and at each broad-arched gate and door fifty archers stood on guard, with bows in their hands. But Death stalked through the royal palace and none could stay his ghostly tread.

On the dais under the golden dome the king cried out again, racked by awful paroxysms. Again his voice came faintly and far away, and again the Devi bent to him, trembling with a fear that was darker than the terror of death.

"Yasmina!" Again that far, weirdly dreeing cry, from realms immeasurable. "Aid me! I am far from my mortal house! Wizards have drawn my soul through the wind-blown darkness. They seek to snap the silver cord that binds me to my dying body. They cluster around me; their hands are taloned, their eyes are red like flame burning in darkness. *Aie*, save me, my sister! Their fingers sear me like fire! They would slay my body and damn my soul! What is this they bring before me?—*Aie!*"

At the terror in his hopeless cry Yasmina screamed uncontrollably and threw herself bodily upon him in the abandon of her anguish. He was torn by a terrible convulsion; foam flew from his contorted lips and his writhing fingers left their marks on the girl's shoulders. But the glassy blankness passed from his eyes like smoke blown from a fire, and he looked up at his sister with recognition.

"Brother!" she sobbed. "Brother—"

"Swift!" he gasped, and his weakening voice was rational. "I know now what brings me to the pyre. I have been on a far journey and I understand. I have been ensorceled by the wizards of the Himelians. They drew my soul out of my body and far away, into a stone room. There they strove to break the silver cord of life, and thrust my soul into the body of a foul night-weird their sorcery summoned up from hell. Ah! I feel their pull upon me now! Your cry and the grip of your fingers brought me back, but I am going fast. My soul clings to my body, but its hold weakens. Quick—kill me, before they can trap my soul for ever!"

"I can not!" she wailed, smiting her naked breasts.

"Swiftly, I command you!" There was the old imperious note in his failing whisper. "You have never disobeyed me—obey my last command! Send my soul clean to Asura! Haste, lest you damn me to spend eternity as a filthy gaunt of darkness. Strike, I command you! *Strike!*"

Sobbing wildly, Yasmina plucked a jeweled dagger from her girdle and plunged it to the hilt in his breast. He stiffened and then went limp, a grim smile curving his dead lips. Yasmina hurled herself face-down on the rush-covered floor, beating the reeds with her clenched hands. Outside, the gongs and conchs brayed and thundered and the priests gashed themselves with copper knives.

2. A Barbarian from the Hills

CHUNDER SHAN, GOVERNOR of Peshkhauri, laid down his golden pen and carefully scanned that which he had written on parchment that bore his offical seal. He had ruled Peshkhauri so long only because he weighed his every word, spoken or written. Danger breeds caution, and only a wary man lives long in that wild country where the hot Vendhyan plains meet the crags of the Himelians. An hour's ride westward or northward and one crossed the border and was among the Hills where men lived by the law of the knife.

The governor was alone in his chamber, seated at his ornately-carven table of inlaid ebony. Through the wide window, open for the coolness, he could see a square of the blue Himelian night, dotted with great white stars. An adjacent parapet was a shadowy line, and further crenelles and embrasures were barely hinted at in the dim starlight. The governor's fortress was strong, and situated outside the walls of the city it guarded. The breeze that stirred the tapestries on the wall brought faint noises from the streets of Peshkhauri—occasional snatches of wailing song, or the thrum of a cithern.

The governor read what he had written, slowly, with his open hand shading his eyes from the bronze butter-lamp, his lips moving. Absently, as he read, he heard the drum of horses' hoofs outside the barbican, the sharp staccato of the guards' challenge. He did not heed, intent upon his letter. It was addressed to the *wazam* of Vendhya, at the royal court of Ayodhya, and it stated, after the customary salutations:

"Let it be known to your excellency that I have faithfully carried out your excellency's instructions. The

63

seven tribesmen are well guarded in their prison, and I have repeatedly sent word into the hills that their chief come in person to bargain for their release. But he has made no move, except to send word that unless they are freed he will burn Peshkhauri and cover his saddle with my hide, begging your excellency's indulgence. This he is quite capable of attempting, and I have tripled the numbers of the lance guards. The man is not a native of Ghulistan. I can not with certainty predict his next move. But since it is the wish of the Devi—"

He was out of his ivory chair and on his feet facing the arched door, all in one instant. He snatched at the curved sword lying in its ornate scabbard on the table, and then checked the movement.

It was a woman who had entered unannounced, a woman whose gossamer robes did not conceal the rich garments beneath any more than they concealed the suppleness and beauty of her tall, slender figure. A filmy veil fell below her breasts, supported by a flowing head-dress bound about with a triple gold braid and adorned with a golden crescent. Her dark eyes regarded the astonished governor over the veil, and then with an imperious gesture of her white hand, she uncovered her face.

"Devi!" The governor dropped to his knee before her, his surprize and confusion somewhat spoiling the stateliness of his obeisance. With a gesture she motioned him to rise, and he hastened to lead her to the ivory chair, all the while bowing level with his girdle. But his first words were of reproof.

"Your Majesty! This was most unwise! The border is unsettled. Raids from the hills are incessant. You came with a large attendance?"

"An ample retinue followed me to Peshkhauri," she answered. "I lodged my people there and came on to the fort with my maid, Gitara."

Chunder Shan groaned in horror.

"Devi! You do not understand the peril. An hour's ride from this spot the hills swarm with barbarians who make a profession of murder and rapine. Women have been stolen and men stabbed between the fort and the city. Peshkhauri is not like your southern provinces—"

"But I am here, and unharmed," she interrupted with a trace of impatience. "I showed my signet ring to the guard at the gate, and to the one outside your door, and they admitted me unannounced, not knowing me, but supposing me to be a secret courier from Ayodhya. Let us not now waste time.

"You have received no word from the chief of the barbarians?"

"None save threats and curses, Devi. He is wary and suspicious. He deems it a trap, and perhaps he is not to be blamed. The Kshatriyas have not always kept their promises to the hill people."

"He must be brought to terms!" broke in Yasmina, the knuckles of her clenched hands showing white.

"I do not understand." The governor shook his head. "When I chanced to capture these seven hillmen, I reported their capture to the *wazam*, as is the custom, and then, before I could hang them, there came an order to hold them and communicate with their chief. This I did, but the man holds aloof, as I have said. These men are of the tribe of Afghulis, but he is a foreigner from the west, and he is called Conan. I have threatened to hang them tomorrow at dawn, if he does not come."

"Good!" exclaimed the Devi. "You have done well. And I will tell you why I have given these orders. My brother—" she faltered, choking, and the governor bowed his head, with the customary gesture of respect for a departed sovereign.

"The king of Vendhya was destroyed by magic," she said at last. "I have devoted my life to the destruction of his murderers. As he died he gave me a clue, and I have followed it. I have read the *Book of Skelos*, and talked with nameless hermits in the caves below Jhelai. I learned how, and by whom, he was destroyed. His enemies were the Black Seers of Mount Yimsha."

"Asura!" whispered Chunder Shan, paling.

Her eyes knifed him through. "Do you fear them?"

"Who does not, your Majesty?" he replied. "They are black devils, haunting the uninhabited hills beyond the Zhaibar. But the sages say that they seldom interfere in the lives of mortal men."

"Why they slew my brother I do not know," she answered. "But I have sworn on the altar of Asura to destroy them! And I need the aid of a man beyond the border. A Kshatriya army, unaided, would never reach Yimsha."

"Aye," muttered Chunder Shan. "You speak the truth there. It would be fight every step of the way, with hairy hillmen hurling down boulders from every height, and rushing us with their long knives in every valley. The Turanians fought their way through the Himelians once, but how many returned to Khurusun? Few of those who escaped the swords of the Kshatriyas, after the king, your brother, defeated their host on the Jhumda River, ever saw Secunderam again."

"And so I must control men across the border," she said, "men who know the way to Mount Yimsha—"

"But the tribes fear the Black Seers and shun the unholy mountain," broke in the governor.

"Does the chief, Conan, fear them?" she asked.

"Well, as to that," muttered the governor, "I doubt if there is anything that devil fears."

"So I have been told. Therefore he is the man I must deal with. He wishes the release of his seven men. Very well; their ransom shall be the heads of the Black Seers!" Her voice thrummed with hate as she uttered the last words, and her hands clenched at her sides. She looked an image of incarnate passion as she stood there with her head thrown high and her bosom heaving.

Again the governor knelt, for part of his wisdom was the knowledge that a woman in such an emotional tempest is as perilous as a blind cobra to any about her.

"It shall be as you wish, your Majesty." Then as she presented a calmer aspect, he rose and ventured to drop a word of warning. "I can not predict what the chief Conan's action will be. The tribesmen are always turbulent, and I have reason to believe that emissaries from the Turanians are stirring them up to raid our borders. As your majesty knows, the Turanians have established themselves in Secunderam and other northern cities, though the hill tribes remain unconquered. King Yezdigerd has long looked southward with greedy lust and perhaps is seeking to gain by treachery what he could not win by force of arms. I have thought that Conan might well be one of his spies."

"We shall see," she answered. "If he loves his followers, he will be at the gates at dawn, to parley. I shall spend the night in the fortress. I came in disguise to Peshkhauri, and lodged my retinue at an inn instead of the palace. Besides my people, only yourself knows of my presence here."

"I shall escort you to your quarters, your Majesty," said the governor, and as they emerged from the doorway, he beckoned the warrior on guard there, and the man fell in behind them, spear held at salute.

The maid waited, veiled like her mistress, outside the

67

door, and the group traversed a wide, winding corridor, lighted by smoky torches, and reached the quarters reserved for visiting notables—generals and viceroys, mostly; none of the royal family had ever honored the fortress before. Chunder Shan had a perturbed feeling that the suite was not suitable to such an exalted personage as the Devi, and though she sought to make him feel at ease in her presence, he was glad when she dismissed him and he bowed himself out. All the menials of the fort had been summoned to serve his royal guest—though he did not divulge her identity—and he stationed a squad of spearmen before her doors, among them the warrior who had guarded his own chamber. In his preoccupation he forgot to replace the man.

The governor had not been gone long from her when Yasmina suddenly remembered something else which she had wished to discuss with him, but had forgotten until that moment. It concerned the past actions of one Kerim Shah, a nobleman from Iranistan, who had dwelt for a while in Peshkhauri before coming on to the court at Ayodhya. A vague suspicion concerning the man had been stirred by a glimpse of him in Peshkhauri that night. She wondered if he had followed her from Ayodhya. Being a truly remarkable Devi, she did not summon the governor to her again, but hurried out into the corridor alone, and hastened toward his chamber.

Chunder Shan, entering his chamber, closed the door and went to his table. There he took the letter he had been writing and tore it to bits. Scarcely had he finished when he heard something drop softly onto the parapet adjacent to the window. He looked up to see a figure loom briefly against the stars, and then a man

68

dropped lightly into the room. The light glinted on a long sheen of steel in his hand.

"Shhhh!" he warned. "Don't make a noise, or I'll send the devil a henchman!"

The governor checked his motion toward the sword on the table. He was within reach of the yard-long Zhaibar knife that glittered in the intruder's fist, and he knew the desperate quickness of a hillman.

The invader was a tall man, at once strong and supple. He was dressed like a hillman, but his dark features and blazing blue eyes did not match his garb. Chunder Shan had never seen a man like him; he was not an Easterner, but some barbarian from the West. But his aspect was as untamed and formidable as any of the hairy tribesmen who haunt the hills of Ghulistan.

"You come like a thief in the night," commented the governor, recovering some of his composure, although he remembered that there was no guard within call. Still, the hillman could not know that.

"I climbed a bastion," snarled the intruder. "A guard thrust his head over the battlement in time for me to rap it with my knife-hilt."

"You are Conan?"

"Who else? You sent word into the hills that you wished for me to come and parley with you. Well, by Crom, I've come! Keep away from that table or I'll gut you."

"I merely wish to seat myself," answered the governor, carefully sinking into the ivory chair, which he wheeled away from the table. Conan moved restlessly before him, glancing suspiciously at the door, thumbing the razor edge of his three-foot knife. He did not walk like an Afghuli, and was bluntly direct where the East is subtle.

"You have seven of my men," he said abruptly. "You

69

refused the ransom I offered. What the devil do you want?"

"Let us discuss terms," answered Chunder Shan cautiously.

"Terms?" There was a timbre of dangerous anger in his voice. "What do you mean? Haven't I offered you gold?"

Chunder Shan laughed.

"Gold? There is more gold in Peshkhauri than you ever saw."

"You're a liar," retorted Conan. "I've seen the *suk* of the goldsmiths in Khurusun."

"Well, more than an Afghuli ever saw," amended Chunder Shan. "And it is but a drop of all the treasure of Vendhya. Why should we desire gold? It would be more to our advantage to hang these seven thieves."

Conan ripped out a sulfurous oath and the long blade quivered in his grip as the muscles rose in ridges on his brown arm.

"I'll split your head like a ripe melon!"

A wild blue flame flickered in the hillman's eyes, but Chunder Shan shrugged his shoulders, though keeping an eye on the keen steel.

"You can kill me easily, and probably escape over the wall afterward. But that would not save the seven tribesmen. My men would surely hang them. And these men are headmen among the Afghulis."

"I know it," snarled Conan. "The tribe is baying like wolves at my heels because I have not procured their release. Tell me in plain words what you want, because, by Crom! if there's no other way, I'll raise a horde and lead it to the very gates of Peshkhauri!"

Looking at the man as he stood squarely, knife in fist and eyes glaring, Chunder Shan did not doubt that he was capable of it. The governor did not believe any hillhorde could take Peshkhauri, but he did not wish a devastated countryside.

"There is a mission you must perform," he said, choosing his words with as much care as if they had been razors. "There—"

Conan had sprung back, wheeling to face the door at the same instant, lips asnarl. His barbarian ears had caught the quick tread of soft slippers outside the door. The next instant the door was thrown open and a slim, silk-robed form entered hastily, pulling the door shut—then stopping short at sight of the hillman.

Chunder Shan sprang up, his heart jumping into his mouth.

"Devi!" he cried involuntarily, losing his head momentarily in his fright.

"*Devi!*" It was like an explosive echo from the hillman's lips. Chunder Shan saw recognition and intent flame up in the fierce blue eyes.

The governor shouted desperately and caught at his sword, but the hillman moved with the devastating speed of a hurricane. He sprang, knocked the governor sprawling with a savage blow of his knife-hilt, swept up the astounded Devi in one brawny arm and leaped for the window. Chunder Shan, struggling frantically to his feet, saw the man poise an instant on the sill in a flutter of silken skirts and white limbs that was his royal captive, and heard his fierce, exultant snarl: "*Now* dare to hang my men!" and then Conan leaped to the parapet and was gone. A wild scream floated back to the governor's ears.

"Guard! *Guard!*" screamed the governor, struggling up and running drunkenly to the door. He tore it open and reeled into the hall. His shouts re-echoed along the

71

corridors, and warriors came running, gaping to see the governor holding his broken head, from which the blood streamed.

"Turn out the lancers!" he roared. "There has been an abduction!" Even in his frenzy he had enough sense left to withhold the full truth. He stopped short as he heard a sudden drum of hoofs outside, a frantic scream and a wild yell of barbaric exultation.

Followed by the bewildered guardsmen, the governor raced for the stair. In the courtyard of the fort a force of lancers always stood by saddled steeds, ready to ride at an instant's notice. Chunder Shan led his squadron flying after the fugitive, though his head swam so he had to hold with both hands to the saddle. He did not divulge the identity of the victim, but said merely that the noblewoman who had borne the royal signet-ring had been carried away by the chief of the Afghulis. The abductor was out of sight and hearing, but they knew the path he would strike—the road that runs straight to the mouth of the Zhaibar. There was no moon; peasant huts rose dimly in the starlight. Behind them fell away the grim bastion of the fort, and the towers of Peshkhauri. Ahead of them loomed the black walls of the Himelians.

3. *Khemsa Uses Magic*

IN THE CONFUSION that reigned in the fortress while the guard was being turned out, no one noticed that the girl who had accompanied the Devi slipped out the great arched gate and vanished in the darkness. She ran straight for the city, her garments tucked high. She did not follow the open road, but cut straight through fields and over slopes, avoiding fences and leaping irrigation ditches as surely as if it were broad daylight, and as easily as if she were a trained masculine runner. The hoof-drum of the guardsmen had faded away up the hill road before she reached the city wall. She did not go to the great gate, beneath whose arch men leaned on spears and craned their necks into the darkness, discussing the unwonted activity about the fortress. She skirted the wall until she reached a certain point where the spire of the tower was visible above the battlements. Then she placed her hands to her mouth and voiced a low weird call that carried strangely.

Almost instantly a head appeared at an embrasure and a rope came wriggling down the wall. She seized it, placed a foot in the loop at the end, and waved her arm. Then quickly and smoothly she was drawn up the sheer stone curtain. An instant later she scrambled over the merlons and stood up on a flat roof which covered a house that was built against the wall. There was an open trap there, and a man in a camel-hair robe who silently coiled the rope, not showing in any way the strain of hauling a full-grown woman up a forty-foot wall.

"Where is Kerim Shah?" she gasped, panting after her long run.

"Asleep in the house below. You have news?"

"Conan has stolen the Devi out of the fortress and carried her away into the hills!" She blurted out her news in a rush, the words stumbling over one another.

Khemsa showed no emotion, but merely nodded his turbaned head. "Kerim Shah will be glad to hear that," he said.

"Wait!" The girl threw her supple arms about his neck. She was panting hard, but not only from exertion. Her eyes blazed like black jewels in the starlight. Her upturned face was close to Khemsa's, but though he submitted to her embrace, he did not return it.

"Do not tell the Hyrkanian!" she panted. "Let us use this knowledge ourselves! The governor has gone into the hills with his riders, but he might as well chase a ghost. He has not told anyone that it was the Devi who was kidnapped. None in Peshkhauri or the fort knows it except us."

"But what good does it do us?" the man expostulated. "My masters sent me with Kerim Shah to aid him in every way—"

"Aid yourself!" she cried fiercely. "Shake off your yoke!"

"You mean—disobey my masters?" he gasped, and she felt his whole body turn cold under her arms.

"Aye!" she shook him in the fury of her emotion. "You too are a magician! Why will you be a slave, using your powers only to elevate others? Use your arts for yourself!"

"That is forbidden!" He was shaking as if with an ague. "I am not one of the Black Circle. Only by the command of the masters do I dare to use the knowledge they have taught me."

"But you *can* use it!" she argued passionately. "Do as I beg you! Of course Conan has taken the Devi to

74

hold as hostage against the seven tribesmen in the governor's prison. Destroy them, so Chunder Shan can not use them to buy back the Devi. Then let us go into the mountains and take her from the Afghulis. They can not stand against your sorcery with their knives. The treasure of the Vendhyan kings will be ours as ransom—and then when we have it in our hands, we can trick them, and sell her to the king of Turan. We shall have wealth beyond our maddest dreams. With it we can buy warriors. We will take Khorbhul, oust the Turanians from the hills, and send our hosts southward; become king and queen of an empire!"

Khemsa too was panting, shaking like a leaf in her grasp; his face showed gray in the starlight, beaded with great drops of perspiration.

"I love you!" she cried fiercely, writhing her body against his, almost strangling him in her wild embrace, shaking him in her abandon. "I will make a king of you! For love of you I betrayed my mistress; for love of me betray your masters! Why fear the Black Seers? By your love for me you have broken one of their laws already! Break the rest! You are as strong as they!"

A man of ice could not have withstood the searing heat of her passion and fury. With an inarticulate cry he crushed her to him, bending her backward and showering gasping kisses on her eyes, face and lips.

"I'll do it!" His voice was thick with laboring emotions. He staggered like a drunken man. "The arts they have taught me shall work for me, not for my masters. We shall be rulers of the world—of the world—"

"Come then!" Twisting lithely out of his embrace, she seized his hand and led him toward the trap-door. "First we must make sure that the governor does not exchange those seven Afghulis for the Devi."

He moved like a man in a daze, until they had descended a ladder and she paused in the chamber below. Kerim Shah lay on a couch motionless, an arm across his face as though to shield his sleeping eyes from the soft light of a brass lamp. She plucked Khemsa's arm and made a quick gesture across her own throat. Khemsa lifted his hand; then his expression changed and he drew away.

"I have eaten his salt," he muttered. "Besides, he can not interfere with us."

He led the girl through a door that opened on a winding stair. After their soft tread had faded into silence, the man on the couch sat up. Kerim Shah wiped the sweat from his face. A knife-thrust he did not dread, but he feared Khemsa as a man fears a poisonous reptile.

"People who plot on roofs should remember to lower their voices," he muttered. "But as Khemsa has turned against his masters, and as he was my only contact between them, I can count on their aid no longer. From now on I play the game in my own way."

Rising to his feet he went quickly to a table, drew pen and parchment from his girdle and scribbled a few succinct lines.

"To Khosru Khan, governor of Secunderam: the Cimmerian Conan has carried the Devi Yasmina to the villages of the Afghulis. It is an opportunity to get the Devi into our hands, as the king has so long desired. Send three thousand horsemen at once. I will meet them in the valley of Gurashah with native guides."

And he signed it with a name that was not in the least like Kerim Shah.

Then from a golden cage he drew forth a carrier pigeon, to whose leg he made fast the parchment, rolled

76

into a tiny cylinder and secured with gold wire. Then he went quickly to a casement and tossed the bird into the night. It wavered on fluttering wings, balanced, and was gone like a flitting shadow. Catching up helmet, sword and cloak, Kerim Shah hurried out of the chamber and down the winding stair.

The prison quarters of Peshkhauri were separated from the rest of the city by a massive wall, in which was set a single iron-bound door under an arch. Over the arch burned a lurid red cresset, and beside the door squatted a warrior with spear and shield.

This warrior, leaning on his spear, and yawning from time to time, started suddenly to his feet. He had not thought he had dozed, but a man was standing before him, a man he had not heard approach. The man wore a camel-hair robe and a green turban. In the flickering light of the cresset his features were shadowy, but a pair of lambent eyes shone surprizingly in the lurid glow.

"Who comes?" demanded the warrior, presenting his spear. "Who are you?"

The stranger did not seem perturbed, though the spear-point touched his bosom. His eyes held the warrior's with strange intensity.

"What are you obliged to do?" he asked, strangely.

"To guard the gate!" The warrior spoke thickly and mechanically; he stood rigid as a statue, his eyes slowly glazing.

"You lie! You are obliged to obey me! You have looked into my eyes, and your soul is no longer your own. Open that door!"

Stiffly, with the wooden features of an image, the guard wheeled about, drew a great key from his girdle, turned it in the massive lock and swung open the door.

77

Then he stood at attention, his unseeing stare straight ahead of him.

A woman glided from the shadows and laid an eager hand on the mesmerist's arm.

"Bid him fetch us horses, Khemsa," she whispered.

"No need of that," answered the Rakhsha. Lifting his voice slightly he spoke to the guardsman. "I have no more use for you. Kill yourself!"

Like a man in a trance the warrior thrust the butt of his spear against the base of the wall, and placed the keen head against his body, just below his ribs. Then slowly, stolidly, he leaned against it with all his weight, so that it transfixed his body and came out between his shoulders. Sliding down the shaft he lay still, the spear jutting above him its full length, like a horrible stalk growing out of his back.

The girl stared down at him in morbid fascination, until Khemsa took her arm and led her through the gate. Torches lighted a narrow space between the outer wall and a lower inner one, in which were arched doors at regular intervals. A warrior paced this enclosure, and when the gate opened he came sauntering up, so secure in his knowledge of the prison's strength that he was not suspicious until Khemsa and the girl emerged from the archway. Then it was too late. The Rahksha did not waste time in hypnotism, though his action savored of magic to the girl. The guard lowered his spear threateningly, opening his mouth to shout an alarm that would bring spearmen swarming out of the guardrooms at either end of the alleyway. Khemsa flicked the spear aside with his left hand, as a man might flick a straw, and his right flashed out and back, seeming gently to caress the warrior's neck in passing. And the guard pitched on his face without a sound, his head lolling on a broken neck.

Khemsa did not glance at him, but went straight to one of the arched doors and placed his open hand against the heavy bronze lock. With a rending shudder the portal buckled inward. As the girl followed him through, she saw that the thick teakwood hung in splinters, the bronze bolts were bent and twisted from their sockets, and the great hinges broken and disjointed. A thousand-pound battering-ram with forty men to swing it could have shattered the barrier no more completely. Khemsa was drunk with freedom and the exercise of his power, glorying in his might and flinging his strength about as a young giant exercises his thews with unnecessary vigor in the exultant pride of his prowess.

The broken door let them into a small courtyard, lit by a cresset. Opposite the door was a wide grille of iron bars. A hairy hand was visible, gripping one of these bars, and in the darkness behind them glimmered the whites of eyes.

Khemsa stood silent for a space, gazing into the shadows from which those glimmering eyes gave back his stare with burning intensity. Then his hand went into his robe and came out again, and from his opening fingers a shimmering feather of sparkling dust sifted to the flags. Instantly a flare of green fire lighted the enclosure. In the brief glare the forms of seven men, standing motionless behind the bars, were limned in vivid detail; tall, hairy men in ragged hillmen's garments. They did not speak, but in their eyes blazed the fear of death, and their hairy fingers gripped the bars.

The fire died out but the glow remained, a quivering ball of lambent green that pulsed and shimmered on the flags before Khemsa's feet. The wide gaze of the tribesmen was fixed upon it. It wavered, elongated; it turned into a luminous green smoke spiraling upward. It twisted and writhed like a great shadowy serpent, then broadened and billowed out in shining folds and whirls. It grew to a cloud moving silently over the flags—straight toward the grille. The men watched its coming with dilated eyes; the bars quivered with the grip of their desperate fingers. Bearded lips parted but no sound came forth. The green cloud rolled on the bars and blotted them from sight; like a fog it oozed through the grille and hid the men within. From the enveloping folds came a strangled gasp, as of a man plunged suddenly under the surface of water. That was all.

Khemsa touched the girl's arm, as she stood with parted lips and dilated eyes. Mechanically she turned away with him, looking back over her shoulder. Already the mist was thinning; close to the bars she saw a pair of sandaled feet, the toes turned upward—she glimpsed the indistinct outlines of seven still, prostrate shapes.

"And now for a steed swifter than the fastest horse ever bred in a mortal stable," Khemsa was saying. "We will be in Afghulistan before dawn."

4. An Encounter in the Pass

YASMINA DEVI could never clearly remember the details of her abduction. The unexpectedness and violence stunned her; she had only a confused impression of a whirl of happenings—the terrifying grip of a mighty arm, the blazing eyes of her abductor, and his hot breath burning on her flesh. The leap through the window to the parapet, the mad race across battlements and roofs when the fear of falling froze her, the reckless descent of a rope bound to a merlon—he went down almost at a run, his captive folded limply over his brawny shoulder—all this was a befuddled tangle in the Devi's mind. She retained a more vivid memory of him running fleetly into the shadows of the trees, carrying her like a child, and vaulting into the saddle of a fierce Bhalkhana stallion which reared and snorted. Then there was a sensation of flying, and the racing hoofs were striking sparks of fire from the flinty road as the stallion swept up the slopes.

As the girl's mind cleared, her first sensations were furious rage and shame. She was appalled. The rulers of the golden kingdoms south of the Himelians were considered little short of divine; and she was the Devi of Vendhya! Fright was submerged in regal wrath. She cried out furiously and began struggling. She, Yasmina, to be carried on the saddle-bow of a hill chief, like a common wench of the market-place! He merely hardened his massive thews slightly against her writhings, and for the first time in her life she experienced the coercion of superior physical strength. His arms felt like iron about her slender limbs. He glanced down at her and grinned hugely. His teeth glimmered whitely in the starlight. The reins lay loose on the stallion's flowing mane, and every thew and fiber of the great beast strained as he hurtled along the boulder-strewn trail. But Conan sat easily, almost carelessly, in the saddle, riding like a centaur.

"You hill-bred dog!" she panted, quivering with the impact of shame, anger, and the realization of helplessness. "You dare—you *dare!* Your life shall pay for this! Where are you taking me?"

"To the villages of Afghulistan," he answered, casting a glance over his shoulder.

Behind them, beyond the slopes they had traversed, torches were tossing on the walls of the fortress, and he glimpsed a flare of light that meant the great gate had been opened. And he laughed, a deep-throated boom gusty as the hill wind.

"The governor has sent his riders after us," he laughed. "By Crom, we will lead him a merry chase! What do you think, Devi—will they pay seven lives for a Kshatriya princess?"

"They will send an army to hang you and your spawn of devils," she promised him with conviction.

He laughed gustily and shifted her to a more comfortable position in his arms. But she took this as a fresh outrage, and renewed her vain struggles, until she saw that her efforts were only amusing him. Besides, her light silken garments, floating on the wind, were being outrageously disarranged by her struggles. She concluded that a scornful submission was the better part of dignity, and lapsed into a smoldering quiescence.

She felt even her anger being submerged by awe as they entered the mouth of the Pass, lowering like a black well mouth in the blacker walls that rose like colossal ramparts to bar their way. It was as if a gigantic knife had cut the Zhaibar out of walls of solid rock. On either hand sheer slopes pitched up for thousands of feet, and the mouth of the Pass was dark as hate. Even Conan could not see with any accuracy, but he knew the road, even by night. And knowing that armed men were racing through the starlight after him, he did not check the stallion's speed. The great brute was not yet showing fatigue. He thundered along the road that followed the valley bed, labored up a slope, swept along a low ridge where treacherous shale on either hand lurked for the unwary, and came upon a trail that followed the lap of the left-hand wall.

Not even Conan could spy, in that darkness, an ambush set by Zhaibar tribesmen. As they swept past the black mouth of a gorge that opened into the Pass, a javelin swished through the air and thudded home behind the stallion's straining shoulder. The great beast let out his life in a shuddering sob and stumbled, going headlong in mid-stride. But Conan had recognized the flight and stroke of the javelin, and he acted with spring-steel quickness.

As the horse fell he leaped clear, holding the girl aloft to guard her from striking boulders. He lit on his feet like a cat, thrust her into a cleft of rock, and wheeled toward the outer darkness, drawing his knife.

Yasmina, confused by the rapidity of events, not quite sure just what had happened, saw a vague shape rush out of the darkness, bare feet slapping softly on the rock, ragged garments whipping on the wind of his haste. She glimpsed the flicker of steel, heard the lightning crack of stroke, parry and counter-stroke, and the crunch of bone as Conan's long knife split the other's skull.

Conan sprang back, crouching in the shelter of the

rocks. Out in the night men were moving and a stentorian voice roared: "What, you dogs! Do you flinch? In, curse you, and take them!"

Conan started, peered into the darkness and lifted his voice.

"Yar Afzal! Is it you?"

There sounded a startled imprecation, and the voice called warily.

"Conan? Is it you, Conan?"

"Aye!" The Cimmerian laughed. "Come forth, you old war-dog. I've slain one of your men."

There was movement among the rocks, a light flared dimly, and then a flame appeared and came bobbing toward him, and as it approached, a fierce bearded countenance grew out of the darkness The man who carried it held it high, thrust forward, and craned his neck to peer among the boulders it lighted; the other hand gripped a great curved tulwar. Conan stepped forward, sheathing his knife, and the other roared a greeting.

"Aye, it is Conan! Come out of your rocks, dogs! It is Conan!"

Others pressed into the wavering circle of light— wild, ragged, bearded men, with eyes like wolves, and long blades in their fists. They did not see Yasmina, for she was hidden by Conan's massive body. But peeping from her covert, she knew icy fear for the first time that night. These men were more like wolves than human beings.

"What are you hunting in the Zhaibar by night, Yar Afzal?" Conan demanded of the burly chief, who grinned like a bearded ghoul.

"Who knows what might come up the Pass after dark? We Wazulis are night-hawks. But what of you, Conan?"

"I have a prisoner," answered the Cimmerian. And moving aside he disclosed the cowering girl. Reaching a long arm into the crevice he drew her trembling forth. Her imperious bearing was gone. She stared timidly at the ring of bearded faces that hemmed her in, and was grateful for the strong arm that clasped her possessively. The torch was thrust close to her, and there was a sucking intake of breath about the ring.

"She is my captive," Conan warned, glancing pointedly at the feet of the man he had slain, just visible within the ring of light. "I was taking her to Afghulistan, but now you have slain my horse, and the Kshatriyas are close behind me."

"Come with us to my village," suggested Yar Afzal. "We have horses hidden in the gorge. They can never follow us in the darkness. They are close behind you, you say?"

"So close that I hear now the clink of their hoofs on the flint," answered Conan grimly.

Instantly there was movement; the torch was dashed out and the ragged shapes melted like phantoms into the darkness. Conan swept up the Devi in his arms, and she did not resist. The rocky ground hurt her slim feet in their soft slippers and she felt very small and helpless in that brutish, primordial blackness among those colossal, nighted crags.

Feeling her shiver in the wind that moaned down the defiles, Conan jerked a ragged cloak from its owner's shoulders and wrapped it about her. He also hissed a warning in her ear, ordering her to make no sound. She did not hear the distant clink of shod hoofs on rock that warned the keen-eared hillmen; but she was far too frightened to disobey, in any event.

She could see nothing but a few faint stars far above, but she knew by the deepening darkness when they

85

entered the gorge mouth. There was a stir about them, the uneasy movement of horses. A few muttered words, and Conan mounted the horse of the man he had killed, lifting the girl up in front of him. Like phantoms except for the click of their hoofs, the band swept away up the shadowy gorge. Behind them on the trail they left the dead horse and the dead man, which were found less than half an hour later by the riders from the fortress, who recognized the man as a Wazuli and drew their own conclusions accordingly.

Yasmina, snuggled warmly in her captor's arms, grew drowsy in spite of herself. The motion of the horse, though it was uneven, uphill and down, yet possessed a certain rhythm which combined with weariness and emotional exhaustion to force sleep upon her. She had lost all sense of time or direction. They moved in soft thick darkness, in which she sometimes glimpsed vaguely gigantic walls sweeping up like black ramparts, or great crags shouldering the stars; at times she sensed echoing depths beneath them, or felt the wind of dizzy heights blowing cold about her. Gradually these things faded into a dreamy unwakefulness in which the clink of hoofs and the creak of saddles were like the irrelevant sounds in a dream.

She was vaguely aware when the motion ceased and she was lifted down and carried a few steps. Then she was laid down on something soft and rustling, and something—a folded coat perhaps—was thrust under her head, and the cloak in which she was wrapped was carefully tucked about her. She heard Yar Afzal laugh.

"A rare prize, Conan; fit mate for a chief of the Afghulis."

"Not for me," came Conan's answering rumble. "This wench will buy the lives of my seven headmen, blast their souls."

86

That was the last she heard as she sank into dreamless slumber.

She slept while armed men rode through the dark hills, and the fate of kingdoms hung in the balance. Through the shadowy gorges and defiles that night there rang the hoofs of galloping horses, and the starlight glimmered on helmets and curved blades, until the ghoulish shapes that haunt the crags stared into the darkness from ravine and boulder and wondered what things were afoot.

A band of these sat gaunt horses in the black pit-mouth of a gorge as the hurrying hoofs swept past. Their leader, a well-built man in a helmet and gilt-braided cloak, held up his hand warningly, until the riders had sped on. Then he laughed softly.

"They must have lost the trail! Or else they have found that Conan has already reached the Afghuli villages. It will take many riders to smoke out that hive. There will be squadrons riding up the Zhaibar by dawn."

"If there is fighting in the hills there will be looting," muttered a voice behind him, in the dialect of the Irakzai.

"There will be looting," answered the man with the helmet. "But first it is our business to reach the valley of Gurashah and await the riders that will be galloping southward from Secunderam before daylight."

He lifted his reins and rode out of the defile, his men falling in behind him—thirty ragged phantoms in the starlight.

5. *The Black Stallion*

THE SUN WAS well up when Yasmina awoke. She did not start and stare blankly, wondering where she was. She awoke with full knowledge of all that had occurred. Her supple limbs were stiff from her long ride, and her firm flesh still seemed to feel the contact of the muscular arm that had borne her so far.

She was lying on a sheepskin covering a pallet of leaves on a hard-beaten dirt floor. A folded sheepskin coat was under her head, and she was wrapped in a ragged cloak. She was in a large room, the walls of which were crudely but strongly built of uncut rocks, plastered with sun-baked mud. Heavy beams supported a roof of the same kind, in which showed a trap-door up to which led a ladder. There were no windows in the thick walls, only loop-holes. There was one door, a sturdy bronze affair that must have been looted from some Vendhyan border tower. Opposite it was a wide opening in the wall, with no door, but several strong wooden bars in place. Beyond them Yasmina saw a magnificent black stallion munching a pile of dried grass. The building was fort, dwelling-place and stable in one.

At the other end of the room a girl in the vest and baggy trousers of a hill-woman squatted beside a small fire, cooking strips of meat on an iron grid laid over blocks of stone. There was a sooty cleft in the wall a few feet from the floor, and some of the smoke found its way out there. The rest floated in blue wisps about the room.

The hill-girl glanced at Yasmina over her shoulder, displaying a bold, handsome face, and then continued her cooking. Voices boomed outside; then the door was kicked open, and Conan strode in. He looked more enormous than ever with the morning sunlight behind him, and Yasmina noted some details that had escaped her the night before. His garments were clean and not ragged. The broad Bakhariot girdle that supported his knife in its ornamented scabbard would have matched the robes of a prince, and there was a glint of fine Turanian mail under his shirt.

"Your captive is awake, Conan," said the Wazuli girl, and he grunted, strode up to the fire and swept the strips of mutton off into a stone dish.

The squatting girl laughed up at him, with some spicy jest, and he grinned wolfishly, and hooking a toe under her haunches, tumbled her sprawling onto the floor. She seemed to derive considerable amusement from this bit of rough horse-play, but Conan paid no more heed to her. Producing a great hunk of bread from somewhere, with a copper jug of wine, he carried the lot to Yasmina, who had risen from her pallet and was regarding him doubtfully.

"Rough fare for a Devi, girl, but our best," he grunted. "It will fill your belly, at least."

He set the platter on the floor, and she was suddenly aware of a ravenous hunger. Making no comment, she seated herself cross-legged on the floor, and taking the dish in her lap, she began to eat, using her fingers, which were all she had in the way of table utensils. After all, adaptability is one of the tests of true aristocracy. Conan stood looking down at her, his thumbs hooked in his girdle. He never sat cross-legged, after the Eastern fashion.

"Where am I?" she asked abruptly.

"In the hut of Yar Afzal, the chief of the Khurum Wazulis," he answered. "Afghulistan lies a good many miles farther on to the west. We'll hide here awhile. The

89

Kshatriyas are beating up the hills for you—several of their squads have been cut up by the tribes already."

"What are you going to do?" she asked.

"Keep you until Chunder Shan is willing to trade back my seven cow-thieves," he grunted. "Women of the Wazulis are crushing ink out of *shoki* leaves, and after a while you can write a letter to the governor."

A touch of her old imperious wrath shook her, as she thought how maddeningly her plans had gone awry, leaving her captive of the very man she had plotted to get into her power. She flung down the dish, with the remnants of her meal, and sprang to her feet, tense with anger.

"I will not write a letter! If you do not take me back, they will hang your seven men, and a thousand more besides!"

The Wazuli girl laughed mockingly, Conan scowled, and then the door opened and Yar Afzal came swaggering in. The Wazuli chief was as tall as Conan, and of greater girth, but he looked fat and slow beside the hard compactness of the Cimmerian. He plucked his red-stained beard and stared meaningly at the Wazuli girl, and that wench rose and scurried out without delay. Then Yar Afzal turned to his guest.

"The damnable people murmur, Conan," quoth he. "They wish me to murder you and take the girl to hold for ransom. They say that anyone can tell by her garments that she is a noble lady. They say why should the Afghuli dogs profit by her, when it is the people who take the risk of guarding her?"

"Lend me your horse," said Conan. "I'll take her and go."

"Pish!" boomed Yar Afzal. "Do you think I can't handle my own people? I'll have them dancing in their shirts if they cross me! They don't love you—or any

90

other outlander—but you saved my life once, and I will not forget. Come out, though, Conan; a scout has returned."

Conan hitched at his girdle and followed the chief outside. They closed the door after them, and Yasmina peeped through a loop-hole. She looked out on a level space before the hut. At the farther end of that space there was a cluster of mud and stone huts, and she saw naked children playing among the boulders, and the slim erect women of the hills going about their tasks.

Directly before the chief's hut a circle of hairy, ragged men squatted, facing the door. Conan and Yar Afzal stood a few paces before the door, and between them and the ring of warriors another man sat cross-legged. This one was addressing his chief in the harsh accents of the Wazuli which Yasmina could scarcely understand, though as part of her royal education she had been taught the languages of Iranistan and the kindred tongues of Ghulistan.

"I taiked with a Dagozai who saw the riders last night," said the scout. "He was lurking near when they came to the spot where we ambushed the lord Conan. He overheard their speech. Chunder Shan was with them. They found the dead horse, and one of the men recognized it as Conan's. Then they found the man Conan slew, and knew him for a Wazuli. It seemed to them that Conan had been slain and the girl taken by the Wazuli; so they turned aside from their purpose of following to Afghulistan. But they did not know from which village the dead man was come, and we had left no trail a Kshatriya could follow.

"So they rode to the nearest Wazuli village, which was the village of Jugra, and burnt it and slew many of the people. But the men of Khojur came upon them in darkness and slew some of them, and wounded the

91

governor. So the survivors retired down the Zhaibar in the darkness before dawn, but they returned with reinforcements before sunrise, and there has been skirmishing and fighting in the hills all morning. It is said that a great army is being raised to sweep the hills about the Zhaibar. The tribes are whetting their knives and laying ambushes in every pass from here to Gurashah valley. Moreover, Kerim Shah has returned to the hills."

A grunt went around the circle, and Yasmina leaned closer to the loop-hole at the name she had begun to mistrust.

"Where went he?" demanded Yar Afzal.

"The Dagozai did not know; with him were thirty Irakzai of the lower villages. They rode into the hills and disappeared."

"These Irakzai are jackals that follow a lion for crumbs," growled Yar Afzal. "They have been lapping up the coins Kerim Shah scatters among the border tribes to buy men like horses. I like him not, for all he is our kinsman from Iranistan."

"He's not even that," said Conan. "I know him of old. He's an Hyrkanian, a spy of Yezdigerd's. If I catch him I'll hang his hide to a tamarisk."

"But the Kshatriyas!" clamored the men in the semicircle. "Are we to squat on our haunches until they smoke us out? They will learn at last in which Wazuli village the wench is held. We are not loved by the Zhaibari; they will help the Kshatriyas hunt us out."

"Let them come," grunted Yar Afzal. "We can hold the defiles against a host."

One of the men leaped up and shook his fist at Conan.

"Are we to take all the risks while he reaps the

92

rewards?" he howled. "Are we to fight his battles for him?"

With a stride Conan reached him and bent slightly to stare full into his hairy face. The Cimmerian had not drawn his long knife, but his left hand grasped the scabbard, jutting the hilt suggestively forward.

"I ask no man to fight my battles," he said softly. "Draw your blade if you dare, you yapping dog!"

The Wazuli started back, snarling like a cat.

"Dare to touch me and here are fifty men to rend you apart!" he screeched.

"What!" roared Yar Afzal, his face purpling with wrath. His whiskers bristled, his belly swelled with his rage. "Are you chief of Khurum? Do the Wazulis take orders from Yar Afzal, or from a low-bred cur?"

The man cringed before his invincible chief, and Yar Afzal, striding up to him, seized him by the throat and choked him until his face was turning black. Then he hurled the man savagely against the ground and stood over him with his tulwar in his hand.

"Is there any who questions my authority?" he roared, and his warriors looked down sullenly as his bellicose glare swept their semicircle. Yar Afzal grunted scornfully and sheathed his weapon with a gesture that was the apex of insult. Then he kicked the fallen agitator with a concentrated vindictiveness that brought howls from his victim.

"Get down the valley to the watchers on the heights and bring word if they have seen anything," commanded Yar Afzal, and the man went, shaking with fear and grinding his teeth with fury.

Yar Afzal then seated himself ponderously on a stone, growling in his beard. Conan stood near him, legs braced apart, thumbs hooked in his girdle,

93

narrowly watching the assembled warriors. They stared at him sullenly, not daring to brave Yar Afzal's fury, but hating the foreigner as only a hillman can hate.

"Now listen to me, you sons of nameless dogs, while I tell you what the lord Conan and I have planned to fool the Kshatriyas"—the boom of Yar Afzal's bull-like voice followed the discomfited warrior as he slunk away from the assembly.

The man passed by the cluster of huts, where women who had seen his defeat laughed at him and called stinging comments, and hastened on along the trail that wound among spurs and rocks toward the valley head.

Just as he rounded the first turn that took him out of sight of the village, he stopped short, gaping stupidly. He had not believed it possible for a stranger to enter the valley of Khurum without being detected by the hawk-eyed watchers along the heights; yet a man sat cross-legged on a low ledge beside the path—a man in a camel-hair robe and a green turban.

The Wazuli's mouth gaped for a yell, and his hand leaped to his knife-hilt. But at that instant his eyes met those of the stranger and the cry died in his throat, his fingers went limp. He stood like a statue, his own eyes glazed and vacant.

For minutes the scene held motionless; then the man on the ledge drew a cryptic symbol in the dust on the rock with his forefinger. The Wazuli did not see him place anything within the compass of that emblem, but presently something gleamed there—a round, shiny black ball that looked like polished jade. The man in the green turban took this up and tossed it to the Wazuli, who mechanically caught it.

"Carry this to Yar Afzal," he said, and the Wazuli

94

turned like an automaton and went back along the path, holding the black jade ball in his outstretched hand. He did not even turn his head to the renewed jeers of the women as he passed the huts. He did not seem to hear.

The man on the ledge gazed after him with a cryptic smile. A girl's head rose above the rim of the ledge and she looked at him with admiration and a touch of fear that had not been present the night before.

"Why did you do that?" she asked.

He ran his fingers through her dark locks caressingly.

"Are you still dizzy from your flight on the horse-of-air, that you doubt my wisdom?" he laughed. "As long as Yar Afzal lives, Conan will bide safe among the Wazuli fighting-men. Their knives are sharp, and there are many of them. What I plot will be safer, even for me, than to seek to slay him and take her from among them. It takes no wizard to predict what the Wazulis will do, and what Conan will do, when my victim hands the globe of Yezud to the chief of Khurum."

Back before the hut, Yar Afzal halted in the midst of some tirade, surprized and displeased to see the man he had sent up the valley, pushing his way through the throng.

"I bade you go to the watchers!" the chief bellowed. "You have not had time to come from them."

The other did not reply; he stood woodenly, staring vacantly into the chief's face, his palm outstretched holding the jade ball. Conan, looking over Yar Afzal's shoulder, murmured something and reached to touch the chief's arm, but as he did so, Yar Afzal, in a paroxysm of anger, struck the man with his clenched fist and felled him like an ox. As he fell, the jade sphere

95

rolled to Yar Afzal's foot, and the chief, seeming to see it for the first time, bent and picked it up. The men, staring perplexedly at their senseless comrade, saw their chief bend, but they did not see what he picked up from the ground.

Yar Afzal straightened, glanced at the jade, and made a motion to thrust it into his girdle.

"Carry that fool to his hut," he growled. "He has the look of a lotus-eater. He returned me a blank stare. I—*aie!*"

In his right hand, moving toward his girdle, he had suddenly felt movement where movement should not be. His voice died away as he stood and glared at nothing; and inside his clenched right hand he felt the quivering of *change*, of *motion*, of *life*. He no longer held a smooth shining sphere in his fingers. And he dared not look; his tongue clove to the roof of his mouth, and he could not open his hand. His astonished warriors saw Yar Afzal's eyes distend, the color ebb from his face. Then suddenly a bellow of agony burst from his bearded lips; he swayed and fell as if struck by lightning, his right arm tossed out in front of him. Face down he lay, and from between his opening fingers crawled a spider—a hideous, black, hairy-legged monster whose body shone like black jade. The men yelled and gave back suddenly, and the creature scuttled into a crevice of the rocks and disappeared.

The warriors started up, glaring wildly, and a voice rose above their clamor, a far-carrying voice of command which came from none knew where. Afterward each man there—who still lived—denied that he had shouted, but all there heard it.

"Yar Afzal is dead! Kill the outlander!"

That shout focused their whirling minds as one. Doubt, bewilderment and fear vanished in the uproaring surge of the blood-lust. A furious yell rent the skies as the tribesmen responded instantly to the suggestion. They came headlong across the open space, cloaks flapping, eyes blazing, knives lifted.

Conan's action was as quick as theirs. As the voice shouted he sprang for the hut door. But they were closer to him than he was to the door, and with one foot on the sill he had to wheel and parry the swipe of a yard-long blade. He split the man's skull—ducked another swinging knife and gutted the wielder—felled a man with his left fist and stabbed another in the belly—and heaved back mightily against the closed door with his shoulders. Hacking blades were nicking chips out of the jambs about his ears, but the door flew open under the impact of his shoulders, and he went stumbling backward into the room. A bearded tribesman, thrusting with all his fury as Conan sprang back, over-reached and pitched head-first through the doorway. Conan stooped, grasped the slack of his garments and hauled him clear, and slammed the door in the faces of the men who came surging into it. Bones snapped under the impact, and the next instant Conan slammed the bolts into place and whirled with desperate haste to meet the man who sprang from the floor and tore into action like a madman.

Yasmina cowered in a corner, staring in horror as the two men fought back and forth across the room, almost trampling her at times; the flash and clangor of their blades filled the room, and outside the mob clamored like a wolf-pack, hacking deafeningly at the bronze door with their long knives, and dashing huge rocks against it. Somebody fetched a tree trunk, and the door began to stagger under the thunderous assault. Yasmina clasped her ears, staring wildly. Violence and fury within, cataclysmic madness without. The stallion in his stall neighed and reared, thundering with his heels against the walls. He wheeled and launched his hoofs through the bars just as the tribesman, backing away from Conan's murderous swipes, stumbled against them. His spine cracked in three places like a rotten branch and he was hurled headlong against the Cimmerian, bearing him backward so that they both crashed to the beaten floor.

Yasmina cried out and ran forward; to her dazed sight it seemed that both were slain. She reached them just as Conan threw aside the corpse and rose. She caught his arm, trembling from head to foot.

"Oh, you live! I thought—I thought you were dead!"

He glanced down at her quickly, into the pale, upturned face and the wide staring dark eyes.

"Why are you trembling?" he demanded. "Why should you care if I live or die?"

A vestige of her poise returned to her, and she drew away, making a rather pitiful attempt at playing the Devi.

"You are preferable to those wolves howling without," she answered, gesturing toward the door, the stone sill of which was beginning to splinter away.

"That won't hold long," he muttered, then turned and went swiftly to the stall of the stallion.

Yasmina clenched her hands and caught her breath as she saw him tear aside the splintered bars and go into the stall with the maddened beast. The stallion reared above him, neighing terribly, hoofs lifted, eyes and teeth flashing and ears laid back, but Conan leaped and caught his mane with a display of sheer strength that seemed impossible, and dragged the beast down on his forelegs. The steed snorted and quivered, but stood still while the man bridled him and clapped on the gold-worked saddle, with the wide silver stirrups.

Wheeling the beast around in the stall, Conan called quickly to Yasmina, and the girl came, sidling nervously past the stallion's heels. Conan was working at the stone wall, talking swiftly as he worked.

"A secret door in the wall here, that not even the Wazuli know about. Yar Afzal showed it to me once when he was drunk. It opens out into the mouth of the ravine behind the hut. Ha!"

As he tugged at a projection that seemed casual, a whole section of the wall slid back on oiled iron runners. Looking through, the girl saw a narrow defile opening in a sheer stone cliff within a few feet of the hut's back wall. Then Conan sprang into the saddle and hauled her up before him. Behind them the great door groaned like a living thing and crashed in, and a yell rang to the roof as the entrance was instantly flooded with hairy faces and knives in hairy fists. And then the great staliion went through the wall like a javelin from a catapult, and thundered into the defile, running low, foam flying from the bit-rings.

That move came as an absolute surprize to the Wazulis. It was a surprize, too, to those stealing down the ravine. It happened so quickly—the hurricane-like charge of the great horse—that a man in a green turban was unable to get out of the way. He went down under the frantic hoofs, and a girl screamed. Conan got one glimpse of her as they thundered by—a slim, dark girl in silk trousers and a jeweled breast-band, flattening herself against the ravine wall. Then the black horse and his riders were gone up the gorge like the spume blown before a storm, and the men who came tumbling through the wall into the defile after them met that which changed their yells of blood-lust to shrill screams of fear and death.

6. *The Mountain of the Black Seers*

"WHERE NOW?" YASMINA was trying to sit erect on the rocking saddle-bow, clutching her captor. She was conscious of a recognition of shame that she should not find unpleasant the feel of his muscular flesh under her fingers.

"To Afghulistan," he answered. "It's a perilous road, but the stallion will carry us easily, unless we fall in with some of your friends, or my tribal enemies. Now that Yar Afzal is dead, those damned Wazulis will be on our heels. I'm surprized we haven't sighted them behind us already."

"Who was that man you rode down?" she asked.

"I don't know. I never saw him before. He's no Ghuli, that's certain. What the devil he was doing there is more than I can say. There was a girl with him, too."

"Yes." Her gaze was shadowed. "I can not understand that. That girl was my maid, Gitara. Do you suppose she was coming to aid me? That the man was a friend? If so, the Wazulis have captured them both."

"Well," he answered, "there's nothing we can do. If we go back, they'll skin us both. I can't understand how a girl like that could get this far into the mountains with only one man—and he a robed scholar, for that's what he looked like. There's something infernally queer in all this. That fellow Yar Afzal beat and sent away—he moved like a man walking in his sleep. I've seen the priests of Zamora perform their abominable rituals in their forbidden temples, and their victims had a stare like that man. The priests looked into their eyes and muttered incantations, and then the people became like walking dead men, with glassy eyes, doing as they were ordered.

"And then I saw what the fellow had in his hand, which Yar Afzal picked up. It was like a big black jade bead, such as the temple girls of Yezud wear when they dance before the black stone spider which is their god. Yar Afzal held it in his hand, and he didn't pick up anything else. Yet when he fell dead, a spider, like the god at Yezud, only smaller, ran out of his fingers. And then, when the Wazulis stood uncertain there, a voice cried out for them to kill me, and I know that voice didn't come from any of the warriors, nor from the women who watched by the huts. It seemed to come from *above*."

Yasmina did not reply. She glanced at the stark outlines of the mountains all about them and shuddered. Her soul shrank from their gaunt brutality. This was a grim, naked land where anything might happen. Age-old traditions invested it with shuddery horror for anyone born in the hot, luxuriant southern plains.

The sun was high, beating down with fierce heat, yet the wind that blew in fitful gusts seemed to sweep off slopes of ice. Once she heard a strange rushing above them that was not the sweep of the wind, and from the way Conan looked up, she knew it was not a common sound to him, either. She thought that a strip of the cold blue sky was momentarily blurred, as if some all but invisible object had swept between it and herself, but she could not be sure. Neither made any comment, but Conan loosened his knife in his scabbard.

They were following a faintly marked path dipping down into ravines so deep the sun never struck bottom, laboring up steep slopes where loose shale threatened to slide from beneath their feet, and following knife-edge ridges with blue-hazed echoing depths on either hand.

The sun had passed its zenith when they crossed a narrow trail winding among the crags. Conan reined the horse aside and followed it southward, going almost at right angles to their former course.

"A Galzai village is at one end of this trail," he explained. "Their women follow it to a well, for water. You need new garments."

Glancing down at her filmy attire, Yasmina agreed with him. Her cloth-of-gold slippers were in tatters, her robes and silken under-garments torn to shreds that scarcely held together decently. Garments meant for the streets of Peshkhauri were scarcely appropriate for the crags of the Himelians.

Coming to a crook in the trail, Conan dismounted, helped Yasmina down and waited. Presently he nodded, though she heard nothing.

"A woman coming along the trail," he remarked. In sudden panic she clutched his arm.

"You will not—not kill her?"

"I don't kill women ordinarily," he grunted; "though some of the hillwomen are she-wolves. No," he grinned as at a huge jest. "By Crom, I'll *pay* for her clothes! How is that?" He displayed a handful of gold coins, and replaced all but the largest. She nodded, much relieved. It was perhaps natural for men to slay and die; her flesh crawled at the thought of watching the butchery of a woman.

Presently a woman appeared around the crook of the trail—a tall, slim Galzai girl, straight as a young sapling, bearing a great empty gourd. She stopped short and the gourd fell from her hands when she saw them; she wavered as though to run, then realized that Conan was too close to her to allow her to escape, and

102

so stood still, staring at them with a mixed expression of fear and curiosity.

Conan displayed the gold coin.

"If you will give this woman your garments," he said, "I will give you this money."

The response was instant. The girl smiled broadly with surprize and delight, and, with the disdain of a hillwoman for prudish conventions, promptly yanked off her sleeveless embroidered vest, slipped down her wide trousers and stepped out of them, twitched off her wide-sleeved shirt, and kicked off her sandals. Bundling them all in a bunch, she proffered them to Conan, who handed them to the astonished Devi.

"Get behind that rock and put these on," he directed, further proving himself no native hillman. "Fold your robes up into a bundle and bring them to me when you come out."

"The money!" clamored the hill girl, stretching out her hands eagerly. "The gold you promised me!"

Conan flipped the coin to her, she caught it, bit, then thrust it into her hair, bent and caught up the gourd and went on down the path, as devoid of self-consciousness as of garments. Conan waited with some impatience while the Devi, for the first time in her pampered life, dressed herself. When she stepped from behind the rock he swore in surprize, and she felt a curious rush of emotions at the unrestrained admiration burning in his fierce blue eyes. She felt shame, embarrassment, yet a stimulation of vanity she had never before experienced, and a tingling when meeting the impact of his eyes. He laid a heavy hand on her shoulder and turned her about, staring avidly at her from all angles.

"By Crom!" said he. "In those smoky, mystic robes you were aloof and cold and far off as a star! Now you

103

are a woman of warm flesh and blood! You went behind that rock as the Devi of Vendhya; you come out as a hill girl—though a thousand times more beautiful than any wench of the Zhaibar! You were a goddess—now you are real!"

He spanked her resoundingly, and she, recognizing this as merely another expression of admiration, did not feel outraged. It was indeed as if the changing of her garments had wrought a change in her personality. The feelings and sensations she had suppressed rose to domination in her now, as if the queenly robes she had cast off had been material shackles and inhibitions.

But Conan, in his renewed admiration, did not forget that peril lurked all about them. The farther they drew away from the region of the Zhaibar, the less likely he was to encounter any Kshatriya troops. On the other hand he had been listening all throughout their flight for sounds that would tell him the vengeful Wazulis of Khurum were on their heels.

Swinging the Devi up, he followed her into the saddle and again reined the stallion westward. The bundle of garments she had given him, he hurled over a cliff, to fall into the depths of a thousand-foot gorge.

"Why did you do that?" she asked. "Why did you not give them to the girl?"

"The riders from Peshkhauri are combing these hills," he said. "They'll be ambushed and harried at every turn, and by way of reprisal they'll destroy every village they can take. They may turn westward any time. If they found a girl wearing your garments, they'd torture her into talking, and she might put them on my trail."

"What will she do?" asked Yasmina.

"Go back to her village and tell her people that a stranger attacked her," he answered. "She'll have them on our track, all right. But she had to go on and get the water first; if she dared go back without it, they'd whip the skin off her. That gives us a long start. They'll never catch us. By nightfall we'll cross the Afghuli border."

"There are no paths or signs of human habitation in these parts," she commented. "Even for the Himelians this region seems singularly deserted. We have not seen a trail since we left the one where we met the Galzai woman."

For answer he pointed to the northwest, where she glimpsed a peak in a notch of the crags.

"Yimsha," grunted Conan. "The tribes build their villages as far from that mountain as they can."

She was instantly rigid with attention.

"Yimsha!" she whispered. "The mountain of the Black Seers!"

"So they say," he answered. "This is as near as I ever approached it. I have swung north to avoid any Kshatriya troops that might be prowling through the hills. The regular trail from Khurum to Afghulistan lies farther south. This is an ancient one, and seldom used."

She was staring intently at the distant peak. Her nails bit into her pink palms.

"How long would it take to reach Yimsha from this point?"

"All the rest of the day, and all night," he answered, and grinned. "Do you want to go there? By Crom, it's no place for an ordinary human, from what the hill people say."

"Why do they not gather and destroy the devils that inhabit it?" she demanded.

"Wipe out wizards with swords? Anyway, they never interfere with people, unless the people interfere with them. I never saw one of them, though I've talked with men who swore they had. They say they've glimpsed

105

people from the tower among the crags at sunset or sunrise—tall, silent men in black robes."

"Would you be afraid to attack them?"

"I?" The idea seemed a new one to him. "Why, if they imposed upon me, it would be my life or theirs. But I have nothing to do with them. I came to these mountains to raise a following of human beings, not to war with wizards."

Yasmina did not at once reply. She stared at the peak as at a human enemy, feeling all her anger and hatred stir in her bosom anew. And another feeling began to take dim shape. She had plotted to hurl against the masters of Yimsha the man in whose arms she was now carried. Perhaps there was another way, besides the method she had planned, to accomplish her purpose. She could not mistake the look that was beginning to dawn in this wild man's eyes as they rested on her. Kingdoms have fallen when a woman's slim white hands pulled the strings of destiny. Suddenly she stiffened, pointing.

"Look!"

Just visible on the distant peak there hung a cloud of peculiar aspect. It was a frosty crimson in color, veined with sparkling gold. This cloud was in motion; it rotated, and as it whirled it contracted. It dwindled to a spinning taper that flashed in the sun. And suddenly it detached itself from the snow-tipped peak, floated out over the void like a gay-hued feather, and became invisible against the cerulean sky.

"What could that have been?" asked the girl uneasily, as a shoulder of rock shut the distant mountain from view; the phenomenon had been disturbing, even its beauty.

"The hillmen call it Yimsha's Carpet, whatever that means," answered Conan. "I've seen five hundred of them running as if the devil were at their heels, to hide themselves in caves and crags, because they saw that crimson cloud float up from the peak. What in—"

They had advanced through a narrow, knife-cut gash between turreted walls and emerged upon a broad ledge, flanked by a series of rugged slopes on one hand, and a gigantic precipice on the other. The dim trail followed this ledge, bent around a shoulder and reappeared at intervals far below, working a tedious way downward. And emerging from the cut that opened upon the ledge, the black stallion halted short, snorting. Conan urged him on impatiently, and the horse snorted and threw his head up and down, quivering and straining as if against an invisible barrier.

Conan swore and swung off, lifting Yasmina down with him. He went forward, with a hand thrown out before him as if expecting to encounter unseen resistance, but there was nothing to hinder him, though when he tried to lead the horse, it neighed shrilly and jerked back. Then Yasmina cried out, and Conan wheeled, hand starting to knife-hilt.

Neither of them had seen him come, but he stood there, with his arms folded, a man in a camel-hair robe and a green turban. Conan grunted with surprize to recognize the man the stallion had spurned in the ravine outside the Wazuli village.

"Who the devil are you?" he demanded.

The man did not answer. Conan noticed that his eyes were wide, fixed, and of a peculiar luminous quality. And those eyes held his like a magnet.

Khemsa's sorcery was based on hypnotism, as is the case with most Eastern magic. The way has been prepared for the hypnotist for untold centuries of generations who have lived and died in the firm conviction of the reality and power of hypnotism, building up, by mass thought and practise, a colossal though intangible atmosphere against which the individual, steeped in the traditions of the land, finds himself helpless.

But Conan was not a son of the East. Its traditions were meaningless to him; he was the product of an utterly alien atmosphere. Hypnotism was not even a myth in Cimmeria. The heritage that prepared a native of the East for submission to the mesmerist was not his.

He was aware of what Khemsa was trying to do to him; but he felt the impact of the man's uncanny power only as a vague impulsion, a tugging and pulling that he could shake off as a man shakes spider-webs from his garments.

Aware of hostility and black magic, he ripped out his long knife and lunged, as quick on his feet as a mountain lion.

But hypnotism was not all of Khemsa's magic. Yasmina, watching, did not see by what roguery of movement or illusion the man in the green turban avoided the terrible disemboweling thrust. But the keen blade whickered between side and lifted arm, and to Yasmina it seemed that Khemsa merely brushed his open palm lightly against Conan's bull-neck. But the Cimmerian went down like a slain ox.

Yet Conan was not dead; breaking his fall with his left hand, he slashed at Khemsa's legs even as he went down, and the Rakhsha avoided the scythe-like swipe only by a most unwizardly bound backward. Then Yasmina cried out sharply as she saw a woman she recognized as Gitara glide out from among the rocks and come up to the man. The greeting died in the Devi's throat as she saw the malevolence in the girl's beautiful face.

108

Conan was rising slowly, shaken and dazed by the cruel craft of that blow which, delivered with an art forgotten of men before Atlantis sank, would have broken like a rotten twig the neck of a lesser man. Khemsa gazed at him cautiously and a trifle uncertainly. The Rakhsha had learned the full flood of his own power when he faced at bay the knives of the maddened Wazulis in the ravine behind Khurum village; but the Cimmerian's resistance had perhaps shaken his new-found confidence a trifle. Sorcery thrives on success, not on failure.

He stepped forward, lifting his hand—then halted as if frozen, head tilted back, eyes wide open, hand raised. In spite of himself Conan followed his gaze, and so did the women—the girl cowering by the trembling stallion, and the girl beside Khemsa.

Down the mountain-slopes, like a whirl of shining dust blown before the wind, a crimson, conoid cloud came dancing. Khemsa's dark face turned ashen; his hand began to tremble, then sank to his side. The girl beside him, sensing the change in him, stared at him inquiringly.

The crimson shape left the mountain-slope and came down in a long arching swoop. It struck the ledge between Conan and Khemsa, and the Rakhsha gave back with a stifled cry. He backed away, pushing the girl Gitara back with groping, fending hands.

The crimson cloud balanced like a spinning top for an instant, whirling in a dazzling sheen on its point. Then without warning it was gone, vanished as a bubble vanishes when burst. There on the ledge stood four men. It was miraculous, incredible, impossible, yet it was true. They were not ghosts or phantoms. They were four tall men, with shaven, vulture-like heads, and black robes that hid their feet. Their hands were concealed by their wide sleeves. They stood in silence, their naked heads nodding slightly in unison. They were facing Khemsa, but behind them Conan felt his own blood turning to ice in his veins. Rising, he backed stealthily away, until he felt the stallion's shoulder trembling against his back, and the Devi crept into the shelter of his arm. There was no word spoken. Silence hung like a stifling pall.

All four of the men in black robes stared at Khemsa. Their vulture-like faces were immobile, their eyes introspective and contemplative. But Khemsa shook like a man in an ague. His feet were braced on the rock, his calves straining as if in physical combat. Sweat ran in streams down his dark face. His right hand locked on something under his brown robe so desperately that the blood ebbed from that hand and left it white. His left hand fell on the shoulder of Gitara and clutched in agony like the grasp of a drowning man. She did not flinch or whimper, though his fingers dug like talons into her firm flesh.

Conan had witnessed hundreds of battles in his wild life, but never one like this, wherein four diabolical wills sought to beat down one lesser but equally devilish will that opposed them. But he only faintly sensed the monstrous quality of that hideous struggle. With his back to the wall, driven to bay by his former masters, Khemsa was fighting for his life with all the dark power, all the frightful knowledge they had taught him through long, grim years of neophytism and vassalage.

He was stronger than even he had guessed, and the free exercise of his powers in his own behalf had tapped unsuspected reservoirs of forces. And he was nerved to super-energy by frantic fear and desperation. He reeled before the merciless impact on those hypnotic eyes, but he held his ground. His features were distorted into a bestial grin of agony, and his limbs were twisted as in a rack. It was a war of souls, of frightful brains steeped in lore forbidden to men for a million years, of mentalities which had plumbed the abysses and explored the dark stars where spawn the shadows.

Yasmina understood this better than did Conan. And she dimly understood why Khemsa could withstand the concentrated impact of those four hellish wills which might have blasted into atoms the very rock on which he stood. The reason was the girl that he clutched with the strength of his despair. She was like an anchor to his staggering soul, battered by the waves of those psychic emanations. His weakness was now his strength. His love for the girl, violent and evil though it might be, was yet a tie that bound him to the rest of humanity, providing an earthly leverage for his will, a chain that his inhuman enemies could not break; at least not break through Khemsa.

They realized that before he did. And one of them turned his gaze from the Rakhsha full upon Gitara. There was no battle there. The girl shrank and wilted like a leaf in the drouth. Irresistibly impelled, she tore herself from her lover's arms before he realized what was happening. Then a hideous thing came to pass. She began to back toward the precipice, facing her tormenters, her eyes wide and blank as dark gleaming glass from behind which a lamp has been blown out. Khemsa groaned and staggered toward her, falling into the trap set for him. A divided mind could not maintain the unequal battle. He was beaten, a straw in their hands. The girl went backward, walking like an automaton, and Khemsa reeled drunkenly after her, hands vainly outstretched, groaning, slobbering in his pain, his feet moving heavily like dead things.

On the very brink she paused, standing stiffly, her heels on the edge, and he fell on his knees and crawled whimpering toward her, groping for her, to drag her back from destruction. And just before his clumsy fingers touched her, one of the wizards laughed, like the sudden, bronze note of a bell in hell. The girl reeled suddenly and, consummate climax of exquisite cruelty, reason and understanding flooded back into her eyes, which flared with awful fear. She screamed, clutched wildly at her lover's straining hand, and then, unable to save herself, fell headlong with a moaning cry.

Khemsa hauled himself to the edge and stared over, haggardly, his lips working as he mumbled to himself. Then he turned and stared for a long minute at his torturers, with wide eyes that held no human light. And then with a cry that almost burst the rocks, he reeled up and came rushing toward them, a knife lifted in his hand.

One of the Rakhshas stepped forward and stamped his foot, and as he stamped, there came a rumbling that grew swiftly to a grinding roar. Where his foot struck, a crevice opened in the solid rock that widened instantly. Then, with a deafening crash, a whole section of the ledge gave way. There was a last glimpse of Khemsa, with arms wildly upflung, and then he vanished amidst the roar of the avalanche that thundered down into the abyss.

The four looked contemplatively at the ragged edge of rock that formed the new rim of the precipice, and then turned suddenly. Conan thrown off his feet by the shudder of the mountain, was rising, lifting Yasmina. He seemed to move as slowly as his brain was working. He was befogged and stupid. He realized that there was desperate need for him to lift the Devi on the black stallion, and ride like the wind, but an unaccountable sluggishness weighted his every thought and action.

And now the wizards had turned toward him; they raised their arms, and to his horrified sight, he saw their outlines fading, dimming, becoming hazy and nebulous, as a crimson smoke billowed around their feet and rose about them. They were blotted out by a sudden whirling cloud—and then he realized that he too was enveloped in a blinding crimson mist—he heard Yasmina scream, and the stallion cried out like a woman in pain. The Devi was torn from his arm, and as he lashed out with his knife blindly, a terrific blow like a gust of storm wind knocked him sprawling against a rock. Dazedly he saw a crimson conoid cloud spinning up and over the mountain slopes. Yasmina was gone, and so were the four men in black. Only the terrified stallion shared the ledge with him.

7. *On to Yimsha*

As MISTS VANISH before a strong wind, the cobwebs vanished from Conan's brain. With a searing curse he leaped into the saddle and the stallion reared neighing beneath him. He glared up the slopes, hesitated, and then turned down the trail in the direction he had been going when halted by Khemsa's trickery. But now he did not ride at a measured gait. He shook loose the reins and the stallion went like a thunderbolt, as if frantic to lose hysteria in violent physical exertion. Across the ledge and around the crag and down the narrow trail threading the great steep they plunged at breakneck speed. The path followed a fold of rock, winding interminably down from tier to tier of striated escarpment, and once, far below, Conan got a glimpse of the ruin that had fallen—a mighty pile of broken stone and boulders at the foot of a gigantic cliff.

The valley floor was still far below him when he reached a long and lofty ridge that led out from the slope like a natural causeway. Out upon this he rode, with an almost sheer drop on either hand. He could trace ahead of him the trail he had to follow; far ahead it dropped down from the ride and made a great horseshoe back into the river-bed at his left hand. He cursed the necessity of traversing those miles, but it was the only way. To try to descend to the lower lap of the trail here would be to attempt the impossible. Only a bird could get to the river-bed with a whole neck.

So he urged on the wearying stallion, until a clink of hoofs reached his ears, welling up from below. Pulling up short and reining to the lip of the cliff, he stared down into the dry river-bed that wound along the foot of the ridge. Along that gorge rode a motley throng—bearded men on half-wild horses, five hundred strong,

114

bristling with weapons. And Conan shouted suddenly, leaning over the edge of the cliff, three hundred feet above them.

At his shout they reined back, and five hundred bearded faces were tilted up toward him; a deep, clamorous roar filled the canyon. Conan did not waste words.

"I was riding for Ghor!" he roared. "I had not hoped to meet you dogs on the trail. Follow me as fast as your nags can push! I'm going to Yimsha, and—"

"Traitor!" The howl was like a dash of ice-water in his face.

"What?" He glared down at them, jolted speechless. He saw wild eyes blazing up at him, faces contorted with fury, fists brandishing blades.

"Traitor!" they roared back, wholeheartedly. "Where are the seven chiefs held captive in Pesh-khauri?"

"Why, in the governor's prison, I suppose," he answered.

A bloodthirsty yell from a hundred throats answered him, with such a waving of weapons and a clamor that he could not understand what they were saying. He beat down the din with a bull-like roar, and bellowed: "What devil's play is this? Let one of you speak, so I can understand what you mean!"

A gaunt old chief elected himself to this position, shook his tulwar at Conan as a preamble, and shouted accusingly: "You would not let us go raiding Pesh-khauri to rescue our brothers!"

"No, you fools!" roared the exasperated Cimmerian. "Even if you'd breached the wall, which is unlikely, they'd have hanged the prisoners before you could reach them."

"And you went alone to traffic with the governor!"

yelled the Afghuli, working himself into a frothing frenzy.

"Well?"

"Where are the seven chiefs?" howled the old chief, making his tulwar into a glimmering wheel of steel about his head. "Where are they? Dead!"

"What!" Conan nearly fell off his horse in his surprize.

"Aye, dead!" five hundred bloodthirsty voices assured him.

The old chief brandished his arms and got the floor again. "They were not hanged!" he screeched. "A Wazuli in another cell saw them die! The governor sent a wizard to slay them by craft!"

"That must be a lie," said Conan. "The governor would not dare. Last night I talked with him—"

The admission was unfortunate. A yell of hate and accusation split the skies.

"Aye! You went to him alone! To betray us! It is no lie. The Wazuli escaped through the doors the wizard burst in his entry, and told the tale to our scouts whom he met in Zhaibar. They had been sent forth to search for you, when you did not return. When they heard the Wazuli's tale, they returned with all haste to Ghor, and we saddled our steeds and girt our swords!"

"And what do you fools mean to do?" demanded the Cimmerian.

"To avenge our brothers!" they howled. "Death to the Kshatriyas! Slay him, brothers, he is a traitor!"

Arrows began to rattle around him. Conan rose in his stirrups, striving to make himself heard above the tumult, and then, with a roar of mingled rage, defiance and disgust, he wheeled and galloped back up the trail. Behind him and below him the Afghulis came pelting, mouthing their rage, too furious even to remember that

116

the only way they could reach the height whereon he rode was to traverse the river-bed in the other direction, make the broad bend and follow the twisting trail up over the ridge. When they did remember this, and turned back, their repudiated chief had almost reached the point where the ridge joined the escarpment.

At the cliff he did not take the trail by which he had descended, but turned off on another, a mere trace along a rock-fault, where the stallion scrambled for footing. He had not ridden far when the stallion snorted and shied back from something lying in the trail. Conan stared down on the travesty of a man, a broken, shredded, bloody heap that gibbered and gnashed splintered teeth.

Only the dark gods that rule over the grim destinies of wizards know how Khemsa dragged his shattered body from beneath that awful cairn of fallen rocks and up the steep slope to the trail.

Impelled by some obscure reason, Conan dismounted and stood looking down at the ghastly shape, knowing that he was witness of a thing miraculous and opposed to nature. The Rakhsha lifted his gory head, and his strange eyes, glazed with agony and approaching death, rested on Conan with recognition.

"Where are they?" It was a racking croak not even remotely resembling a human voice.

"Gone back to their damnable castle on Yimsha," grunted Conan. "They took the Devi with them."

"I will go!" muttered the man. "I will follow them! They killed Gitara; I will kill them—the acolytes, the Four of the Black Circle, the Master himself! Kill—kill them all!" He strove to drag his mutilated frame along the rock, but not even his indomitable will could animate that gory mass longer, where the splintered bones hung together only by torn tissue and ruptured fiber.

"Follow them!" raved Khemsa, drooling a bloody slaver. "Follow!"

"I'm going to," growled Conan. "I went to fetch my Afghulis, but they've turned on me. I'm going on to Yimsha alone. I'll have the Devi back if I have to tear down that damned mountain with my bare hands. I didn't think the governor would dare kill my headmen, when I had the Devi, but it seems he did. I'll have his head for that. She's no use to me now as a hostage, but—"

"The curse of Yizil on them!" gasped Khemsa. "Go! I am dying. Wait—take my girdle."

He tried to fumble with a mangled hand at his tatters, and Conan, understanding what he sought to convey, bent and drew from about his gory waist a girdle of curious aspect.

"Follow the golden vein through the abyss," muttered Khemsa. "Wear the girdle. I had it from a Stygian priest. It will aid you, though it failed me at last. Break the crystal globe with the four golden pomegranates. Beware of the Master's transmutations—I am going to Gitara—she is waiting for me in hell—*aie, ya Skelos yar!*" And so he died.

Conan stared down at the girdle. The hair of which it was woven was not horsehair. He was convinced that it was woven of the thick black tresses of a woman. Set in the thick mesh were tiny jewels such as he had never seen before. The buckle was strangely made, in the form of a golden serpent head, flat, wedge-shaped and scaled with curious art. A strong shudder shook Conan as he handled it, and he turned as though to cast it over the precipice; then he hesitated, and finally buckled it about his waist, under the Bakhariot girdle. Then he

118

mounted and pushed on.

The sun had sunk behind the crags. He climbed the trail in the vast shadow of the cliffs that was thrown out like a dark blue mantle over valleys and ridges far below. He was not far from the crest when, edging around the shoulder of a jutting crag, he heard the clink of shod hoofs ahead of him. He did not turn back. Indeed, so narrow was the path that the stallion could not have wheeled his great body upon it. He rounded the jut of the rock and came upon a portion of the path that broadened somewhat. A chorus of threatening yells broke on his ear, but his stallion pinned a terrified horse hard against the rock, and Conan caught the arm of the rider in an iron grip, checking the lifted sword in midair.

"Kerim Shah!" muttered Conan, red glints smoldering luridly in his eyes. The Turanian did not struggle; they sat their horses almost breast to breast, Conan's fingers locking the other's sword-arm. Behind Kerim Shah filed a group of lean Irakzai on gaunt horses. They glared like wolves, fingering bows and knives, but rendered uncertain because of the narrowness of the path and the perilous proximity of the abyss that yawned beneath them.

"Where is the Devi?" demanded Kerim Shah.

"What's it to you, you Hyrkanian spy?" snarled Conan.

"I know you have her," answered Kerim Shah. "I was on my way northward with some tribesmen when we were ambushed by enemies in Shalizah Pass. Many of my men were slain, and the rest of us harried through the hills like jackals. When we had beaten off our pursuers, we turned westward, toward Amir Jehun Pass, and this morning we came upon a Wazuli wandering through the hills. He was quite mad, but I learned much from his incoherent gibberings before he died. I learned that he was the sole survivor of a band which followed a chief of the Afghulis and a captive Kshatriya woman into a gorge behind Khurum village. He babbled much of a man in a green turban whom the Afghuli rode down, but who, when attacked by the Wazulis who pursued, smote them with a nameless doom that wiped them out as a gust of wind-driven fire wipes out a cluster of locusts.

"How that one man escaped, I do not know, nor did he; but I knew from his maunderings that Conan of Ghor had been in Khurum with his royal captive. And as we made our way through the hills, we overtook a naked Galzai girl bearing a gourd of water, who told us a tale of having been stripped and ravished by a giant foreigner in the garb of an Afghuli chief, who, she said, gave her garments to a Vendhyan woman who accompanied him. She said you rode westward."

Kerim Shah did not consider it necessary to explain that he had been on his way to keep his rendezvous with the expected troops from Secunderam when he found his way barred by hostile tribesmen. The road to Gurashah valley through Shalizah Pass was longer than the road that wound through Amir Jehun Pass, but the latter traversed part of the Afghuli country, which Kerim Shah had been anxious to avoid until he came with an army. Barred from the Shalizah road, however, he had turned to the forbidden route, until news that Conan had not yet reached Afghulistan with his captive had caused him to turn southward and push on recklessly in the hope of overtaking the Cimmerian in the hills.

"So you had better tell me where the Devi is," suggested Kerim Shah. "We outnumber you—"

"Let one of your dogs nock a shaft and I'll throw you

120

over the cliff," Conan promised. "It wouldn't do you any good to kill me, anyhow. Five hundred Afghulis are on my trail, and if they find you've cheated them, they'll flay you alive. Anyway, I haven't got the Devi. She's in the hands of the Black Seers of Yimsha."

"*Tarim!*" swore Kerim Shah softly, shaken out of his poise for the first time. "Khemsa—"

"Khemsa's dead," grunted Conan. "His masters sent him to hell on a landslide. And now get out of my way. I'd be glad to kill you if I had the time, but I'm on my way to Yimsha."

"I'll go with you," said the Turanian abruptly.

Conan laughed at him. "Do you think I'd trust you, you Hyrkanian dog?"

"I don't ask you to," returned Kerim Shah. "We both want the Devi. You know my reason; King Yezdigerd desires to add her kingdom to his empire, and herself in his seraglio. And I knew you, in the days when you were a hetman of the *kozak* steppes; so I know your ambition is wholesale plunder. You want to loot Vendhya, and to twist out a huge ransom for Yasmina. Well, let us for the time being, without any illusion about each other, unite our forces, and try to rescue the Devi from the Seers. If we succeed, and live, we can fight it out to see who keeps her."

Conan narrowly scrutinized the other for a moment, and then nodded, releasing the Turanian's arm. "Agreed; what about your men?"

Kerim Shah turned to the silent Irakzai and spoke briefly: "This chief and I are going to Yimsha to fight the wizards. Will you go with us, or stay here to be flayed by the Afghulis who are following this man?"

They looked at him with eyes grimly fatalistic. They were doomed and they knew it—had known it ever since the singing arrows of the ambushed Dagozai had driven them back from the pass of Shalizah. The men of the lower Zhaibar had too many reeking bloodfeuds among the crag-dwellers. They were too small a band to fight their way back through the hills to the villages of the lower Zhaibar had too many reeking blood-feuds among the crag-dwellers. They were too small a band to fight their way back through the hills to the villages of the border, without the guidance of the crafty Turanian. They counted themselves as dead already, so they made the reply that only dead men would make: "We will go with thee and die on Yimsha."

"Then in Crom's name let us be gone," grunted Conan, fidgeting with impatience as he stared into the blue gulfs of the deepening twilight. "My wolves were hours behind me, but we've lost a devilish lot of time."

Kerim Shah backed his steed from between the black stallion and the cliff, sheathed his sword and cautiously turned the horse. Presently the band was filing up the path as swiftly as they dared. They came out upon the crest nearly a mile east of the spot where Khemsa had halted the Cimmerian and the Devi. The path they had traversed was a perilous one, even for hillmen, and for that reason Conan had avoided it that day when carrying Yasmina, though Kerim Shah, following him, had taken it supposing the Cimmerian had done likewise. Even Conan sighed with relief when the horses scrambled up over the last rim. They moved like phantom riders through an enchanted realm of shadows. The soft creak of leather, the clink of steel marked their passing, then again the dark mountain slopes lay naked and silent in the starlight.

8. *Yasmina Knows Stark Terror*

YASMINA HAD TIME but for one scream when she felt herself enveloped in that crimson whirl and torn from her protector with appalling force. She screamed once, and then she had no breath to scream. She was blinded, deafened, rendered mute and eventually senseless by the terrific rushing of the air about her. There was a dazed consciousness of dizzy height and numbing speed, a confused impression of natural sensations gone mad, and then vertigo and oblivion.

A vestige of these sensations clung to her as she recovered consciousness; so she cried out and clutched wildly as though to stay a headlong and involuntary flight. Her fingers closed on soft fabric, and a relieving sense of stability pervaded her. She took cognizance of her surroundings.

She was lying on a dais covered with black velvet. This dais stood in a great, dim room whose walls were hung with dusky tapestries across which crawled dragons reproduced with repellent realism. Floating shadows merely hinted at the lofty ceiling, and gloom that lent itself to illusion lurked in the corners. There seemed to be neither windows nor doors in the walls, or else they were concealed by the nighted tapestries. Where the dim light came from, Yasmina could not determine. The great room was a realm of mysteries, of shadows, and shadowy shapes in which she could not have sworn to observe movement, yet which invaded her mind with a dim and formless terror.

But her gaze fixed itself on a tangible object. On another, smaller dais of jet, a few feet away, a man sat cross-legged, gazing contemplatively at her. His long black velvet robe, embroidered with gold thread, fell loosely about him, masking his figure. His hands were folded in his sleeves. There was a velvet cap upon his head. His face was calm, placid, not unhandsome, his eyes lambent and slightly oblique. He did not move a muscle as he sat regarding her, nor did his expression alter when he saw she was conscious.

Yasmina felt fear crawl like a trickle of ice-water down her supple spine. She lifted herself on her elbows and stared apprehensively at the stranger.

"Who are you?" she demanded. Her voice sounded brittle and inadequate.

"I am the Master of Yimsha." The tone was rich and resonant, like the mellow notes of a temple bell.

"Why did you bring me here?" she demanded.

"Were you not seeking me?"

"If you are one of the Black Seers—yes!" she answered recklessly, believing that he could read her thoughts anyway.

He laughed softly, and chills crawled up and down her spine again.

"You would turn the wild children of the hills against the Seers of Yimsha!" he smiled. "I have read it in your mind, princess. Your weak, human mind, filled with petty dreams of hate and revenge."

"You slew my brother!" A rising tide of anger was vying with her fear; her hands were clenched, her lithe body rigid. "Why did you persecute him? He never harmed you. The priests say the Seers are above meddling in human affairs. Why did you destroy the king of Vendhya?"

"How can an ordinary human understand the motives of a Seer?" returned the Master calmly. "My acolytes in the temples of Turan, who are the priests behind the priests of Tarim, urged me to bestir myself in behalf of Yezdigerd. For reasons of my own, I

124

complied. How can I explain my mystic reasons to your puny intellect? You could not understand."

"I understand this: that my brother died!" Tears of grief and rage shook in her voice. She rose upon her knees and stared at him with wide blazing eyes, as supple and dangerous in that moment as a she-panther.

"As Yezdigerd desired," agreed the Master calmly. "For a while it was my whim to further his ambitions."

"Is Yezdigerd your vassal?" Yasmina tried to keep the timbre of her voice unaltered. She had felt her knee pressing something hard and symmetrical under a fold of velvet. Subtly she shifted her position, moving her hand under the fold.

"Is the dog that licks up the offal in the temple yard the vassal of the god?" returned the Master.

He did not seem to notice the actions she sought to dissemble. Concealed by the velvet, her fingers closed on what she knew was the golden hilt of a dagger. She bent her head to hide the light of triumph in her eyes.

"I am weary of Yezdigerd," said the Master. "I have turned to other amusements—ha!"

With a fierce cry Yasmina sprang like a jungle cat, stabbing murderously. Then she stumbled and slid to the floor, where she cowered, staring up at the man on the dais. He had not moved; his cryptic smile was unchanged. Tremblingly she lifted her hand and stared at it with dilated eyes. There was no dagger in her fingers; they grasped a stalk of golden lotus, the crushed blossoms drooping on the bruised stem.

She dropped it as if it had been a viper, and scrambled away from the proximity of her tormenter. She returned to her own dais, because that was at least more dignified for a queen than groveling on the floor at the feet of a sorcerer, and eyed him apprehensively, expecting reprisals.

But the Master made no move.

"All substance is one to him who holds the key of the cosmos," he said cryptically. "To an adept nothing is immutable. At will, steel blossoms bloom in unnamed gardens, or flower-swords flash in the moonlight."

"You are a devil," she sobbed.

"Not I!" he laughed. "I was born on this planet, long ago. Once I was a common man, nor have I lost all human attributes in the numberless eons of my adeptship. A human steeped in the dark arts is greater than a devil. I am of human origin, but I rule demons. You have seen the Lords of the Black Circle—it would blast your soul to hear from what far realm I summoned them and from what doom I guard them with ensorceled crystal and golden serpents.

"But only I can rule them. My foolish Khemsa thought to make himself great—poor fool, bursting material doors and hurtling himself and his mistress through the air from hill to hill! Yet if he had not been destroyed his power might have grown to rival mine."

He laughed again. "And you, poor, silly thing! Plotting to send a hairy hill chief to storm Yimsha! It was such a jest that I myself could have designed, had it occurred to me, that you should fall in his hands. And I read in your childish mind an intention to seduce by your feminine wiles to attempt your purpose, anyway.

"But for all your stupidity, you are a woman fair to look upon. It is my whim to keep you for my slave."

The daughter of a thousand proud emperors gasped with shame and fury at the word.

"You dare not!"

His mocking laughter cut her like a whip across her naked shoulders.

"The king dares not trample a worm in the road? Little fool, do you not realize that your royal pride is no

126

more to me than a straw blown on the wind? I, who have known the kisses of the queens of Hell! You have seen how I deal with a rebel!"

Cowed and awed, the girl crouched on the velvet-covered dais. The light grew dimmer and more phantom-like. The features of the Master became shadowy. His voice took on a newer tone of command.

"I will never yield to you!" Her voice trembled with fear but it carried a ring of resolution.

"You will yield," he answered with horrible conviction. "Fear and pain shall teach you. I will lash you with horror and agony to the last quivering ounce of your endurance, until you become as melted wax to be bent and molded in my hands as I desire. You shall know such discipline as no mortal woman ever knew, until my slightest command is to you as the unalterable will of the gods. And first, to humble your pride, you shall travel back through the lost ages, and view all the shapes that have been you. *Aie, yil la khosa!*"

At these words the shadowy room swam before Yasmina's affrighted gaze. The roots of her hair prickled her scalp, and her tongue clove to her palate. Somewhere a gong sounded a deep, ominous note. The dragons on the tapestries glowed like blue fire, and then faded out. The Master on his dais was but a shapeless shadow. The dim light gave way to soft, thick darkness, almost tangible, that pulsed with strange radiations. She could no longer see the Master. She could see nothing. She had a strange sensation that the walls and ceiling had withdrawn immensely from her.

Then somewhere in the darkness a glow began, like a firefly that rhythmically dimmed and quickened. It grew to a golden ball, and as it expanded its light grew more intense, flaming whitely. It burst suddenly, showering the darkness with white sparks that did not

127

illumine the shadows. But like an impression left in the gloom, a faint luminance remained, and revealed a slender dusky shaft shooting up from the shadowy floor. Under the girl's dilated gaze it spread, took shape; stems and broad leaves appeared, and great black poisonous blossoms that towered above her as she cringed against the velvet. A subtle perfume pervaded the atmosphere. It was the dread figure of the black lotus that had grown up as she watched, as it grows in the haunted, forbidden jungles of Khitai.

The broad leaves were murmurous with evil life. The blossoms bent toward her like sentient things, nodding serpent-like on pliant stems. Etched against soft, impenetrable darkness it loomed over her, gigantic, blackly visible in some mad way. Her brain reeled with the drugging scent and she sought to crawl from the dais. Then she clung to it as it seemed to be pitching at an impossible slant. She cried out with terror and clung to the velvet, but she felt her fingers ruthlessly torn away. There was a sensation as of all sanity and stability crumbling and vanishing. She was a quivering atom of sentiency driven through a black, roaring, icy void by a thundering wind that threatened to extinguish her feeble flicker of animate life like a candle blown out in a storm.

Then there came a period of blind impulse and movement, when the atom that was she mingled and merged with myriad other atoms of spawning life in the yeasty morass of existence, molded by formative forces until she emerged again a conscious individual, whirling down an endless spiral of lives.

In a mist of terror she relived all her former existences, recognized and *was* again all the bodies that had carried her ego throughout the changing ages. She bruised her feet again over the long, weary road of life that stretched out behind her into the immemorial Past. Back beyond the dimmest dawns of Time she crouched shuddering in primordial jungles, hunted by slavering beasts of prey. Skin-clad, she waded thigh-deep in rice-swamps, battling with squawking water-fowl for the precious grains. She labored with the oxen to drag the pointed stick through the stubborn soil, and she crouched endlessly over looms in peasant huts.

She saw walled cities burst into flame, and fled screaming before the slayers. She reeled naked and bleeding over burning sands, dragged at the slaver's stirrup, and she knew the grip of hot, fierce hands on her writhing flesh, the shame and agony of brutal lust. She screamed under the bite of the lash, and moaned on the rack; mad with terror she fought against the hands that forced her head inexorably down on the bloody block.

She knew the agonies of childbirth, and the bitterness of love betrayed. She suffered all the woes and wrongs and brutalities that man has inflicted on woman throughout the eons; and she endured all the spite and malice of woman for woman. And like the flick of a fiery whip throughout was the consciousness she retained of her Devi-ship. She was all the women she had ever been, yet in her knowing she was Yasmina. This consciousness was not lost in the throes of reincarnation. At one and the same time she was a naked slave-wench groveling under the whip, and the proud Devi of Vendhya. And she suffered not only as the slave-girl suffered, but as Yasmina, to whose pride the whip was like a white-hot brand.

Life merged into life in flying chaos, each with its burden of woe and shame and agony, until she dimly heard her own voice screaming unbearably, like one long-drawn cry of suffering echoing down the ages.

Then she awakened on the velvet-covered dais in the mystic room.

In a ghostly gray light she saw again the dais and the cryptic robed figure seated upon it. The hooded head was bent, the high shoulders faintly etched against the uncertain dimness. She could make out no details clearly, but the hood, where the velvet cap had been, stirred a formless uneasiness in her. As she stared, there stole over her a nameless fear that froze her tongue to her palate—a feeling that it was not the Master who sat so silently on that black dais.

Then the figure moved and rose upright, towering above her. It stooped over her and the long arms in their wide black sleeves bent about her. She fought against them in speechless fright, surprized by their lean hardness. The hooded head bent down toward her averted face. And she screamed, and screamed again in poignant fear and loathing. Bony arms gripped her lithe body, and from that hood looked forth a countenance of death and decay—features like rotting parchment on a moldering skull.

She screamed again, and then, as those champing, grinning jaws bent toward her lips, she lost consciousness. . . .

9. The Castle of the Wizards

THE SUN HAD risen over the white Himelian peaks. At the foot of a long slope a group of horsemen halted and stared upward. High above them a stone tower poised on the pitch of the mountainside. Beyond and above that gleamed the walls of a greater keep, near the line where the snow began that capped Yimsha's pinnacle. There was a touch of unreality about the whole—purple slopes pitching up to that fantastic castle, toy-like with distance, and above it the white glistening peak shouldering the cold blue.

"We'll leave the horses here," grunted Conan. "That treacherous slope is safer for a man on foot. Besides, they're done."

He swung down from the black stallion which stood with wide-braced legs and drooping head. They had pushed hard throughout the night, gnawing at scraps from saddle-bags, and pausing only to give the horses the rests they had to have.

"That first tower is held by the acolytes of the Black Seers," said Conan. "Or so men say; watch-dogs for their masters—lesser sorcerers. They won't sit sucking their thumbs as we climb this slope."

Kerim Shah glanced up the mountain, then back the way they had come; they were already far up on Yimsha's side, and a vast expanse of lesser peaks and crags spread out beneath them. Among those laby-rinths the Turanian sought in vain for a movement of color that would betray men. Evidently the pursuing Afghulis had lost their chief's trail in the night.

"Let us go, then." They tied the weary horses in a clump of tamarisk and without further comment turned up the slope. There was no cover. It was a naked incline, strewn with boulders not big enough to conceal a man. But they did conceal something else.

The party had not gone fifty steps when a snarling shape burst from behind a rock. It was one of the gaunt savage dogs that infested the hill villages, and its eyes glared redly, its jaws dripped foam. Conan was leading, but it did not attack him. It dashed past him and leaped at Kerim Shah. The Turanian leaped aside, and the great dog flung itself upon the Irakzai behind him. The man yelled and threw up his arm, which was torn by the brute's fangs as it bore him backward, and the next instant half a dozen tulwars were hacking at the beast. Yet not until it was literally dismembered did the hideous creature cease its efforts to seize and rend its attackers.

Kerim Shah bound up the wounded warrior's gashed arm, looked at him narrowly, and then turned away without a word. He rejoined Conan, and they renewed the climb in silence.

Presently Kerim Shah said: "Strange to find a village dog in this place."

"There's no offal here," grunted Conan.

Both turned their heads to glance back at the wounded warrior toiling after them among his companions. Sweat glistened on his dark face and his lips were drawn back from his teeth in a grimace of pain. Then both looked again at the stone tower squatting above them.

A slumberous quiet lay over the uplands. The tower showed no sign of life, nor did the strange pyramidal structure beyond it. But the men who toiled upward went with the tenseness of men walking on the edge of a crater. Kerim Shah had unslung the powerful Turanian bow that killed at five hundred paces, and the Irakzai looked to their own lighter and less lethal bows.

But they were not within bow-shot of the tower when something shot down out of the sky without warning. It passed so close to Conan that he felt the wind of the rushing wings, but it was an Irakzai who staggered and fell, blood jetting from a severed jugular. A hawk with wings like burnished steel shot up again, blood dripping from the simitar-beak, to reel against the sky as Kerim Shah's bowstring twanged. It dropped like a plummet, but no man saw where it struck the earth.

Conan bent over the victim of the attack, but the man was already dead. No one spoke; useless to comment on the fact that never before had a hawk been known to swoop on a man. Red rage began to vie with fatalistic lethargy in the wild souls of the Irakzai. Hairy fingers nocked arrows and men glared vengefully at the tower whose very silence mocked them.

But the next attack came swiftly. They all saw it—a white puffball of smoke that tumbled over the tower-rim and came drifting and rolling down the slope toward them. Others followed it. They seemed harmless, mere woolly globes of cloudy foam, but Conan stepped aside to avoid contact with the first. Behind him one of the Irakzai reached out and thrust his sword into the unstable mass. Instantly a sharp report shook the mountainside. There was a burst of blinding flame, and then the puffball had vanished, and of the too-curious warrior remained only a heap of charred and blackened bones. The crisped hand still gripped the ivory sword-hilt, but the blade was gone— melted and destroyed by that awful heat. Yet men standing almost within reach of the victim had not suffered except to be dazzled and half blinded by the sudden flare.

"Steel touches it off," grunted Conan. "Look out—

here they come!"

The slope above them was almost covered by the billowing spheres. Kerim Shah bent his bow and sent a shaft into the mass, and those touched by the arrow burst like bubbles in spurting flame. His men followed his example and for the next few minutes it was as if a thunderstorm raged on the mountain slope, with bolts of lightning striking and bursting in showers of flame. When the barrage ceased, only a few arrows were left in the quivers of the archers.

They pushed on grimly, over soil charred and blackened, where the naked rock had in places been turned to lava by the explosion of those diabolical bombs.

Now they were almost within arrow-flight of the silent tower, and they spread their line, nerves taut, ready for any horror that might descend upon them.

On the tower appeared a single figure, lifting a ten-foot bronze horn. Its strident bellow roared out across the echoing slopes, like the blare of trumpets on Judgment Day. And it began to be fearfully answered. The ground trembled under the feet of the invaders, and rumblings and grindings welled up from the subterranean depths.

The Irakzai screamed, reeling like drunken men on the shuddering slope, and Conan, eyes glaring, charged recklessly up the incline, knife in hand, straight at the door that showed in the tower-wall. Above him the great horn roared and bellowed in brutish mockery. And then Kerim Shah drew a shaft to his ear and loosed.

Only a Turanian could have made that shot. The bellowing of the horn ceased suddenly, and a high, thin scream shrilled in its place. The green-robed figure on the tower staggered, clutching at the long shaft which

134

quivered in its bosom, and then pitched across the parapet. The great horn tumbled upon the battlement and hung precariously, and another robed figure rushed to seize it, shrieking in horror. Again the Turanian bow twanged, and again it was answered by a death-howl. The second acolyte, in falling, struck the horn with his elbow and knocked it clattering over the parapet to shatter on the rocks far below.

At such headlong speed had Conan covered the ground that before the clattering echoes of that fall had died away, he was hacking at the door. Warned by his savage instinct, he gave back suddenly as a tide of molten lead splashed down from above. But the next instant he was back again, attacking the panels with redoubled fury. He was galvanized by the fact that his enemies had resorted to earthly weapons. The sorcery of the acolytes was limited. Their necromantic resources might well be exhausted.

Kerim Shah was hurrying up the slope, his hillmen behind him in a straggling crescent. They loosed as they ran, their arrows splintering against the walls or arching over the parapet.

The heavy teak portal gave way beneath the Cimmerian's assault, and he peered inside warily, expecting anything. He was looking into a circular chamber from which a stair wound upward. On the opposite side of the chamber a door gaped open, revealing the outer slope—and the backs of half a dozen green-robed figures in full retreat.

Conan yelled, took a step into the tower, and then native caution jerked him back, just as a great block of stone fell crashing to the floor where his foot had been an instant before. Shouting to his followers, he raced around the tower.

The acolytes had evacuated their first line of defense.

As Conan rounded the tower he saw their green robes twinkling up the mountain ahead of him. He gave chase, panting with earnest blood-lust, and behind him Kerim Shah and the Irakzai came pelting, the latter yelling like wolves at the flight of their enemies, their fatalism momentarily submerged by temporary triumph.

The tower stood on the lower edge of a narrow plateau whose upward slant was barely perceptible. A few hundred yards away this plateau ended abruptly in a chasm which had been invisible farther down the mountain. Into this chasm the acolytes apparently leaped without checking their speed. Their pursuers saw the green robes flutter and disappear over the edge.

A few moments later they themselves were standing on the brink of the mighty moat that cut them off from the castle of the Black Seers. It was a sheer-walled ravine that extended in either direction as far as they could see, apparently girdling the mountain, some four hundred yards in width and five hundred feet deep. And in it, from rim to rim, a strange, translucent mist sparkled and shimmered.

Looking down, Conan grunted. Far below him, moving across the glimmering floor, which shone like burnished silver, he saw the forms of the green-robed acolytes. Their outline was wavering and indistinct, like figures seen under deep water. They walked in single file, moving toward the opposite wall.

Kerim Shah nocked an arrow and sent it singing downward. But when it struck the mist that filled the chasm it seemed to lose momentum and direction, wandering widely from its course.

"If they went down, so can we!" grunted Conan, while Kerim Shah stared after his shaft in amazement. "I saw them last at this spot—"

Squinting down he saw something shining like a golden thread across the canyon floor far below. The acolytes seemed to be following this thread, and there suddenly came to him Khemsa's cryptic words— "Follow the golden vein!" On the brink, under his very hand as he crouched, he found it, a thin vein of sparkling gold running from an outcropping of ore to the edge and down across the silvery floor. And he found something else, which had before been invisible to him because of the peculiar refraction of the light. The gold vein followed a narrow ramp which slanted down into the ravine, fitted with niches for hand and foot hold.

"Here's where they went down," he grunted to Kerim Shah. "They're no adepts, to waft themselves through the air! We'll follow them—"

It was at that instant that the man who had been bitten by the mad dog cried out horribly and leaped at Kerim Shah, foaming and gnashing his teeth. The Turanian, quick as a cat on his feet, sprang aside and the madman pitched head-first over the brink. The others rushed to the edge and glared after him in amazement. The maniac did not fall plummet-like. He floated slowly down through the rosy haze like a man sinking in deep water. His limbs moved like a man trying to swim, and his features were purple and convulsed beyond the contortions of his madness. Far down at last on the shining floor his body settled and lay still.

"There's death in that chasm," muttered Kerim Shah, drawing back from the rosy mist that shimmered almost at his feet. "What now, Conan?"

"On!" answered the Cimmerian grimly. "Those acolytes are human; if the mist doesn't kill them, it won't kill me."

He hitched his belt, and his hands touched the girdle Khemsa had given him; he scowled, then smiled bleakly. He had forgotten that girdle; yet thrice had death passed him by to strike another victim.

The acolytes had reached the farther wall and were moving up it like great green flies. Letting himself upon the ramp, he descended warily. The rosy cloud lapped about his ankles, ascending as he lowered himself. It reached his knees, his thighs, his waist, his arm-pits. He felt it as one feels a thick heavy fog on a damp night. With it lapping about his chin he hesitated, and then ducked under. Instantly his breath ceased; all air was shut off from him and he felt his ribs caving in on his vitals. With a frantic effort he heaved himself up, fighting for life. His head rose above the surface and he drank air in great gulps.

Kerim Shah leaned down toward him, spoke to him, but Conan neither heard nor heeded. Stubbornly, his mind fixed on what the dying Khemsa had told him, the Cimmerian groped for the gold vein, and found that he had moved off it in his descent. Several series of hand-holds were niched in the ramp. Placing himself directly over the thread, he began climbing down once more. The rosy mist rose about him, engulfed him. Now his head was under, but he was still drinking pure air. Above him he saw his companions staring down at him, their features blurred by the haze that shimmered over his head. He gestured for them to follow, and went down swiftly, without waiting to see whether they complied or not.

Kerim Shah sheathed his sword without comment and followed, and the Irakzai, more fearful of being left alone than of the terrors that might lurk below, scrambled after him. Each man clung to the golden thread as they saw the Cimmerian do.

Down the slanting ramp they went to the ravine floor and moved out across the shining level, treading the gold vein like rope-walkers. It was as if they walked along an invisible tunnel through which air circulated freely. They felt death pressing in on them above and on either hand, but it did not touch them.

The vein crawled up a similar ramp on the other wall up which the acolytes had disappeared, and up it they went with taut nerves, not knowing what might be waiting for them among the jutting spurs of rock that fanged the lip of the precipice.

It was the green-robed acolytes who awaited them, with knives in their hands. Perhaps they had reached the limits to which they could retreat. Perhaps the Stygian girdle about Conan's waist could have told why their necromantic spells had proven so weak and so quickly exhausted. Perhaps it was knowledge of death decreed for failure that sent them leaping from among the rocks, eyes glaring and knives glittering, resorting in their desperation to material weapons.

There among the rocky fangs on the precipice lip was no war of wizard craft. It was a whirl of blades, where real steel bit and real blood spurted, where sinewy arms dealt forthright blows that severed quivering flesh, and men went down to be trodden under foot as the fight raged over them.

One of the Irakzai bled to death among the rocks, but the acolytes were down—slashed and hacked asunder or hurled over the edge to float sluggishly down to the silver floor that shone so far below.

Then the conquerors shook blood and sweat from their eyes, and looked at one another. Conan and Kerim Shah still stood upright, and four of the Irakzai.

They stood among the rocky teeth that serrated the precipice brink, and from that spot a path wound up a gentle slope to a broad stair, consisting of half a dozen steps, a hundred feet across, cut out of a green jade-like substance. They led up to a broad stage or roofless gallery of the same polished stone, and above it rose, tier upon tier, the castle of the Black Seers. It seemed to have been carved out of the sheer stone of the mountain. The architecture was faultless, but unadorned. The many casements were barred and masked with curtains within. There was no sign of life, friendly or hostile.

They went up the path in silence, and warily as men treading the lair of a serpent. The Irakzai were dumb, like men marching to a certain doom. Even Kerim Shah was silent. Only Conan seemed unaware what a monstrous dislocating and uprooting of accepted thought and action their invasion constituted, what an unprecedented violation of tradition. He was not of the East; and he came of a breed who fought devils and wizards as promptly and matter-of-factly as they battled human foes.

He strode up the shining stairs and across the wide green gallery straight toward the great golden-bound teak door that opened upon it. He cast but a single glance upward at the higher tiers of the great pyramidal structure towering above him. He reached a hand for the bronze prong that jutted like a handle from the door—then checked himself, grinning hardly. The handle was made in the shape of a serpent, head lifted on arched neck; and Conan had a suspicion that that metal head would come to grisly life under his hand.

He struck it from the door with one blow, and its bronze clink on the glassy floor did not lessen his caution. He flipped it aside with his knife-point, and again turned to the door. Utter silence reigned over the towers. Far below them the mountain slopes fell away into a purple haze of distance. The sun glittered on snow-clad peaks on either hand. High above, a vulture hung like a black dot in the cold blue of the sky. But for it, the men before the gold-bound door were the only evidence of life, tiny figures on a green jade gallery poised on the dizzy height, with that fantastic pile of stone towering above them.

A sharp wind off the snow slashed them, whipping their tatters about. Conan's long knife splintering through the teak panels roused the startled echoes. Again and again he struck, hewing through polished wood and metal bands alike. Through the sundered ruins he glared into the interior, alert and suspicious as a wolf. He saw a broad chamber, the polished stone walls untapestried, the mosaic floor uncarpeted. Square, polished ebon stools and a stone dais formed the only furnishings. The room was empty of human life. Another door showed in the opposite wall.

"Leave a man on guard outside," grunted Conan. "I'm going in."

Kerim Shah designated a warrior for that duty, and the man fell back toward the middle of the gallery, bow in hand. Conan strode into the castle, followed by the Turanian and the three remaining Irakzai. The one outside spat, grumbled in his beard, and started suddenly as a low mocking laugh reached his ears.

He lifted his head and saw, on the tier above him, a tall, black-robed figure, naked head nodding slightly as he stared down. His whole attitude suggested mockery and malignity. Quick as a flash the Irakzai bent his bow and loosed, and the arrow streaked upward to strike full in the black-robed breast. The mocking smile did not alter. The Seer plucked out the missile and threw it back at the bowman, not as a weapon is hurled, but with a contemptuous gesture. The Irakzai dodged, instinctively throwing up his arm. His fingers closed on the revolving shaft.

Then he shrieked. In his hand the wooden shaft suddenly *writhed*. Its rigid outline became pliant, melting in his grasp. He tried to throw it from him, but it was too late. He held a living serpent in his naked hand, and already it had coiled about his wrist and its wicked wedge-shaped head darted at his muscular arm. He screamed again and his eyes became distended, his features purple. He went to his knees shaken by an awful convulsion, and then lay still.

The men inside had wheeled at his first cry. Conan took a swift stride toward the open doorway, and then halted short, baffled. To the men behind him it seemed that he strained against empty air. But though he could see nothing, there was a slick, smooth, hard surface under his hands, and he knew that a sheet of crystal had been let down in the doorway. Through it he saw the Irakzai lying motionless on the glassy gallery, an ordinary arrow sticking in his arm.

Conan lifted his knife and smote, and the watchers were dumfounded to see his blow checked apparently in midair, with the loud clang of steel that meets an unyielding substance. He wasted no more effort. He knew that not even the legendary tulwar of Amir Khurum could shatter that invisible curtain.

In a few words he explained the matter to Kerim Shah, and the Turanian shrugged his shoulders. "Well, if our exit is barred, we must find another. In the meanwhile our way lies forward, does it not?"

With a grunt the Cimmerian turned and strode across the chamber to the opposite door, with a feeling of treading on the threshold of doom. As he lifted his knife to shatter the door, it swung silently open as if of its own accord. He strode into a great hall, flanked with tall glassy columns. A hundred feet from the door began the broad jade-green steps of a stair that tapered toward the top like the side of a pyramid. What lay beyond that stair he could not tell. But between him and its shimmering foot stood a curious altar of gleaming black jade. Four great golden serpents twined their tails about this altar and reared their wedge-shaped heads in the air, facing the four quarters of the compass like the enchanted guardians of a fabled treasure. But on the altar, between the arching necks, stood only a crystal globe filled with a cloudy smoke-like substance, in which floated four golden pomegranates.

The sight stirred some dim recollection in his mind; then Conan heeded the altar no longer, for on the lower steps of the stair stood four black-robed figures. He had not seen them come. They were simply there, tall, gaunt, their vulture-heads nodding in unison, their feet and hands hidden by their flowing garments.

One lifted his arm and the sleeve fell away revealing his hand—and it was not a hand at all. Conan halted in mid-stride, compelled against his will. He had encountered a force differing subtly from Khemsa's mesmerism, and he could not advance, though he felt it in his power to retreat if he wished. His companions had likewise halted, and they seemed even more helpless than he, unable to move in either direction.

The seer whose arm was lifted beckoned to one of the Irakzai, and the man moved toward him like one in a trance, eyes staring and fixed, blade hanging in limp fingers. As he pushed past Conan, the Cimmerian threw an arm across his breast to arrest him. Conan was so much stronger than the Irakzai that in ordinary circumstances he could have broken his spine between his hands. But now the muscular arm was brushed

143

aside like a straw and the Irakzai moved toward the stair, treading jerkily and mechanically. He reached the steps and knelt stiffly, proffering his blade and bending his head. The Seer took the sword. It flashed as he swung it up and down. The Irakzai's head tumbled from his shoulders and thudded heavily on the black marble floor. An arch of blood jetted from the severed arteries and the body slumped over and lay with arms spread wide.

Again a malformed hand lifted and beckoned, and another Irakzai stumbled stiffly to his doom. The ghastly drama was re-enacted and another headless form lay beside the first.

As the third tribesman clumped his way past Conan to his death, the Cimmerian, his veins bulging in his temples with his efforts to break past the unseen barrier that held him, was suddenly aware of allied forces, unseen, but waking into life about him. This realization came without warning, but so powerfully that he could not doubt his instinct. His left hand slid involuntarily under his Bakhariot belt and closed on the Stygian girdle. And as he gripped it he felt new strength flood his numbed limbs; the will to live was a pulsing white-hot fire, matched by the intensity of his burning rage.

The third Irakzai was a decapitated corpse, and the hideous finger was lifting again when Conan felt the bursting of the invisible barrier. A fierce, involuntary cry burst from his lips as he leaped with the explosive suddenness of pent-up ferocity. His left hand gripped the sorcerer's girdle as a drowning man grips a floating log, and the long knife was a sheen of light in his right. The men on the steps did not move. They watched calmly, cynically; if they felt surprise they did not show it. Conan did not allow himself to think what might

144

chance when he came within knife-reach of them. His blood was pounding in his temples, a mist of crimson swam before his sight. He was afire with the urge to kill—to drive his knife deep into flesh and bone, and twist the blade in blood and entrails.

Another dozen strides would carry him to the steps where the sneering demons stood. He drew his breath deep, his fury rising redly as his charge gathered momentum. He was hurtling past the altar with its golden serpents when like a levin-flash there shot across his mind again as vividly as if spoken in his external ear, the cryptic words of Khemsa: "*Break the crystal ball!*"

His reaction was almost without his own volition. Execution followed impulse so spontaneously that the greatest sorcerer of the age would not have had time to read his mind and prevent his action. Wheeling like a cat from his headlong charge, he brought his knife crashing down upon the crystal. Instantly the air vibrated with a peal of terror, whether from the stairs, the altar, or the crystal itself he could not tell. Hisses filled his ears as the golden serpents, suddenly vibrant with hideous life, writhed and smote at him. But he was fired to the speed of a maddened tiger. A whirl of steel sheared through the hideous trunks that waved toward him, and he smote the crystal sphere again and yet again. And the globe burst with a noise like a thunder-clap, raining fiery shards on the black marble, and the gold pomegranates, as if released from captivity, shot upward toward the lofty roof and were gone.

A mad screaming, bestial and ghastly, was echoing through the great hall. On the steps writhed four black-robed figures, twisting in convulsions, froth dripping from their livid mouths. Then with one frenzied

145

crescendo of inhuman ululation they stiffened and lay still, and Conan knew that they were dead. He stared down at the altar and the crystal shards. Four headless golden serpents still coiled about the altar, but no alien life now animated the dully gleaming metal.

Kerim Shah was rising slowly from his knees, whither he had been dashed by some unseen force. He shook his head to clear the ringing from his ears.

"Did you hear that crash when you struck? It was as if a thousand crystal panels shattered all over the castle as that globe burst. Were the souls of the wizards imprisoned in those golden balls?—Ha!"

Conan wheeled as Kerim Shah drew his sword and pointed.

Another figure stood at the head of the stair. His robe, too, was black, but of richly embroidered velvet, and there was a velvet cap on his head. His face was calm, and not unhandsome.

"Who the devil are you?" demanded Conan, staring up at him, knife in hand.

"I am the Master of Yimsha!" His voice was like the chime of a temple bell, but a note of cruel mirth ran through it.

"Where is Yasmina?" demanded Kerim Shah.

The Master laughed down at him.

"What is that to you, dead man? Have you so quickly forgotten my strength, once lent to you, that you come armed against me, you poor fool? I think I will take your heart, Kerim Shah!"

He held out his hand as if to receive something, and the Turanian cried out sharply like a man in mortal agony. He reeled drunkenly, and then, with a splintering of bones, a rending of flesh and muscle and a snapping of mail-links, his breast burst outward with a shower of blood, and through the ghastly aperture something red and dripping shot through air into the Master's outstretched hand, as a bit of steel leaps to the magnet. The Turanian slumped to the floor and lay motionless, and the Master laughed and hurled the object to fall before Conan's feet—a still-quivering human heart.

With a roar and a curse Conan charged the stair. From Khemsa's girdle he felt strength and deathless hate flow into him to combat the terrible emanation of power that met him on the steps. The air filled with a shimmering steely haze through which he plunged like a swimmer, head lowered, left arm bent about his face, knife gripped low in his right hand. His half-blinded eyes, glaring over the crook of his elbow, made out the hated shape of the Seer before and above him, the outline wavering as a reflection wavers in disturbed water.

He was racked and torn by forces beyond his comprehension, but he felt a driving power outside and beyond his own lifting him inexorably upward and onward, despite the wizard's strength and his own agony.

Now he had reached the head of the stairs, and the Master's face floated in the steely haze before him, and a strange fear shadowed the inscrutable eyes. Conan waded through the mist as through a surf, and his knife lunged upward like a live thing. The keen point ripped the Master's robe as he sprang back with a low cry. Then before Conan's gaze, the wizard vanished—simply disappeared like a burst bubble, and something long and undulating darted up one of the smaller stairs that led up to left and right from the landing.

Conan charged after it, up the left-hand stair,

uncertain as to just what he had seen whip up those steps, but in a berserk mood that drowned the nausea and horror whispering at the back of his consciousness.

He plunged out into a broad corridor whose uncarpeted floor and untapestried walls were of polished jade, and something long and swift whisked down the corridor ahead of him, and into a curtained door. From within the chamber rose a scream of urgent terror. The sound lent wings to Conan's flying feet and he hurtled through the curtains and headlong into the chamber within.

A frightful scene met his glare. Yasmina cowered on the farther edge of a velvet-covered dais, screaming her loathing and horror, an arm lifted as if to ward off attack, while before her swayed the hideous head of a giant serpent, shining neck arching up from dark-gleaming coils. With a choked cry Conan threw his knife.

Instantly the monster whirled and was upon him like the rush of wind through tall grass. The long knife quivered in its neck, point and a foot of blade showing on one side, and the hilt and a hand's-breadth of steel on the other, but it only seemed to madden the giant reptile. The great head towered above the man who faced it, and then darted down, the venom-dripping jaws gaping wide. But Conan had plucked a dagger from his girdle and he stabbed upward as the head dipped down. The point tore through the lower jaw and transfixed the upper, pinning them together. The next instant the great trunk had looped itself about the Cimmerian as the snake, unable to use its fangs, employed its remaining form of attack.

Conan's left arm was pinioned among the bone-crushing folds, but his right was free. Bracing his feet to keep upright, he stretched forth his hand, gripped the hilt of the long knife jutting from the serpent's neck, and tore it free in a shower of blood. As if divining his purpose with more than bestial intelligence, the snake writhed and knotted, seeking to cast its loops about his right arm. But with the speed of light the long knife rose and fell, shearing half-way through the reptile's giant trunk.

Before he could strike again, the great pliant loops fell from him and the monster dragged itself across the floor, gushing blood from its ghastly wounds. Conan sprang after it, knife lifted, but his vicious swipe cut empty air as the serpent writhed away from him and struck its blunt nose against a paneled screen of sandalwood. One of the panels gave inward and the long, bleeding barrel whipped through it and was gone.

Conan instantly attacked the screen. A few blows rent it apart and he glared into the dim alcove beyond. No horrific shape coiled there; there was blood on the marble floor, and bloody tracks led to a cryptic arched door. Those tracks were of a man's bare feet....

"*Conan!*" He wheeled back into the chamber just in time to catch the Devi of Vendhya in his arms as she rushed across the room and threw herself upon him, catching him about the neck with a frantic clasp, half hysterical with terror and gratitude and relief.

His wild blood had been stirred to its uttermost by all that had passed. He caught her to him in a grasp that would have made her wince at another time, and crushed her lips with his. She made no resistance; the Devi was drowned in the elemental woman. She closed her eyes and drank in his fierce, hot, lawless kisses with all the abandon of passionate thirst. She was panting with his violence when he ceased for breath, and glared down at her lying limp in his mighty arms.

"I knew you'd come for me," she murmured. "You would not leave me in this den of devils."

At her words recollection of their environment came to him suddenly. He lifted his head and listened intently. Silence reigned over the castle of Yimsha, but it was a silence impregnated with menace. Peril crouched in every corner, leered invisibly from every hanging.

"We'd better go while we can," he muttered. "Those cuts were enough to kill any common beast—or *man*—but a wizard has a dozen lives. Wound one, and he writhes away like a crippled snake to soak up fresh venom from some source of sorcery."

He picked up the girl and carrying her in his arms like a child, he strode out into the gleaming jade corridor and down the stairs, nerves tautly alert for any sign or sound.

"I met the Master," she whispered, clinging to him and shuddering. "He worked his spells on me to break my will. The most awful was a moldering corpse which seized me in its arms—I fainted then and lay as one dead, I do not know how long. Shortly after I regained consciousness I heard sounds of strife below, and cries, and then that snake came slithering through the curtains—ah!" She shook at the memory of that horror. "I knew somehow that it was not an illusion, but a real serpent that sought my life."

"It was not a shadow, at least," answered Conan cryptically. "He knew he was beaten, and chose to slay you rather than let you be rescued."

"What do you mean, *he*?" she asked uneasily, and then shrank against him, crying out, and forgetting her question. She had seen the corpses at the foot of the stairs. Those of the Seers were not good to look at; as they lay twisted and contorted, their hands and feet were exposed to view, and at the sight Yasmina went livid and hid her face against Conan's powerful shoulder.

10. Yasmina and Conan

CONAN PASSED THROUGH the hall quickly enough, traversed the outer chamber and approached the door that let upon the gallery. Then he saw the floor sprinkled with tiny, glittering shards. The crystal sheet that had covered the doorway had been shivered to bits, and he remembered the crash that had accompanied the shattering of the crystal globe. He believed that every piece of crystal in the castle had broken at that instant, and some dim instinct or memory of esoteric lore vaguely suggested the truth of the monstrous connection between the Lords of the Black Circle and the golden pomegranates. He felt the short hair bristle chilly at the back of his neck and put the matter hastily out of his mind.

He breathed a deep sigh of relief as he stepped out upon the green jade gallery. There was still the gorge to cross, but at least he could see the white peaks glistening in the sun, and the long slopes falling away into the distant blue hazes.

The Irakzai lay where he had fallen, an ugly blotch on the glassy smoothness. As Conan strode down the winding path, he was surprised to note the position of the sun. It had not yet passed its zenith; and yet it seemed to him that hours had passed since he plunged into the castle of the Black Seers.

He felt an urge to hasten, not a mere blind panic, but an instinct of peril growing behind his back. He said nothing to Yasmina, and she seemed content to nestle her dark head against his arching breast and find security in the clasp of his iron arms. He paused an instant on the brink of the chasm, frowning down. The haze which danced in the gorge was no longer rose-hued and sparkling. It was smoky, dim, ghostly, like the life-tide that flickered thinly in a wounded man. The thought came vaguely to Conan that the spells of magicians were more closely bound to their personal beings than were the actions of common men to the actors.

But far below, the floor shone like tarnished silver, and the gold thread sparkled undimmed. Conan shifted Yasmina across his shoulder, where she lay docilely, and began the descent. Hurriedly he descended the ramp, and hurriedly he fled across the echoing floor. He had a conviction that they were racing with time, that their chances of survival depended upon crossing that gorge of horrors before the wounded Master of the castle should regain enough power to loose some other doom upon them.

When he toiled up the farther ramp and came out upon the crest, he breathed a gusty sigh of relief and stood Yasmina upon her feet.

"You walk from here," he told her; "it's downhill all the way."

She stole a glance at the gleaming pyramid across the chasm; it reared up against the snowy slope like the citadel of silence and immemorial evil.

"Are you a magician, that you have conquered the Black Seers of Yimsha, Conan of Ghor?" she asked, as they went down the path, with his heavy arm about her supple waist.

"It was a girdle Khemsa gave me before he died," Conan answered. "Yes, I found him on the trail. It is a curious one, which I'll show you when I have time. Against some spells it was weak, but against others it was strong, and a good knife is always a hearty incantation."

"But if the girdle aided you in conquering the Master," she argued, "why did it not aid Khemsa?"

He shook his head. "Who knows? But Khemsa had been the Master's slave; perhaps that weakened its magic. He had no hold on me as he had on Khemsa. Yet I can't say that I conquered him. He retreated, but I have a feeling that we haven't seen the last of him. I want to put as many miles between us and his lair as we can."

He was further relieved to find horses tethered among the tamarisks as he had left them. He loosed them swiftly and mounted the black stallion, swinging the girl up before him. The others followed, freshened by their rest.

"And what now?" she asked. "To Afghulistan?"

"Not just now!" He grinned hardly. "Somebody—maybe the governor—killed my seven headmen. My idiotic followers think I had something to do with it, and unless I am able to convince them otherwise, they'll hunt me like a wounded jackal."

"Then what of me? If the headmen are dead, I am useless to you as a hostage. Will you slay me, to avenge them?"

He looked down at her, with eyes fiercely aglow, and laughed at the suggestion.

"Then let us ride to the border," she said. "You'll be safe from the Afghulis there—"

"Yes, on a Vendhyan gibbet."

"I am queen of Vendhya," she reminded him with a touch of her old imperiousness. "You have saved my life. You shall be rewarded."

She did not intend it as it sounded, but he growled in his throat, ill pleased.

"Keep your bounty for your city-bred dogs, princess! If you're a queen of the plains, I'm a chief of the hills, and not one foot toward the border will I take you!"

"But you would be safe—" she began bewilderedly.

"And you'd be the Devi again," he broke in. "No, girl; I prefer you as you are now—a woman of flesh and blood, riding on my saddle-bow."

"But you can't *keep* me!" she cried. "You can't—"

"Watch and see!" he advised grimly.

"But I will pay you a vast ransom—"

"Devil take your ransom!" he answered roughly, his arms hardening about her supple figure. "The kingdom of Vendhya could give me nothing I desire half so much as I desire you. I took you at the risk of my neck; if your courtiers want you back, let them come up the Zhaibar and fight for you."

"But you have no followers now!" she protested. "You are hunted! How can you preserve your own life, much less mine?"

"I still have friends in the hills," he answered. "There is a chief of the Khurakzai who will keep you safely while I bicker with the Afghulis. If they will have none of me, by Crom! I will ride northward with you to the steppes of the *kozaki*. I was a hetman among the Free Companions before I rode southward. I'll make you a queen on the Zaporoska River!"

"But I can not!" she objected. "You must not hold me—"

"If the idea's so replusive," he demanded, "why did you yield your lips to me so willingly?"

"Even a queen is human," she answered, coloring. "But because I am a queen, I must consider my kingdom. Do not carry me away into some foreign country. Come back to Vendhya with me!"

"Would you make me your king?" he asked sardonically.

155

"Well, there are customs—" she stammered, and he interrupted her with a hard laugh.

"Yes, civilized customs that won't let you do as you wish. You'll marry some withered old king of the plains, and I can go my way with only the memory of a few kisses snatched from your lips. Ha!"

"But I must return to my kingdom!" she repeated helplessly.

"Why?" he demanded angrily. "To chafe your rump on gold thrones, and listen to the plaudits of smirking, velvet-skirted fools? Where is the gain? Listen: I was born in the Cimmerian hills where the people are all barbarians. I have been a mercenary soldier, a corsair, a *kozak*, and a hundred other things. What king has roamed the countries, fought the battles, loved the women, and won the plunder that I have?

"I came into Ghulistan to raise a horde and plunder the kingdoms to the south—your own among them. Being chief of the Afghulis was only a start. If I can conciliate them, I'll have a dozen tribes following me within a year. But if I can't I'll ride back to the steppes and loot the Turanian borders with the *kozaki*. And you'll go with me. To the devil with your kingdom; they fended for themselves before you were born."

She lay in his arms looking up at him, and she felt a tug at her spirit, a lawless, reckless urge that matched his own and was by it called into being. But a thousand generations of sovereignship rode heavy upon her.

"I can't! I can't!" she repeated helplessly.

"You haven't any choice," he assured her. "You— what the devil!"

They had left Yimsha some miles behind them, and were riding along a high ridge that separated two deep valleys. They had just topped a steep crest where they could gaze down into the valley on their right hand.

156

And there a running fight was in progress. A strong wind was blowing away from them, carrying the sound from their ears, but even so the clashing of steel and thunder of hoofs welled up from far below.

They saw the glint of the sun on lance-tip and spired helmet. Three thousand mailed horsemen were driving before them a ragged band of turbaned riders, who fled snarling and striking like fleeing wolves.

"Turanians!" muttered Conan. "Squadrons from Secunderam. What the devil are they doing here?"

"Who are the men they pursue?" asked Yasmina. "And why do they fall back so stubbornly? They can not stand against such odds."

"Five hundred of my mad Afghulis," he growled, scowling down into the vale. "They're in a trap, and they know it."

The valley was indeed a cul-de-sac at that end. It narrowed to a high-walled gorge, opening out further into a round bowl, completely rimmed with lofty, unscalable walls.

The turbaned riders were being forced into this gorge, because there was nowhere else for them to go, and they went reluctantly, in a shower of arrows and a whirl of swords. The helmeted riders harried them, but did not press in too rashly. They knew the desperate fury of the hill tribes, and they knew too that they had their prey in a trap from which there was no escape. They had recognized the hillmen as Afghulis, and they wished to hem them in and force a surrender. They needed hostages for the purpose they had in mind.

Their emir was a man of decision and initiative. When he reached Gurashah valley, and found neither guides nor emissary waiting for him, he pushed on, trusting to his own knowledge of the country. All the way from Secunderam there had been fighting, and

157

tribesmen were licking their wounds in many a crag-perched village. He knew there was a good chance that neither he nor any of his helmeted spearmen would ever ride through the gates of Secunderam again, for the tribes would all be up behind him now, but he was determined to carry out his orders—which were to take Yasmina Devi from the Afghulis at all costs, and to bring her captive to Secunderam, or if confronted by impossibility, to strike off her head before he himself died.

Of all this, of course, the watchers on the ridge were not aware. But Conan fidgeted with nervousness.

"Why the devil did they get themselves trapped?" he demanded of the universe at large. "I know what they're doing in these parts—they were hunting me, the dogs! Poking into every valley—and found themselves penned in before they knew it. The poor fools! They're making a stand in the gorge, but they can't hold out for long. When the Turanians have pushed them back into the bowl, they'll slaughter them at their leisure."

The din welling up from below increased in volume and intensity. In the strait of the narrow gut, the Afghulis, fighting desperately, were for the time holding their own against the mailed riders, who could not throw their whole weight against them.

Conan scowled darkly, moved restlessly, fingering his hilt, and finally spoke bluntly: "Devi, I must go down to them. I'll find a place for you to hide until I come back to you. You spoke of your kingdom—well, I don't pretend to look on those hairy devils as my children, but after all, such as they are, they're my henchmen. A chief should never desert his followers, even if they desert him first. They think they were right in kicking me out—hell, I won't be cast off! I'm still chief of the Afghulis, and I'll prove it! I can climb down

158

on foot into the gorge."

"But what of me?" she queried. "You carried me away forcibly from *my* people; now will you leave me to die in the hills alone while you go down and sacrifice yourself uselessly?"

His veins swelled with the conflict of his emotions.

"That's right," he muttered helplessly. "Crom knows what I *can* do."

She turned her head slightly, a curious expression dawning on her beautiful face. Then:

"Listen!" she cried. "Listen!"

A distant fanfare of trumpets was borne faintly to their ears. They stared into the deep valley on the left, and caught a glint of steel on the farther side. A long line of lances and polished helmets moved along the vale, gleaming in the sunlight.

"The riders of Vendhya!" she cried exultingly.

"There are thousands of them!" muttered Conan. "It has been long since a Kshatriya host has ridden this far into the hills."

"They are searching for me!" she exclaimed. "Give me your horse! I will ride to my warriors! The ridge is not so precipitous on the left, and I can reach the valley floor. Go to your men and make them hold out a little longer. I will lead my horsemen into the valley at the upper end and fall upon the Turanians! We will crush them in the vise! Quick, Conan! Will you sacrifice your men to your own desire?"

The burning hunger of the steppes and the wintry forests glared out of his eyes, but he shook his head and swung off the stallion, placing the reins in her hands.

"You win!" he grunted. "Ride like the devil!"

She wheeled away down the left-hand slope and he ran swiftly along the ridge until he reached the long ragged cleft that was the defile in which the fight raged.

Down the rugged wall he scrambled like an ape, clinging to projections and crevices, to fall at last, feet first, into the mêlée that raged in the mouth of the gorge. Blades were whickering and clanging about him, horses rearing and stamping, helmet plumes nodding among turbans that were stained crimson.

As he hit, he yelled like a wolf, caught a gold-worked rein, and dodging the sweep of a simitar, drove his long knife upward through the rider's vitals. In another instant he was in the saddle, yelling ferocious orders to the Afghulis. They stared at him stupidly for an instant; then as they saw the havoc his steel was wreaking among their enemies, they fell to their work again, accepting him without comment. In that inferno of licking blades and spurting blood there was no time to ask or answer questions.

The riders in their spired helmets and gold-worked hauberks swarmed about the gorge mouth, thrusting and slashing, and the narrow defile was packed and jammed with horses and men, the warriors crushed breast to breast, stabbing with shortened blades, slashing murderously when there was an instant's room to swing a sword. When a man went down he did not get up from beneath the stamping, swirling hoofs. Weight and sheer strength counted heavily there, and the chief of the Afghulis did the work of ten. At such times accustomed habits sway men strongly, and the warriors, who were used to seeing Conan in their vanguard, were heartened mightily, despite their distrust of him.

But superior numbers counted too. The pressure of the men behind forced the horsemen of Turan deeper and deeper into the gorge, in the teeth of the flickering tulwars. Foot by foot the Afghulis were shoved back, leaving the defile-floor carpeted with dead, on which the riders trampled. As he hacked and smote like a man possessed, Conan had time for some chilling doubts—would Yasmina keep her word? She had but to join her warriors, turn southward and leave him and his band to perish.

But at last, after what seemed centuries of desperate battling, in the valley outside there rose another sound above the clash of steel and yells of slaughter. And then with a burst of trumpets that shook the walls, and rushing thunder of hoofs, five thousand riders of Vendhya smote the hosts of Secunderam.

That stroke split the Turanian squadrons asunder, shattered, tore and rent them and scattered their fragments all over the valley. In an instant the surge had ebbed back out of the gorge; there was a chaotic, confused swirl of fighting, horsemen wheeling and smiting singly and in clusters, and then the emir went down with a Kshatriya lance through his breast, and the riders in their spired helmets turned their horses down the valley, spurring like mad and seeking to slash a way through the swarms which had come upon them from the rear. As they scattered in flight, the conquerors scattered in pursuit, and all across the valley floor, and up on the slopes near the mouth and over the crests streamed the fugitives and the pursuers. The Afghulis, those left to ride, rushed out of the gorge and joined in the harrying of their foes, accepting the unexpected alliance as unquestioningly as they had accepted the return of their repudiated chief.

The sun was sinking toward the distant crags when Conan, his garments hacked to tatters and the mail under them reeking and clotted with blood, his knife dripping and crusted to the hilt, strode over the corpses to where Yasmina Devi sat her horse among her nobles on the crest of the ridge, near a lofty precipice.

161

"You kept your word, Devi!" he roared. "By Crom, though, I had some bad seconds down in that gorge— *look out!*"

Down from the sky swooped a vulture of tremendous size with a thunder of wings that knocked men sprawling from their horses.

The simitar-like beak was slashing for the Devi's soft neck, but Conan was quicker—a short run, a tigerish leap, the savage thrust of a dripping knife, and the vulture voiced a horribly human cry, pitched sideways and went tumbling down the cliffs to the rocks and river a thousand feet below. As it dropt, its black wings thrashing the air, it took on the semblance, not of a bird, but of a black-robed human body that fell, arms in wide black sleeves thrown abroad.

Conan turned to Yasmina, his red knife still in his hand, his blue eyes smoldering, blood oozing from wounds on his thickly-muscled arms and thighs.

"You are the Devi again," he said, grinning fiercely at the gold-clasped gossamer robe she had donned over her hill-girl attire, and awed not at all by the imposing array of chivalry about him. "I have you to thank for the lives of some three hundred and fifty of my rogues, who are at least convinced that I didn't betray them. You have put my hands on the reins of conquest again."

"I still owe you my ransom," she said, her dark eyes glowing as they swept over him. "Ten thousand pieces of gold I will pay you—"

He made a savage, impatient gesture, shook the blood from his knife and thrust it back in its scabbard, wiping his hands on his mail.

"I will collect your ransom in my own way, at my own time," he said. "I will collect it in your palace at Ayodhya, and I will come with fifty thousand men to

162

see that the scales are fair."

She laughed, gathering her reins into her hands. "And I will meet you on the shores of the Jhumda with a hundred thousand!"

His eyes shone with fierce appreciation and admiration, and stepping back, he lifted his hand with a gesture that was like the assumption of kingship, indicating that her road was clear before her.

A Witch Shall Be Born

1. The Blood-Red Crescent

TARAMIS, QUEEN OF KHAURAN, awakened from a dream-haunted slumber to a silence that seemed more like the stillness of nighted catacombs than the normal quiet of a sleeping palace. She lay staring into the darkness, wondering why the candles in their golden candelabra had gone out. A flecking of stars marked a gold-barred casement that lent no illumination to the interior of the chamber. But as Taramis lay there, she became aware of a spot of radiance glowing in the darkness before her. She watched, puzzled. It grew and its intensity deepened as it expanded, a widening disk of lurid light hovering against the dark velvet hangings of the opposite wall. Taramis caught her breath, starting up to a sitting position. A dark object was visible in that circle of light—*a human head.*

In a sudden panic the queen opened her lips to cry out for her maids; then she checked herself. The glow was more lurid, the head more vividly limned. It was a woman's head, small, delicately molded, superbly poised, with a high-piled mass of lustrous black hair. The face grew distinct as she stared—and it was the sight of this face which froze the cry in Taramis' throat. The features were her own! She might have been looking into a mirror which subtly altered her reflection, lending it a tigerish gleam of eye, a vindictive curl of lip.

"Ishtar!" gasped Taramis. "I am bewitched!"

Appallingly, the apparition spoke, and its voice was like honeyed venom.

"Bewitched? No, sweet sister! Here is no sorcery."

"Sister?" stammered the bewildered girl. "I have no sister."

"You never had a sister?" came the sweet, poisonously mocking voice. "Never a twin sister whose flesh was as soft as yours to caress or hurt?"

"Why, once I had a sister," answered Taramis, still convinced that she was in the grip of some sort of nightmare. "But she died."

The beautiful face in the disk was convulsed with the aspect of a fury; so hellish became its expression that Taramis, cowering back, half expected to see snaky locks writhe hissing about the ivory brow.

"You lie!" The accusation was spat from between the snarling red lips. "She did not die! Fool! Oh, enough of this mummery! Look—and let your sight be blasted!"

Light ran suddenly along the hangings like flaming serpents, and incredibly the candles in the golden sticks flared up again. Taramis crouched on her velvet couch, her lithe legs flexed beneath her, staring wide-eyed at the pantherish figure which posed mockingly before her. It was as if she gazed upon another Taramis, identical with herself in every contour of feature and limb, yet animated by an alien and evil personality. The face of this stranger waif reflected the opposite of every characteristic the countenance of the queen denoted. Lust and mystery sparkled in her scintillant eyes, cruelty lurked in the curl of her full red lips. Each movement of her supple body was subtly suggestive. Her coiffure imitated that of the queen's, on her feet were gilded sandals such as Taramis wore in her

166

boudoir. The sleeveless, low-necked silk tunic, girdled at the waist with a cloth-of-gold cincture, was a duplicate of the queen's night-garment.

"Who are you?" gasped Taramis, an icy chill she could not explain creeping along her spine. "Explain your presence before I call my ladies-in-waiting to summon the guard!"

"Scream until the roof-beams crack," callously answered the stranger. "Your sluts will not wake till dawn, though the palace spring into flames about them. Your guardsmen will not hear your squeals; they have been sent out of this wing of the palace."

"What!" exclaimed Taramis, stiffening with out-raged majesty. "Who dared give my guardsmen such a command?"

"I did, sweet sister," sneered the other girl. "A little while ago, before I entered. They thought it was their darling adored queen. Ha! How beautifully I acted the part! With what imperious dignity, softened by womanly sweetness, did I address the great louts who knelt in their armor and plumed helmets!"

Taramis felt as if a stifling net of bewilderment were being drawn about her.

"Who are you?" she cried desperately. "What madness is this? Why do you come here?"

"Who am I?" There was the spite of a she-cobra's hiss in the soft response. The girl stepped to the edge of the couch, grasped the queen's white shoulders with fierce fingers, and bent to glare full into the startled eyes of Taramis. And under the spell of that hypnotic glare, the queen forgot to resent the unprecedented outrage of violent hands laid on regal flesh.

"Fool!" gritted the girl between her teeth. "Can you ask? Can you wonder? I am Salome!"

"Salome!" Taramis breathed the word, and the hairs
167

prickled on her scalp as she realized the incredible, numbing truth of the statement. "I thought you died within the hour of your birth," she said feebly.

"So thought many," answered the woman who called herself Salome. "They carried me into the desert to die, damn them! I, a mewing, puling babe whose life was so young it was scarcely the flicker of a candle. And do you know why they bore me forth to die?"

"I—I have heard the story—" faltered Taramis.

Salome laughed fiercely, and slapped her bosom. The low-necked tunic left the upper parts of her firm breasts bare, and between them there shone a curious mark—a crescent, red as blood.

"The mark of the witch!" cried Taramis, recoiling.

"Aye!" Salome's laughter was dagger-edged with hate. "The curse of the kings of Khauran! Aye, they tell the tale in the market-places, with wagging beards and rolling eyes, the pious fools! They tell how the first queen of our line had traffic with a fiend of darkness and bore him a daughter who lives in foul legendry to this day. And thereafter in each century a girl baby was born into the Askhaurian dynasty, with a scarlet half-moon between her breasts, that signified her destiny.

"'Every century a witch shall be born.' So ran the ancient curse. And so it has come to pass. Some were slain at birth, as they sought to slay me. Some walked the earth as witches, proud daughters of Khauran, with the moon of hell burning upon their ivory bosoms. Each was named Salome. I too am Salome. It was always Salome, the witch. It will always be Salome, the witch, even when the mountains of ice have roared down from the pole and ground the civilizations to ruin, and a new world has risen from the ashes and dust—even then there shall be Salomes to walk the earth, to trap men's hearts by their sorcery, to dance before the kings of the world, and see the heads of the wise men fall at their pleasure."

"But—but you—" stammered Taramis.

"I?" The scintillant eyes burned like dark fires of mystery. "They carried me into the desert far from the city, and laid me naked on the hot sand, under the flaming sun. And then they rode away and left me for the jackals and the vultures and the desert wolves.

"But the life in me was stronger than the life in common folk, for it partakes of the essence of the forces that seethe in the black gulfs beyond mortal ken. The hours passed, and the sun slashed down like the molten flames of hell, but I did not die—aye, something of that torment I remember, faintly and far away, as one remembers a dim, formless dream. Then there were camels, and yellow-skinned men who wore silk robes and spoke in a weird tongue. Strayed from the caravan road, they passed close by, and their leader saw me, and recognized the scarlet crescent on my bosom. He took me up and gave me life.

"He was a magician from far Khitai, returning to his native kingdom after a journey to Stygia. He took me with him to purple-towering Paikang, its minarets rising amid the vine-festooned jungles of bamboo, and there I grew to womanhood under his teaching. Age had steeped him deep in black wisdom, not weakened his powers of evil. Many things he taught me—"

She paused, smiling enigmatically, with wicked mystery gleaming in her dark eyes. Then she tossed her head.

"He drove me from him at last, saying that I was but a common witch in spite of his teachings, and not fit to command the mighty sorcery he would have taught me. He would have made me queen of the world and ruled the nations through me, he said, but I was only a harlot

169

of darkness. But what of it? I could never endure to seclude myself in a golden tower, and spend the long hours staring into a crystal globe, mumbling over incantations written on serpent's skin in the blood of virgins, poring over musty volumes in forgotten languages.

"He said I was but an earthly sprite, knowing naught of the deeper gulfs of cosmic sorcery. Well, this world contains all I desire—power, and pomp, and glittering pageantry, handsome men and soft women for my paramours and my slaves. He had told me who I was, of the curse and my heritage. I have returned to take that to which I have as much right as you. Now it is mine by right of possession."

"What do you mean?" Taramis sprang up and faced her sister, stung out of her bewilderment and fright. "Do you imagine that by drugging a few of my maids and tricking a few of my guardsmen you have established a claim to the throne of Khauran? Do not forget that I am queen of Khauran! I shall give you a place of honor, as my sister, but—"

Salome laughed hatefully.

"How generous of you, dear, sweet sister! But before you begin putting me in my place—perhaps you will tell me whose soldiers camp in the plain outside the city walls?"

"They are the Shemitish mercenaries of Constantius, the Kothic *voivode* of the Free Companies."

"And what do they in Khauran?" cooed Salome.

Taramis felt that she was being subtly mocked, but she answered with an assumption of dignity which she scarcely felt.

"Constantius asked permission to pass along the borders of Khauran on his way to Turan. He himself is hostage for their good behavior as long as they are

170

within my domains."

"And Constantius," pursued Salome. "Did he not ask your hand today?"

Taramis shot her a clouded glance of suspicion.

"How did you know that?"

An insolent shrug of the slim naked shoulders was the only reply.

"You refused, dear sister?"

"Certainly I refused!" exclaimed Taramis angrily. "Do you, an Askhaurian princess yourself, suppose that the queen of Khauran could treat such a proposal with anything but disdain? Wed a bloody-handed adventurer, a man exiled from his own kingdom because of his crimes, and the leader of organized plunderers and hired murderers?

"I should never have allowed him to bring his black-bearded slayers into Khauran. But he is virtually a prisoner in the south tower, guarded by my soldiers. Tomorrow I shall bid him order his troops to leave the kingdom. He himself shall be kept captive until they are over the border. Meantime, my soldiers man the walls of the city, and I have warned him that he will answer for any outrages perpetrated on the villagers or shepherds by his mercenaries."

"He is confined in the south tower?" asked Salome.

"That is what I said. Why do you ask?"

For answer Salome clapped her hands, and lifting her voice, with a gurgle of cruel mirth in it, called: "The queen grants you an audience, Falcon!"

A gold-arabesqued door opened and a tall figure entered the chamber, at the sight of which Taramis cried out in amazement and anger.

"Constantius! You dare enter my chamber!"

"As you see, Your Majesty!" He bent his dark, hawk-like head in mock humility.

Constantius, whom men called Falcon, was tall, broad-shouldered, slim-waisted, lithe and strong as pliant steel. He was handsome in an aquiline, ruthless way. His face was burnt dark by the sun, and his hair, which grew far back from his high, narrow forehead, was black as a raven. His dark eyes were penetrating and alert, the hardness of his thin lips not softened by his thin black mustache. His boots were of Kordavan leather, his hose and doublet of plain, dark silk, tarnished with the wear of the camps and the stains of armor rust.

Twisting his mustache, he let his gaze travel up and down the shrinking queen with an effrontery that made her wince.

"By Ishtar, Taramis," he said silkily, "I find you more alluring in your night-tunic than in your queenly robes. Truly, this is an auspicious night!"

Fear grew in the queen's dark eyes. She was no fool; she knew that Constantius would never dare this outrage unless he was sure of himself.

"You are mad!" she said. "If I am in your power in this chamber, you are no less in the power of my subjects, who will rend you to pieces if you touch me. Go at once, if you would live."

Both laughed mockingly, and Salome made an impatient gesture.

"Enough of this farce; let us on to the next act in the comedy. Listen, dear sister: it was I who sent Constantius here. When I decided to take the throne of Khauran, I cast about for a man to aid me, and chose the Falcon, because of his utter lack of all characteristics men call good."

"I am overwhelmed, princess," murmured Constantius sardonically, with a profound bow.

"I sent him to Khauran, and, once his men were

camped in the plain outside, and he was in the palace, I entered the city by that small gate in the west wall—the fools guarding it thought it was you returning from some nocturnal adventure—"

"You hell-cat!" Taramis' cheeks flamed and her resentment got the better of her regal reserve.

Salome smiled hardly.

"They were properly surprised and shocked, but admitted me without question. I entered the palace the same way, and gave the order to the surprised guards that sent them marching away, as well as the men who guarded Constantius in the south tower. Then I came here, attending to the ladies-in-waiting on the way."

Taramis' fingers clenched and she paled.

"Well, what next?" she asked in a shaky voice.

"Listen!" Salome inclined her head. Faintly through the casement there came the clank of marching men in armor; gruff voices shouted in an alien tongue, and cries of alarm mingled with the shouts.

"The people awaken and grow fearful," said Constantius sardonically. "You had better go and reassure them, Salome!"

"Call me Taramis," answered Salome. "We must become accustomed to it."

"What have you done?" cried Taramis. "What have you done?"

"I have gone to the gates and ordered the soldiers to open them," answered Salome. "They were astounded, but they obeyed. That is the Falcon's army you hear, marching into the city."

"You devil!" cried Taramis. "You have betrayed my people, in my guise! You have made me seem a traitor! Oh, I shall go to them—"

With a cruel laugh Salome caught her wrist and jerked her back. The magnificent suppleness of the

173

queen was helpless against the vindictive strength that steeled Salome's slender limbs.

"You know how to reach the dungeons from the palace, Constantius?" said the witch-girl. "Good. Take this spitfire and lock her into the strongest cell. The jailers are all sound in drugged sleep. I saw to that. Send a man to cut their throats before they can awaken. None must ever know what has occurred tonight. Thenceforward I am Taramis, and Taramis is a nameless prisoner in an unknown dungeon."

Constantius smiled with a glint of strong white teeth under his thin mustache.

"Very good; but you would not deny me a little— ah—amusement first?"

"Not I! Tame the scornful hussy as you will." With a wicked laugh Salome flung her sister into the Kothian's arms, and turned away through the door that opened into the outer corridor.

Fright widened Taramis' lovely eyes, her supple figure rigid and straining against Constantius' embrace. She forgot the men marching in the streets, forgot the outrage to her queenship, in the face of the menace to her womanhood. She forgot all sensations but terror and shame as she faced the complete cynicism of Constantius' burning, mocking eyes, felt his hard arms crushing her writhing body.

Salome, hurrying along the corridor outside, smiled spitefully as a scream of despair and agony rang suddering through the palace.

2. The Tree of Death

THE YOUNG SOLDIER's hose and shirt were smeared with dried blood, wet with sweat and gray with dust. Blood oozed from the deep gash in his thigh, from the cuts on his breast and shoulder. Perspiration glistened on his livid face and his fingers were knotted in the cover of the divan on which he lay. Yet his words reflected mental suffering that outweighed physical pain.

"She must be mad!" he repeated again and again, like one still stunned by some monstrous and incredible happening. "It's like a nightmare! Taramis, whom all Khauran loves, betraying her people to that devil from Koth! Oh, Ishtar, why was I not slain? Better die than live to see our queen turn traitor and harlot!"

"Lie still, Valerius," begged the girl who was washing and bandaging his wounds with trembling hands. "Oh, please lie still, darling! You will make your wounds worse. I dared not summon a leech—"

"No," muttered the wounded youth. "Constantius' blue-bearded devils will be searching the quarters for wounded Khaurani; they'll hang every man who has wounds to show he fought against them. Oh, Taramis, how could you betray the people who worshipped you?" In his fierce agony he writhed, weeping in rage and shame, and the terrified girl caught him in her arms, straining his tossing head against her bosom, imploring him to be quiet.

"Better death than the black shame that has come upon Khauran this day," he groaned. "Did you see it, Ivga?"

"No, Valerius." Her soft, nimble fingers were again at work, gently cleansing and closing the gaping edges of his raw wounds. "I was awakened by the noise of fighting in the streets—I looked out a casement and saw the Shemites cutting down people; then presently I heard you calling me faintly from the alley door."

"I had reached the limits of my strength," he muttered. "I fell in the alley and could not rise. I knew they'd find me soon if I lay there—I killed three of the blue-bearded beasts, by Ishtar! They'll never swagger through Khauran's streets, by the gods! The fiends are tearing their hearts in hell!"

The trembling girl crooned soothingly to him, as to a wounded child, and closed his panting lips with her own cool sweet mouth. But the fire that raged in his soul would not allow him to lie silent.

"I was not on the wall when the Shemites entered," he burst out. "I was asleep in the barracks, with the others not on duty. It was just before dawn when our captain entered, and his face was pale under his helmet. 'The Shemites are in the city,' he said. 'The queen came to the southern gate and gave orders that they should be admitted. She made the men come down from the walls, where they've been on guard since Constantius entered the kingdom. I don't understand it, and neither does anyone else, but I heard her give the order, and we obeyed as we always do. We are ordered to assemble in the square before the palace. Form ranks outside the barracks and march—leave your arms and armor here. Ishtar knows what this means, but it is the queen's order.'

"Well, when we came to the square the Shemites were drawn up on foot opposite the palace, ten thousand of the blue-bearded devils, fully armed, and people's heads were thrust out of every window and door on the square. The streets leading into the square were thronged by bewildered folk. Taramis was standing on the steps of the palace, alone except for

Constantius, who stood stroking his mustache like a great lean cat who has just devoured a sparrow. But fifty Shemites with bows in their hands were ranged below them.

"That's where the queen's guard should have been, but they were drawn up at the foot of the palace stair, as puzzled as we, though they had come fully armed, in spite of the queen's order.

"Taramis spoke to us then, and told us that she had reconsidered the proposal made her by Constantius— why, only yesterday she threw it in his teeth in open court!—and that she had decided to make him her royal consort. She did not explain why she had brought the Shemites into the city so treacherously. But she said that, as Constantius had control of a body of professional fighting-men, the army of Khauran would no longer be needed, and therefore she disbanded it, and ordered us to go quietly to our homes.

"Why, obedience to our queen is second nature to us, but we were struck dumb and found no word to answer. We broke ranks almost before we knew what we were doing, like men in a daze.

"But when the palace guard was ordered to disarm likewise and disband, the captain of the guard, Conan, interrupted. Men said he was off duty the night before, and drunk. But he was wide awake now. He shouted to the guardsmen to stand as they were until they received an order from him—and such is his dominance of his men, that they obeyed in spite of the queen. He strode up to the palace steps and glared at Taramis—and then he roared: 'This is not the queen! This isn't Taramis! It's some devil in masquerade!'

"Then hell was to pay! I don't know just what happened. I think a Shemite struck Conan, and Conan killed him. The next instant the square was a

177

battleground. The Shemites fell on the guardsmen, and their spears and arrows struck down many soldiers who had already disbanded.

"Some of us grabbed up such weapons as we could and fought back. We hardly knew what we were fighting for, but it was against Constantius and his devils—not against Taramis, I swear it! Constantius shouted to cut the traitors down. We were not traitors!" Despair and bewilderment shook his voice. The girl murmured pityingly, not understanding it all, but aching in sympathy with her lover's suffering.

"The people did not know which side to take. It was a madhouse of confusion and bewilderment. We who fought didn't have a chance, in no formation, without armor and only half armed. The guards were fully armed and drawn up in a square, but there were only five hundred of them. They took a heavy toll before they were cut down, but there could be only one conclusion to such a battle. And while her people were being slaughtered before her, Taramis stood on the palace steps, with Constantius' arm about her waist, and laughed like a heartless, beautiful fiend! Gods, it's all mad—mad!

"I never saw a man fight as Conan fought. He put his back to the courtyard wall, and before they overpowered him the dead men were strewn in heaps thigh-deep about him. But at last they dragged him down, a hundred against one. When I saw him fall I dragged myself away feeling as if the world had burst under my very fingers. I heard Constantius call to his dogs to take the captain alive—stroking his mustache, with that hateful smile on his lips!"

That smile was on the lips of Constantius at that very moment. He sat his horse among a cluster of his men—

178

thick-bodied Shemites with curled blue-black beards and hooked noses; the low-swinging sun struck glints from their peaked helmets and the silvered scales of their corselets. Nearly a mile behind, the walls and towers of Khauran rose sheer out of the meadowlands.

By the side of the caravan road a heavy cross had been planted, and on this grim tree a man hung, nailed there by iron spikes through his hands and feet. Naked but for a loin-cloth, the man was almost a giant in stature, and his muscles stood out in thick corded ridges on limbs and body, which the sun had long ago burned brown. The perspiration of agony beaded his face and his mighty breast, but from under the tangled black mane that fell over his low, broad forehead, his blue eyes blazed with an unquenched fire. Blood oozed sluggishly from the lacerations in his hands and feet.

Constantius saluted him mockingly.

"I am sorry, captain," he said, "that I can not remain to ease your last hours, but I have duties to perform in yonder city—I must not keep our delicious queen waiting!" He laughed softly. "So I leave you to your own devices—and those beauties!" He pointed meaningly at the black shadows which swept incessantly back and forth, high above.

"Were it not for them, I imagine that a powerful brute like yourself should live on the cross for days. Do not cherish any illusions of rescue because I am leaving you unguarded. I have had it proclaimed that anyone seeking to take your body, living or dead, from the cross, will be flayed alive together with all the members of his family, in the public square. I am so firmly established in Khauran that my order is as good as a regiment of guardsmen. I am leaving no guard, because the vultures will not approach as long as anyone is near, and I do not wish them to feel any constraint.

179

That is also why I brought you so far from the city. These desert vultures approach the walls no closer than this spot.

"And so, brave captain, farewell! I will remember you when, in an hour, Taramis lies in my arms."

Blood started afresh from the pierced palms as the victim's mallet-like fists clenched convulsively on the spike-heads. Knots and bunches of muscle started out of the massive arms, and Conan bent his head forward and spat savagely at Constantius' face. The *voivode* laughed coolly, wiped the saliva from his gorget and reined his horse about.

"Remember me when the vultures are tearing at your living flesh," he called mockingly. "The desert scavengers are a particularly voracious breed. I have seen men hang for hours on a cross, eyeless, earless, and scalpless, before the sharp beaks had eaten their way into his vitals."

Without a backward glance he rode toward the city, a supple, erect figure, gleaming in his burnished armor, his stolid, bearded henchmen jogging beside him. A faint rising of dust from the worn trail marked their passing.

The man hanging on the cross was the one touch of sentient life in a landscape that seemed desolate and deserted in the late evening. Khauran, less than a mile away, might have been on the other side of the world, and existing in another age.

Shaking the sweat out of his eyes, Conan stared blankly at the familiar terrain. On either side of the city, and beyond it, stretched the fertile meadowlands, with cattle browsing in the distance where fields and vineyards checkered the plain. The western and northern horizons were dotted with villages, miniature in the distance. A lesser distance to the southeast a

180

silvery gleam marked the course of a river, and beyond that river sandy desert began abruptly to stretch away and away beyond the horizon. Conan stared at that expanse of empty waste shimmering tawnily in the late sunlight as a trapped hawk stares at the open sky. A revulsion shook him when he glanced at the gleaming towers of Khauran. The city had betrayed him— trapped him into circumstances that left him hanging to a wooden cross like a hare nailed to a tree.

A red lust for vengeance swept away the thought. Curses ebbed fitfully from the man's lips. All his universe contracted, focused, became incorporated in the four iron spikes that held him from life and freedom. His great muscles quivered, knotting like iron cables. With the sweat starting out on his graying skin, he sought to gain leverage, to tear the nails from the wood. It was useless. They had been driven deep. Then he tried to tear his hands off the spikes, and it was not the knifing, abysmal agony that finally caused him to cease his efforts, but the futility of it. The spike-heads were broad and heavy; he could not drag them through the wounds. A surge of helplessness shook the giant, for the first time in his life. He hung motionless, his head resting on his breast, shutting his eyes against the aching glare of the sun.

A beat of wings caused him to look, just as a feathered shadow shot down out of the sky. A keen beak, stabbing at his eyes, cut his cheek, and he jerked his head aside, shutting his eyes involuntarily. He shouted, a croaking, desperate shout of menace, and the vultures swerved away and retreated, frightened by the sound. They resumed their wary circling above his head. Blood trickled over Conan's mouth, and he licked his lips involuntarily, spat at the salty taste.

Thirst assailed him savagely. He had drunk deeply

181

of wine the night before, and no water had touched his lips since before the battle in the square, that dawn. And killing was thirsty, salt-sweaty work. He glared at the distant river as a man in hell glares through the opened grille. He thought of gushing freshets of white water he had breasted, laved to the shoulders in liquid jade. He remembered great horns of foaming ale, jacks of sparkling wine gulped carelessly or spilled on the tavern floor. He bit his lip to keep from bellowing in intolerable anguish as a tortured animal bellows.

The sun sank, a lurid ball in a fiery sea of blood. Against a crimson rampart that banded the horizon the towers of the city floated unreal as a dream. The very sky was tinged with blood to his misted glare. He licked his blackened lips and stared with bloodshot eyes at the distant river. It too seemed crimson like blood, and the shadows crawling up from the east seemed black as ebony.

In his dulled ears sounded the louder beat of wings. Lifting his head he watched with the burning glare of a wolf the shadows wheeling above him. He knew that his shouts would frighten them away no longer. One dipped—dipped—lower and lower. Conan drew his head back as far as he could, waiting with terrible patience. The vulture swept in with a swift roar of wings. Its beak flashed down, ripping the skin on Conan's chin as he jerked his head aside; then before the bird could flash away, Conan's head lunged forward on his mighty neck muscles, and his teeth, snapping like those of a wolf, locked on the bare, wattled neck.

Instantly the vulture exploded into squawking, flapping hysteria. Its thrashing wings blinded the man, and its talons ripped his chest. But grimly he hung on, the muscles starting out in lumps on his jaws. And the

182

scavenger's neck-bones crunched between those powerful teeth. With a spasmodic flutter the bird hung limp. Conan let go, spat blood from his mouth. The other vultures, terrified by the fate of their companion, were in full flight to a distant tree, where they perched like black demons in conclave.

Ferocious triumph surged through Conan's numbed brain. Life beat strongly and savagely through his veins. He could still deal death; he still lived. Every twinge of sensation, even of agony, was a negation of death.

"By Mitra!" Either a voice spoke, or he suffered from hallucination. "In all my life I have never seen such a thing!"

Shaking the sweat and blood from his eyes, Conan saw four horsemen sitting their steeds in the twilight and staring up at him. Three were lean, white-robed hawks, Zuagir tribesmen without a doubt, nomads from beyond the river. The other was dressed like them in a white, girdled *khalat* and a flowing head-dress which, banded about the temples with a triple circlet of braided camel-hair, fell to his shoulders. But he was not a Shemite. The dusk was not so thick, nor Conan's hawk-like sight so clouded, that he could not perceive the man's facial characteristics.

He was as tall as Conan, though not so heavy-limbed. His shoulders were broad and his supple figure was hard as steel and whalebone. A short black beard did not altogether mask the aggressive jut of his lean jaw, and gray eyes cold and piercing as a sword gleamed from the shadow of the *kafieh*. Quieting his restless steed with a quick, sure hand, this man spoke: "By Mitra, I should know this man!"

"Aye!" It was the guttural accents of a Zuagir. "It is the Cimmerian who was captain of the queen's guard!"

183

"She must be casting off all her old favorites," muttered the rider. "Who'd have ever thought it of Queen Taramis? I'd rather have had a long, bloody war. It would have given us desert folk a chance to plunder. As it is we've come this close to the walls and found only this nag"—he glanced at a fine gelding led by one of the nomads—"and this dying dog."

Conan lifted his bloody head.

"If I could come down from this beam I'd make a dying dog out of you, you Zaporoskan thief!" he rasped through blackened lips.

"Mitra, the knave knows me!" exclaimed the other. "How, knave, do you know me?"

"There's only one of your breed in these parts," muttered Conan. "You are Olgerd Vladislav, the outlaw chief."

"Aye! and once a hetman of the *kozaki* of the Zaporoskan River, as you have guessed. Would you like to live?"

"Only a fool would ask that question," panted Conan.

"I am a hard man," said Olgerd, "and toughness is the only quality I respect in a man. I shall judge if you are a man, or only a dog after all, fit only to lie here and die."

"If we cut him down we may be seen from the walls," objected one of the nomads.

Olgerd shook his head.

"The dusk is too deep. Here, take this ax, Djebal, and cut down the cross at the base."

"If it falls forward it will crush him," objected Djebal. "I can cut it so it will fall backward, but then the shock of the fall may crack his skull and tear loose all his entrails."

"If he's worthy to ride with me he'll survive it,"

184

answered Olgerd imperturbably. "If not, then he doesn't deserve to live. Cut!"

The first impact of the battle-ax against the wood and its accompanying vibrations sent lances of agony through Conan's swollen feet and hands. Again and again the blade fell, and each stroke reverberated on his bruised brain, setting his tortured nerves aquiver. But he set his teeth and made no sound. The ax cut through, the cross reeled on its splintered base and toppled backward. Conan made his whole body a solid knot of iron-hard muscle, jammed his head back hard against the wood and held it rigid there. The beam struck the ground heavily and rebounded slightly. The impact tore his wounds and dazed him for an instant. He fought the rushing tide of blackness, sick and dizzy, but realized that the iron muscles that sheathed his vitals had saved him from permanent injury.

And he had made no sound, though blood oozed from his nostrils and his belly-muscles quivered with nausea. With a grunt of approval Djebal bent over him with a pair of pincers used to draw horse-shoe nails, and gripped the head of the spike in Conan's right hand, tearing the skin to get a grip on the deeply embedded head. The pincers were small for that work. Djebal sweated and tugged, swearing and wrestling with the stubborn iron, working it back and forth—in swollen flesh as well as in wood. Blood started, oozing over the Cimmerian's fingers. He lay so still he might have been dead, except for the spasmodic rise and fall of his great chest. The spike gave way, and Djebal held up the blood-stained thing with a grunt of satisfaction, then flung it away and bent over the other.

The process was repeated, and then Djebal turned his attention to Conan's skewered feet. But the Cimmerian, struggling up to a sitting posture,

185

wrenched the pincers from his fingers and sent him staggering backward with a violent shove. Conan's hands were swollen to almost twice their normal size. His fingers felt like misshapen thumbs, and closing his hands was an agony that brought blood streaming from under his grinding teeth. But somehow, clutching the pincers clumsily with both hands, he managed to wrench out first one spike and then the other. They were not driven so deeply into the wood as the others had been.

He rose stiffly and stood upright on his swollen, lacerated feet, swaying drunkenly, the icy sweat dripping from his face and body. Cramps assailed him and he clamped his jaws against the desire to retch.

Olgerd, watching him impersonally, motioned him toward the stolen horse. Conan stumbled toward it, and every step was a stabbing, throbbing hell that flecked his lips with bloody foam. One misshapen, groping hand fell clumsily on the saddle-bow, a bloody foot somehow found the stirrup. Setting his teeth, he swung up, and he almost fainted in midair; but he came down in the saddle—and as he did so, Olgerd struck the horse sharply with his whip. The startled beast reared, and the man in the saddle swayed and slumped like a sack of sand, almost unseated. Conan had wrapped a rein about each hand, holding it in place with a clamping thumb. Drunkenly he exerted the strength of his knotted biceps, wrenching the horse down; it screamed, its jaw almost dislocated.

One of the Shemites lifted a water-flask questioningly.

Olgerd shook his head.

"Let him wait until we get to camp. It's only ten miles. If he's fit to live in the desert he'll live that long without a drink."

The group rode like swift ghosts toward the river; among them Conan swayed like a drunken man in the saddle, bloodshot eyes glazed, foam drying on his blackened lips.

3. A Letter to Nemedia

THE SAVANT ASTREAS, traveling in the East in his never-tiring search for knowledge, wrote a letter to his friend and fellow-philosopher Alcemides, in his native Nemedia, which constitutes the entire knowledge of the Western nations concerning the events of that period in the East, always a hazy, half-mythical region in the minds of the Western folk.

Astreas wrote, in part: "You can scarcely conceive, my dear old friend, of the conditions now existing in this tiny kingdom since Queen Taramis admitted Constantius and his mercenaries, an event which I briefly described in my last, hurried letter. Seven months have passed since then, during which time it seems as though the devil himself had been loosed in this unfortunate realm. Taramis seems to have gone quite mad; whereas formerly she was famed for her virtue, justice and tranquillity, she is now notorious for qualities precisely opposite to those just enumerated. Her private life is a scandal—or perhaps 'private' is not the correct term, since the queen makes no attempt to conceal the debauchery of her court. She constantly indulges in the most infamous revelries, in which the unfortunate ladies of the court are forced to join, young married women as well as virgins.

"She herself has not bothered to marry her paramour, Constantius, who sits on the throne beside her and reigns as her royal consort, and his officers follow his example, and do not hesitate to debauch any woman they desire, regardless of her rank or station. The wretched kingdom groans under exorbitant taxation, the farms are stripped to the bone, and the merchants go in rags which are all that is left them by the tax-gatherers. Nay, they are lucky if they escape with a whole skin.

"I sense your incredulity, good Alcemides; you will fear that I exaggerate conditions in Khauran. Such conditions would be unthinkable in any of the Western countries, admittedly. But you must realize the vast difference that exists between West and East, especially this part of the East. In the first place, Khauran is a kingdom of no great size, one of the many principalities which at one time formed the eastern part of the empire of Koth, and which later regained the independence which was theirs at a still earlier age. This part of the world is made up of these tiny realms, diminutive in comparison with the great kingdoms of the West, or the great sultanates of the farther East, but important in their control of the caravan routes, and in the wealth concentrated in them.

"Khauran is the most southeasterly of these principalities, bordering on the very deserts of eastern Shem. The city of Khauran is the only city of any magnitude in the realm, and stands within sight of the river which separates the grasslands from the sandy desert, like a watch-tower to guard the fertile meadows behind it. The land is so rich that it yields three and four crops a year, and the plains north and west of the city are dotted with villages. To one accustomed to the great plantations and stock-farms of the West, it is strange to see these tiny fields and vineyards; yet wealth in grain and fruit pours from them as from a horn of plenty. The villagers are agriculturists, nothing else. Of a mixed, aboriginal race, they are unwarlike, unable to protect themselves, and forbidden the possession of arms. Dependent wholly upon the soldiers of the city for protection, they are helpless under the present conditions. So the savage revolt of the rural sections, which would be a certainty in any Western nation, is here impossible.

"They toil supinely under the iron hand of Constantius, and his black-bearded Shemites ride incessantly through the fields, with whips in their hands, like the slave-drivers of the black serfs who toil in the plantations of southern Zingara.

"Nor do the people of the city fare any better. Their wealth is stripped from them, their fairest daughters taken to glut the insatiable lust of Constantius and his mercenaries. These men are utterly without mercy or compassion, possessed of all the characteristics our armies learned to abhor in our wars against the Shemitish allies of Argos—inhuman cruelty, lust, and wild-beast ferocity. The people of the city are Khauran's ruling caste, predominantly Hyborian, and valorous and war-like. But the treachery of their queen delivered them into the hands of their oppressors. The Shemites are the only armed force in Khauran, and the most hellish punishment is inflicted on any Khauran found possessing weapons. A systematic persecution to destroy the young Khaurani men able to bear arms has been savagely pursued. Many have ruthlessly been slaughtered, others sold as slaves to the Turanians. Thousands have fled the kingdom and either entered the service of other rulers, or become outlaws, lurking in numerous bands along the borders.

"At present there is some possibility of invasion from the desert, which is inhabited by tribes of Shemitish nomads. The mercenaries of Constantius are men from the Shemitish cities of the west, Pelishtim, Anakim, Akkharim, and are ardently hated by the Zuagirs and other wandering tribes. As you know, good Alcemides, the countries of these bar-barians are divided into the western meadowlands

190

which stretch to the distant ocean, and in which rise the cities of the town-dwellers, and the eastern deserts, where the lean nomads hold sway; there is incessant warfare between the dwellers of the cities and the dwellers of the desert.

"The Zuagirs have fought with and raided Khauran for centuries, without success, but they resent its conquest by their western kin. It is rumored that their natural antagonism is being fomented by the man who was formerly the captain of the queen's guard, and who, somehow escaping the hate of Constantius, who actually had him upon the cross, fled to the nomads. He is called Conan, and is himself a barbarian, one of those gloomy Cimmerians whose ferocity our soldiers have more than once learned to their bitter cost. It is rumored that he has become the right-hand man of Olgerd Vladislav, the *kozak* adventurer who wandered down from the northern steppes and made himself chief of a band of Zuagirs. There are also rumors that this band has increased vastly in the last few months, and that Olgerd, incited no doubt by this Cimmerian, is even considering a raid on Khauran.

"It can not be anything more than a raid, as the Zuagirs are without siege-machines, or the knowledge of investing a city, and it has been proven repeatedly in the past that the nomads in their loose formation, or rather lack of formation, are no match in hand-to-hand fighting for the well-disciplined, fully-armed warriors of the Shemitish cities. The natives of Khauran would perhaps welcome this conquest, since the nomads could deal with them no more harshly than their present masters, and even total extermination would be preferable to the suffering they have to endure. But they are so cowed and helpless that they could give no aid to the invaders.

"Their plight is most wretched. Taramis, apparently possessed of a demon, stops at nothing. She has abolished the worship of Ishtar, and turned the temple into a shrine of idolatry. She has destroyed the ivory image of the goddess which these eastern Hyborians worship (and which, inferior as it is to the true religion of Mitra which we Western nations recognize, is still superior to the devil-worship of the Shemites) and filled the temple of Ishtar with obscene images of every imaginable sort—gods and goddesses of the night, portrayed in all the salacious and perverse poses and with all the revolting characteristics that a degenerate brain could conceive. Many of these images are to be identified as foul deities of the Shemites, the Turanians, the Vendhyans, and the Khitans, but others are reminiscent of a hideous and half-remembered antiquity, vile shapes forgotten except in the most obscure legends. Where the queen gained the knowledge of them I dare not even hazard a guess.

"She has instituted human sacrifice, and since her mating with Constantius, no less than five hundred men, women and children have been immolated. Some of these have died on the altar she has set up in the temple, herself wielding the sacrificial dagger, but most have met a more horrible doom.

"Taramis has placed some sort of monster in a crypt in the temple. What it is, and whence it came, none knows. But shortly after she had crushed the desperate revolt of her soldiers against Constantius, she spent a night alone in the desecrated temple, alone except for a dozen bound captives, and the shuddering people saw thick, foul-smelling smoke curling up from the dome, heard all night the frenetic chanting of the queen, and the agonized cries of her tortured captives; and toward dawn another voice mingled with these sounds—a strident, inhuman croaking that froze the blood of all who heard.

"In the full dawn Taramis reeled drunkenly from the temple, her eyes blazing with demoniac triumph. The captives were never seen again, nor the croaking voice heard. But there is a room in the temple into which none ever goes but the queen, driving a human sacrifice before her. And this victim is never seen again. All know that in that grim chamber lurks some monster from the black night of ages, which devours the shrieking humans Taramis delivers up to it.

"I can no longer think of her as a mortal woman, but as a rabid she-fiend, crouching in her blood-fouled lair amongst the bones and fragments of her victims, with taloned, crimsoned fingers. That the gods allow her to pursue her awful course unchecked almost shakes my faith in divine justice.

"When I compare her present conduct with her deportment when first I came to Khauran, seven months ago, I am confused with bewilderment, and almost inclined to the belief held by many of the people—that a demon has possessed the body of Taramis. A young soldier, Valerius, had another belief. He believed that a witch had assumed a form identical with that of Khauran's adored ruler. He believed that Taramis had been spirited away in the night, and confined in some dungeon, and that this being ruling in her place was but a female sorcerer. He swore that he would find the real queen, if she still lived, but I greatly fear that he himself has fallen victim to the cruelty of Constantius. He was implicated in the revolt of the palace guards, escaped and remained in hiding for some time, stubbornly refusing to seek safety abroad, and it was during this time that I encountered him and he told me his beliefs.

193

"But he has disappeared, as so many have, whose fate one dares not conjecture, and I fear he has been apprehended by the spies of Constantius.

"But I must conclude this letter and slip it out of the city by means of a swift carrier-pigeon, which will carry it to the post whence I purchased it, on the borders of Koth. By rider and camel-train it will eventually come to you. I must haste, before dawn. It is late, and the stars gleam whitely on the gardened roofs of Khauran. A shuddering silence envelops the city, in which I hear the throb of a sullen drum from the distant temple. I doubt not that Taramis is there, concocting more deviltry."

But the savant was incorrect in his conjecture concerning the whereabouts of the woman he called Taramis. The girl whom the world knew as queen of Khauran stood in a dungeon, lighted only by a flickering torch which played on her features, etching the diabolical cruelty of her beautiful countenance.

On the bare stone floor before her crouched a figure whose nakedness was scarcely covered with tattered rags.

This figure Salome touched contemptuously with the upturned toe of her gilded sandal, and smiled vindictively as her victim shrank away.

"You do not love my caresses, sweet sister?"

Taramis was still beautiful, in spite of her rags and the imprisonment and abuse of seven weary months. She did not reply to her sister's taunts, but bent her head as one grown accustomed to mockery.

This resignation did not please Salome. She bit her red lip, and stood tapping the toe of her shoe against the flags as she frowned down at the passive figure. Salome was clad in the barbaric splendor of a woman of Shushan. Jewels glittered in the torchlight on her gilded sandals, on her gold breast-plates and the slender chains that held them in place. Gold anklets clashed as she moved, jeweled bracelets weighted her bare arms. Her tall coiffure was that of a Shemitish woman, and jade pendants hung from gold hoops in her ears, flashing and sparkling with each impatient movement of her haughty head. A gem-crusted girdle supported a silk skirt so transparent that it was in the nature of a cynical mockery of convention.

Suspended from her shoulders and trailing down her back hung a darkly scarlet cloak, and this was thrown carelessly over the crook of one arm and the bundle that arm supported.

Salome stooped suddenly and with her free hand grasped her sister's disheveled hair and forced back the girl's head to stare into her eyes. Taramis met that tigerish glare without flinching.

"You are not so ready with your tears as formerly, sweet sister," muttered the witch-girl.

"You shall wring no more tears from me," answered Taramis. "Too often you have reveled in the spectacle of the queen of Khauran sobbing for mercy on her knees. I know that you have spared me only to torment me; that is why you have limited your tortures to such torments as neither slay nor permanently disfigure. But I fear you no longer; you have strained out the last vestige of hope, fright and shame from me. Slay me and be done with it, for I have shed my last tear for your enjoyment, you she-devil from hell!"

"You flatter yourself, my dear sister," purred Salome. "So far it is only your handsome body that I have caused to suffer, only your pride and self-esteem that I have crushed. You forget that, unlike myself, you are capable of mental torment. I have observed this

195

when I have regaled you with narratives concerning the comedies I have enacted with some of your stupid subjects. But this time I have brought more vivid proof of these farces. Did you know that Krallides, your faithful councillor, had come skulking back from Turan and been captured?"

Taramis turned pale.

"What—what have you done to him?"

For answer Salome drew the mysterious bundle from under her cloak. She shook off the silken swathings and held it up—the head of a young man, the features frozen in a convulsion as if death had come in the midst of inhuman agony.

Taramis cried out as if a blade had pierced her heart.

"Oh, Ishtar! Krallides!"

"Aye! He was seeking to stir up the people against me, poor fool, telling them that Conan spoke the truth when he said I was not Taramis. How would the people rise against the Falcon's Shemites? With sticks and pebbles? Bah! Dogs are eating his headless body in the marketplace, and this foul carrion shall be cast into the sewer to rot.

"How, sister!" She paused, smiling down at her victim. "Have you discovered that you still have unshed tears? Good! I reserved the mental torment for the last. Hereafter I shall show you many such sights as—this!"

Standing there in the torchlight with the severed head in her hand she did not look like anything ever born by a human woman, in spite of her awful beauty. Taramis did not look up. She lay face down on the slimy floor, her slim body shaken in sobs of agony, beating her clenched hands against the stones. Salome sauntered toward the door, her anklets clashing at each step, her ear pendants winking in the torch-glare.

A few moments later she emerged from a door under a sullen arch that let into a court which in turn opened upon a winding alley. A man standing there turned toward her—a giant Shemite, with somber eyes and shoulders like a bull, his great black beard falling over his mighty, silver-mailed breast.

"She wept?" His rumble was like that of a bull, deep. low-pitched and stormy. He was the general of the mercenaries, one of the few even of Constantius' associates who knew the secret of the queens of Khauran.

"Aye, Khumbanigash. There are whole sections of her sensibilities that I have not touched. When one sense is dulled by continual laceration, I will discover a newer, more poignant pang.—Here, dog!" A trembling, shambling figure in rags, filth and matted hair approached, one of the beggars that slept in the alleys and open courts. Salome tossed the head to him. "Here, deaf one; cast that in the nearest sewer.—Make the sign with your hands, Khumbanigash. He can not hear."

The general complied, and the tousled head bobbed, as the man turned painfully away.

"Why do you keep up this farce?" rumbled Khumbanigash. "You are so firmly established on the throne that nothing can unseat you. What if the Khaurani fools learn the truth? They can do nothing. Proclaim yourself in your true identity! Show them their beloved ex-queen—and cut off her head in the public square!"

"Not yet, good Khumbanigash—"

The arched door slammed on the hard accents of Salome, the stormy reverberations of Khumbanigash. The mute beggar crouched in the courtyard, and there was none to see that the hands which held the severed

197

head were quivering strongly—brown, sinewy hands, strangely incongruous with the bent body and filthy tatters.

"I knew it!" It was a fierce, vibrant whisper, scarcely audible. "She lives! Oh, Krallides, your martyrdom was not in vain! They have her locked in that dungeon! Oh, Ishtar, if you love true men, aid me now!"

4. Wolves of the Desert

OLGERD VLADISLAV FILLED his jeweled goblet with crimson wine from a golden jug and thrust the vessel across the ebony table to Conan the Cimmerian. Olgerd's apparel would have satisfied the vanity of any Zaporoskan hetman.

His *khalat* was of white silk, with pearls sewn on the bosom. Girdled at the waist with a Bakhauriot belt, its skirts were drawn back to reveal his wide silken breeches, tucked into short boots of soft green leather, adorned with gold thread. On his head was a green silk turban, wound about a spired helmet chased with gold. His only weapon was a broad curved Cherkees knife in an ivory sheath girdled high on his left hip, *kozak* fashion. Throwing himself back in his gilded chair with its carven eagles, Olgerd spread his booted legs before him, and gulped down the sparkling wine noisily.

To his splendor the huge Cimmerian opposite him offered a strong contrast, with his square-cut black mane, brown scarred countenance and burning blue eyes. He was clad in black mesh-mail, and the only glitter about him was the broad gold buckle of the belt which supported his sword in its worn leather scabbard.

They were alone in the silk-walled tent, which was hung with gilt-worked tapestries and littered with rich carpets and velvet cushions, the loot of the caravans. From outside came a low, incessant murmur, the sound that always accompanies a great throng of men, in camp or otherwise. An occasional gust of desert wind rattled the palm-leaves.

"Today in the shadow, tomorrow in the sun," quoth Olgerd, loosening his crimson girdle a trifle and

199

reaching again for the wine-jug. "That's the way of life. Once I was a hetman on the Zaporoska; now I'm a desert chief. Seven months ago you were hanging on a cross outside Khauran. Now you're lieutenant to the most powerful raider between Turan and the western meadows. You should be thankful to me!"

"For recognizing my usefulness?" Conan laughed and lifted the jug. "When you allow the elevation of a man, one can be sure that you'll profit by his advancement. I've earned everything I've won, with my blood and sweat." He glanced at the scars on the insides of his palms. There were scars, too, on his body, scars that had not been there seven months ago.

"You fight like a regiment of devils," conceded Olgerd. "But don't get to thinking that you've had anything to do with the recruits who've swarmed in to join us. It was our success at raiding, guided by my wit, that brought them in. These nomads are always looking for a successful leader to follow, and they have more faith in a foreigner than in one of their own race.

"There's no limit to what we may accomplish! We have eleven thousand men now. In another year we may have three times that number. We've contented ourselves, so far, with raids on the Turanian outposts and the city-states to the west. With thirty or forty thousand men we'll raid no longer. We'll invade and conquer and establish ourselves as rulers. I'll be emperor of all Shem yet, and you'll be my vizier, so long as you carry out my orders unquestioningly. In the meantime, I think we'll ride eastward and storm that Turanian outpost at Vezek, where the caravans pay toll."

Conan shook his head. "I think not."

Olgerd glared, his quick temper irritated.

"What do you mean, *you* think not? I do the

200

thinking for this army!"

"There are enough men in this band now for my purpose," answered the Cimmerian. "I'm sick of waiting. I have a score to settle."

"Oh!" Olgerd scowled, and gulped wine, then grinned. "Still thinking of that cross, eh? Well, I like a good hater. But that can wait."

"You told me once you'd aid me in taking Khauran," said Conan.

"Yes, but that was before I began to see the full possibilities of our power," answered Olgerd. "I was only thinking of the loot in the city. I don't want to waste our strength unprofitably. Khauran is too strong a nut for us to crack now. Maybe in a year—"

"Within the week," answered Conan, and the *kozak* stared at the certainty in his voice.

"Listen," said Olgerd, "even if I were willing to throw away men on such a hare-brained attempt— what could you expect? Do you think these wolves could besiege and take a city like Khauran?"

"There'll be no siege," answered the Cimmerian. "I know how to draw Constantius out into the plain."

"And what then?" cried Olgerd with an oath. "In the arrow-play our horsemen would have the worst of it, for the armor of the *asshuri* is the better, and when it came to sword-strokes their close-marshaled ranks of trained swordsmen would cleave through our loose lines and scatter our men like chaff before the wind."

"Not if there were three thousand desperate Hyborian horsemen fighting in a solid wedge such as I could teach them," answered Conan.

"And where would you secure three thousand Hyborians?" asked Olgerd with vast sarcasm. "Will you conjure them out of the air?"

"I *have* them," answered the Cimmerian imperturb-

201

ably. "Three thousand men of Khauran camp at the oasis of Akrel awaiting my orders."

"*What?*" Olgerd glared like a startled wolf.

"Aye. Men who had fled from the tyranny of Constantius. Most of them have been living the lives of outlaws in the deserts east of Khauran, and are gaunt and hard and desperate as man-eating tigers. One of them will be a match for any three squat mercenaries. It takes oppression and hardship to stiffen men's guts and put the fire of hell into their thews. They were broken up into small bands; all they needed was a leader. They believed the word I sent them by my riders, and assembled at the oasis and put themselves at my disposal."

"All this without my knowledge?" A feral light began to gleam in Olgerd's eyes. He hitched at his weapon-girdle.

"It was *I* they wished to follow, not *you.*"

"And what did you tell these outcasts to gain their allegiance?" There was a dangerous ring in Olgerd's voice.

"I told them that I'd use this horde of desert wolves to help them destroy Constantius and give Khauran back into the hands of its citizens."

"You fool!" whispered Olgerd. "Do you deem yourself chief already?"

The men were on their feet, facing each other across the ebony board, devil-lights dancing in Olgerd's cold gray eyes, a grim smile on the Cimmerian's hard lips.

"I'll have you torn between four palm-trees," said the *kozak* calmly.

"Call the men and bid them do it!" challenged Conan. "See if they obey you!"

Baring his teeth in a snarl, Olgerd lifted his hand— then paused. There was something about the confidence in the Cimmerian's dark face that shook him. His eyes began to burn like those of a wolf.

"You scum of the western hills," he muttered, "have you dared seek to undermine my power?"

"I didn't have to," answered Conan. "You lied when you said I had nothing to do with bringing in the new recruits. I had everything to do with it. They took your orders, but they fought for me. There is not room for two chiefs of the Zuagirs. They know I am the stronger man. I understand them better than you, and they, me; because I am a barbarian too."

"And what will they say when you ask them to fight for the Khaurani?" asked Olgerd sardonically.

"They'll follow me. I'll promise them a camel-train of gold from the palace. Khauran will be willing to pay that as a guerdon for getting rid of Constantius. After that, I'll lead them against the Turanians as you have planned. They want loot, and they'd as soon fight Constantius for it as anybody."

In Olgerd's eyes grew a recognition of defeat. In his red dreams of empire he had missed what was going on about him. Happenings and events that had seemed meaningless before now flashed into his mind, with their true significance, bringing a realization that Conan spoke no idle boast. The giant black-mailed figure before him was the real chief of the Zuagirs.

"Not if you die!" muttered Olgerd, and his hand flickered toward his hilt. But quick as the stroke of a great cat Conan's arm shot across the table and his fingers locked on Olgerd's forearm. There was a snap of breaking bones, and for a tense instant the scene held: the men facing each other as motionless as images, perspiration starting out on Olgerd's forehead. Conan laughed, never easing his grip on the broken arm.

"Are you fit to live, Olgerd?"

His smile did not alter as the corded muscles rippled in knotting ridges along his forearm and his fingers ground into the *kozak's* quivering flesh. There was the sound of broken bones grating together and Olgerd's face turned the color of ashes; blood oozed from his lip where his teeth sank, but he uttered no sound.

With a laugh Conan released him and drew back, and the *kozak* swayed, caught the table edge with his good hand to steady himself.

"I give you life, Olgerd, as you gave it to me," said Conan tranquilly, "though it was for your own ends that you took me down from the cross. It was a bitter test you gave me then; you couldn't have endured it; neither could anyone, but a western barbarian.

"Take your horse and go. It's tied behind the tent, and food and water are in the saddle-bags. None will see your going, but go quickly. There's no room for a fallen chief on the desert. If the warriors see you, maimed and deposed, they'll never let you leave the camp alive."

Olgerd did not reply. Slowly, without a word, he turned and stalked across the tent, through the flapped opening. Unspeaking he climbed into the saddle of the great white stallion that stood tethered there in the shade of a spreading palm-tree; and unspeaking, with his broken arm thrust in the bosom of his *khalat*, he reined the steed about and rode eastward into the open desert, out of the life of the people of the Zuagir.

Inside the tent Conan emptied the wine-jug and smacked his lips with relish. Tossing the empty vessel into a corner, he braced his belt and strode out through the front opening, halting for a moment to let his gaze sweep over the lines of camel-hair tents that stretched before him, and the white-robed figures that moved among them, arguing, singing, mending bridles or whetting tulwars.

He lifted his voice in a thunder that carried to the farthest confines of the encampment: "*Aie*, you dogs, sharpen your ears and listen! Gather around here. I have a tale to tell you."

5. The Voice From the Crystal

IN A CHAMBER in a tower near the city wall a group of men listened attentively to the words of one of their number. They were young men, but hard and sinewy, with the bearing that comes only to men rendered desperate by adversity. They were clad in mail shirts and worn leather; swords hung at their girdles.

"I knew that Conan spoke the truth when he said it was not Taramis!" the speaker exclaimed. "For months I have haunted the outskirts of the palace, playing the part of a deaf beggar. At last I learned what I had believed—that our queen was a prisoner in the dungeons that adjoin the palace. I watched my opportunity and captured a Shemitish jailer—knocked him senseless as he left the courtyard late one night— dragged him into a cellar near by and questioned him. Before he died he told me what I have just told you, and what we have suspected all along—that the woman ruling Khauran is a witch: Salome. Taramis, he said, is imprisoned in the lowest dungeon.

"This invasion of the Zuagirs gives us the opportunity we sought. What Conan means to do, I can not say. Perhaps he merely wishes vengeance on Constantius. Perhaps he intends sacking the city and destroying it. He is a barbarian and no one can understand their minds.

"But this is what we must do: rescue Taramis while the battle rages! Constantius will march out into the plain to give battle. Even now his men are mounting. He will do this because there is not sufficient food in the city to stand a siege. Conan burst out of the desert so suddenly that there was no time to bring in supplies. And the Cimmerian is equipped for a siege. Scouts have reported that the Zuagirs have siege engines, built, undoubtedly, according to the instructions of Conan, who learned all the arts of war among the Western nations.

"Constantius does not desire a long siege; so he will march with his warriors into the plain, where he expects to scatter Conan's forces at one stroke. He will leave only a few hundred men in the city, and they will be on the walls and in the towers commanding the gates.

"The prison will be left all but unguarded. When we have freed Taramis our next actions will depend upon circumstances. If Conan wins, we must show Taramis to the people and bid them rise—they will! Oh, they will! With their bare hands they are enough to overpower the Shemites left in the city and close the gates against both the mercenaries and the nomads. Neither must get within the walls! Then we will parley with Conan. He was always loyal to Taramis. If he knows the truth, and she appeals to him, I believe he will spare the city. If, which is more probable, Constantius prevails, and Conan is routed, we must steal out of the city with the queen and seek safety in flight.

"Is all clear?"

They replied with one voice.

"Then let us loosen our blades in our scabbards, commend our souls to Ishtar, and start for the prison, for the mercenaries are already marching through the southern gate."

This was true. The dawnlight glinted on peaked helmets pouring in a steady stream through the broad arch, on the bright housings of the chargers. This would be a battle of horsemen, such as is possible only

207

in the lands of the East. The riders flowed through the gates like a river of steel—somber figures in black and silver mail, with their curled beards and hooked noses, and their inexorable eyes in which glimmered the fatality of their race—the utter lack of doubt or of mercy.

The streets and the walls were lined with throngs of people who watched silently these warriors of an alien race riding forth to defend their native city. There was no sound; dully, expressionless they watched, those gaunt people in shabby garments, their caps in their hands.

In a tower that overlooked the broad street that led to the southern gate, Salome lolled on a velvet couch cynically watching Constantius as he settled his broad sword-belt about his lean hips and drew on his gauntlets. They were alone in the chamber. Outside, the rhythmical clank of harness and shuffle of horses' hoofs welled up through the gold-barred casements.

"Before nightfall," quoth Constantius, giving a twirl to his thin mustache, "you'll have some captives to feed to your temple-devil. Does it not grow weary of soft, city-bred flesh? Perhaps it would relish the harder thews of a desert man."

"Take care you do not fall prey to a fiercer beast than Thaug," warned the girl. "Do not forget who it is that leads these desert animals."

"I am not likely to forget," he answered. "That is one reason why I am advancing to meet him. The dog has fought in the West and knows the art of siege. My scouts had some trouble in approaching his columns, for his outriders have eyes like hawks; but they did get close enough to see the engines he is dragging on ox-cart wheels drawn by camels—catapults, rams, ballistas, mangonels—by Ishtar! he must have had ten

208

thousand men working day and night for a month. Where he got the material for their construction is more than I can understand. Perhaps he has a treaty with the Turanians, and gets supplies from them.

"Anyway, they won't do him any good. I've fought these desert wolves before—an exchange of arrows for awhile, in which the armor of my warriors protects them—then a charge and my squadrons sweep through the loose swarms of the nomads, wheel and sweep back through, scattering them to the four winds. I'll ride back through the south gate before sunset, with hundreds of naked captives staggering at my horse's tail. We'll hold a fête tonight, in the great square. My soldiers delight in flaying their enemies alive—we will have a wholesale skinning, and make these weak-kneed townsfolk watch. As for Conan, it will afford me intense pleasure, if we take him alive, to impale him on the palace steps."

"Skin as many as you like," answered Salome indifferently. "I would like a dress made of human hide. But at least a hundred captives you must give to me—for the altar, and for Thaug."

"It shall be done," answered Constantius, with his gauntleted hand brushing back the thin hair from his high bald forehead, burned dark by the sun. "For victory and the fair honor of Taramis!" he said sardonically, and, taking his vizored helmet under his arm, he lifted a hand in salute, and strode clanking from the chamber. His voice drifted back, harshly lifted in orders to his officers.

Salome leaned back on the couch, yawned, stretched herself like a great supple cat, and called: "Zang!"

A cat-footed priest, with features like yellowed parchment stretched over a skull, entered noiselessly. Salome turned to an ivory pedestal on which stood two crystal globes, and taking from it the smaller, she handed the glistening sphere to the priest.

"Ride with Constantius," she said. "Give me the news of the battle. Go!"

The skull-faced man bowed low, and hiding the globe under his dark mantle, hurried from the chamber.

Outside in the city there was no sound, except the clank of hoofs and after a while the clang of a closing gate. Salome mounted a wide marble stair that led to the flat, canopied, marble-battlemented roof. She was above all other buildings of the city. The streets were deserted, the great square in front of the palace was empty. In normal times folk shunned the grim temple which rose on the opposite side of that square, but now the town looked like a dead city. Only on the southern wall and the roofs that overlooked it was there any sign of life. There the people massed thickly. They made no demonstration, did not know whether to hope for the victory or defeat of Constantius. Victory meant further misery under his intolerable rule; defeat probably meant the sack of the city and red massacre. No word had come from Conan. They did not know what to expect at his hands. They remembered that he was a barbarian.

The squadrons of the mercenaries were moving out into the plain. In the distance, just this side of the river, other dark masses were moving, barely recognizable as men on horses. Objects dotted the farther bank; Conan had not brought his siege engines across the river, apparently fearing an attack in the midst of the crossing. But he had crossed with his full force of horsemen. The sun rose and struck glints of fire from the dark multitudes. The squadrons from the city broke into a gallop; a deep roar reached the ears of the people on the wall.

The rolling masses merged, intermingled; at that distance it was a tangled confusion in which no details stood out. Charge and countercharge were not to be identified. Clouds of dust rose from the plains, under the stamping hoofs, veiling the action. Through these swirling clouds masses of riders loomed, appearing and disappearing, and spears flashed.

Salome shrugged her shoulders and descended the stair. The palace lay silent. All the slaves were on the wall, gazing vainly southward with the citizens.

She entered the chamber where she had talked with Constantius, and approached the pedestal, noting that the crystal globe was clouded, shot with bloody streaks of crimson. She bent over the ball, swearing under her breath.

"Zang!" she called. "Zang!"

Mists swirled in the sphere, resolving themselves into billowing dust-clouds through which black figures rushed unrecognizably; steel glinted like lightning in the murk. Then the face of Zang leaped into startling distinctness; it was as if the wide eyes gazed up at Salome. Blood trickled from a gash in the skull-like head, the skin was gray with sweat-runneled dust. The lips parted, writhing; to other ears than Salome's it would have seemed that the face in the crystal contorted silently. But sound to her came as plainly from those ashen lips as if the priest had been in the same room with her, instead of miles away, shouting into the smaller crystal. Only the gods of darkness knew what unseen, magic filaments linked together those shimmering spheres.

"Salome!" shrieked the bloody head. "*Salome!*"

"I hear!" she cried. "Speak! How goes the battle?"

211

"Doom is upon us!" screamed the skull-like apparition. "Khauran is lost! *Aie*, my horse is down and I can not win clear! Men are falling around me! They are dying like flies, in their silvered mail!"

"Stop yammering and tell me what happened!" she cried harshly.

"We rode at the desert-dogs and they came on to meet us!" yowled the priest. "Arrows flew in clouds between the hosts, and the nomads wavered. Constantius ordered the charge. In even ranks we thundered upon them.

"Then the masses of their horde opened to right and left, and through the cleft rushed three thousand Hyborian horsemen whose presence we had not even suspected. Men of Khauran, mad with hate! Big men in full armor on massive horses! In a solid wedge of steel they smote us like a thunderbolt. They split our ranks asunder before we knew what was upon us, and then the desert-men swarmed on us from either flank.

"They have ripped our ranks apart, broken and scattered us! It is a trick of that devil Conan! The siege engines are false—mere frames of palm trunks and painted silk, that fooled our scouts who saw them from afar. A trick to draw us out to our doom! Our warriors flee! Khumbanigash is down—Conan slew him. I do not see Constantius. The Khaurani rage through our milling masses like blood-mad lions, and the desert-men feather us with arrows. I—ahh!"

There was a flicker as of lightning, or trenchant steel, a burst of bright blood—then abruptly the image vanished, like a bursting bubble, and Salome was staring into an empty crystal ball that mirrored only her own furious features.

She stood perfectly still for a few moments, erect and staring into space. Then she clapped her hands and

212

another skull-like priest entered, as silent and immobile as the first.

"Constantius is beaten," she said swiftly. "We are doomed. Conan will be crashing at our gates within the hour. If he catches me, I have no illusions as to what I can expect. But first I am going to make sure that my cursed sister never ascends the throne again. Follow me! Come what may, we shall give Thaug a feast."

As she descended the stairs and galleries of the palace, she heard a faint rising echo from the distant walls. The people there had begun to realize that the battle was going against Constantius. Through the dust clouds masses of horsemen were visible, racing toward the city.

Palace and prison were connected by a long closed gallery, whose vaulted roof rose on gloomy arches. Hurrying along this, the false queen and her slave passed through a heavy door at the other end that let them into the dim-lit recesses of the prison. They had emerged into a wide, arched corridor at a point near where a stone stair descended into the darkness. Salome recoiled suddenly, swearing. In the gloom of the hall lay a motionless form—a Shemitish jailer, his short beard tilted toward the roof as his head hung on a half-severed neck. As panting voices from below reached the girl's ears, she shrank back into the black shadow of an arch, pushing the priest behind her, her hand groping in her girdle.

6. The Vulture's Wings

IT WAS THE smoky light of a torch which roused Taramis, queen of Khauran, from the slumber in which she sought forgetfulness. Lifting herself on her hand she raked back her tangled hair and blinked up, expecting to meet the mocking countenance of Salome, malign with new torments. Instead a cry of pity and horror reached her ears.

"Taramis! Oh, my queen!"

The sound was so strange to her ears that she thought she was still dreaming. Behind the torch she could make out figures now, the glint of steel, then five countenances bent toward her, not swarthy and hook-nosed, but lean, aquiline faces, browned by the sun. She crouched in her tatters, staring wildly.

One of the figures sprang forward and fell on one knee before her, arms stretched appealingly toward her.

"Oh, Taramis! Thank Ishtar we have found you! Do you not remember me, Valerius? Once with your own lips you praised me, after the battle of Korveka!"

"Valerius!" she stammered. Suddenly tears welled into her eyes. "Oh, I dream! It is some magic of Salome's to torment me!"

"No!" The cry rang with exultation. "It is your own true vassals come to rescue you! Yet we must hasten. Constantius fights in the plain against Conan, who has brought the Zuagirs across the river, but three hundred Shemites yet hold the city. We slew the jailer and took his keys, and have seen no other guards. But we must be gone. Come!"

The queen's legs gave way, not from weakness but from the reaction. Valerius lifted her like a child, and

214

with the torch-bearer hurrying before them, they left the dungeon and went up a slimy stone stair. It seemed to mount endlessly, but presently they emerged into a corridor.

They were passing a dark arch when the torch was suddenly struck out, and the bearer cried out in fierce, brief agony. A burst of blue fire glared in the dark corridor, in which the furious face of Salome was limned momentarily, with a beast-like figure crouching beside her—then the eyes of the watchers were blinded by that blaze.

Valerius tried to stagger along the corridor with the queen; dazedly he heard the sound of murderous blows driven deep in flesh, accompanied by gasps of death and a bestial grunting. Then the queen was torn brutally from his arms, and a savage blow on his helmet dashed him to the floor.

Grimly he crawled to his feet, shaking his head in an effort to rid himself of the blue flame which seemed still to dance devilishly before him. When his blinded sight cleared, he found himself alone in the corridor—alone except for the dead. His four companions lay in their blood, heads and bosoms cleft and gashed. Blinded and dazed in that hell-born glare, they had died without an opportunity of defending themselves. The queen was gone.

With a bitter curse Valerius caught up his sword, tearing his cleft helmet from his head to clatter on the flags; blood ran down his cheek from a cut in his scalp.

Reeling, frantic with indecision, he heard a voice calling his name in desperate urgency: "Valerius! *Valerius!*"

He staggered in the direction of the voice, and rounded a corner just in time to have his arms filled with a soft, supple figure which flung itself frantically at him.

"Ivga! Are you mad!"

"I had to come!" she sobbed. "I followed you—hid in an arch of the outer court. A moment ago I saw *her* emerge with a brute who carried a woman in his arms. I knew it was Taramis, and that you had failed! Oh, you are hurt!"

"A scratch!" He put aside her clinging hands. "Quick, Ivga, tell me which way they went!"

"They fled across the square toward the temple."

He paled. "Ishtar! Oh, the fiend! She means to give Taramis to the devil she worships! Quick, Ivga! Run to the south wall where the people watch the battle! Tell them that their real queen has been found—that the impostor has dragged her to the temple! Go!"

Sobbing, the girl sped away, her light sandals pattering on the cobblestones, and Valerius raced across the court, plunged into the street, dashed into the square upon which it debouched, and raced for the great structure that rose on the opposite side.

His flying feet spurned the marble as he darted up the broad stair and through the pillared portico. Evidently their prisoner had given them some trouble. Taramis, sensing the doom intended for her, was fighting against it with all the strength of her splendid young body. Once she had broken away from the brutish priest, only to be dragged down again.

The group was half-way down the broad nave, at the other end of which stood the grim altar and beyond that the great metal door, obscenely carven, through which many had gone, but from which only Salome had ever emerged. Taramis' breath came in panting gasps; her tattered garment had been torn from her in the struggle. She writhed in the grasp of her apish

216

captor like a white, naked nymph in the arms of a satyr. Salome watched cynically, though impatiently, moving toward the carven door, and from the dusk that lurked along the lofty walls the obscene gods and gargoyles leered down, as if imbued with salacious life.

Choking with fury, Valerius rushed down the great hall, sword in hand. At a sharp cry from Salome, the skull-faced priest looked up, then released Taramis, drew a heavy knife, already smeared with blood, and ran at the oncoming Khaurani.

But cutting down men blinded by the devil's-flame loosed by Salome was different from fighting a wiry young Hyborian afire with hate and rage.

Up went the dripping knife, but before it could fall Valerius' keen narrow blade slashed through the air, and the fist that held the knife jumped from its wrist in a shower of blood. Valerius, berserk, slashed again and yet again before the crumpling figure could fall. The blade licked through flesh and bone. The skull-like head fell one way, the half-sundered torso the other.

Valerius whirled on his toes, quick and fierce as a jungle-cat, glaring about for Salome. She must have exhausted her fire-dust in the prison. She was bending over Taramis, grasping her sister's black locks in one hand, in the other lifting a dagger. Then with a fierce cry Valerius' sword was sheathed in her breast with such fury that the point sprang out between her shoulders. With an awful shriek the witch sank down, writhing in convulsions, grasping at the naked blade as it was withdrawn, smoking and dripping. Her eyes were unhuman; with a more than human vitality she clung to the life that ebbed through the wound that split the crimson crescent on her ivory bosom. She groveled on the floor, clawing and biting at the naked stones in her agony.

Sickened at the sight, Valerius stooped and lifted the half-fainting queen. Turning his back on the twisting figure upon the floor, he ran toward the door, stumbling in his haste. He staggered out upon the portico, halted at the head of the steps. The square thronged with people. Some had come at Ivga's incoherent cries; others had deserted the walls in fear of the onsweeping hordes out of the desert, fleeing unreasoningly toward the center of the city. Dumb resignation had vanished. The throng seethed and milled, yelling and screaming. About the road there sounded somewhere the splintering of stone and timbers.

A band of grim Shemites cleft the crowd—the guards of the northern gates, hurrying toward the south gate to reinforce their comrades there. They reined up short at sight of the youth on the steps, holding the limp, naked figure in his arms. The heads of the throng turned toward the temple; the crowd gaped, a new bewilderment added to their swirling confusion.

"Here is your queen!" yelled Valerius, straining to make himself understood above the clamor. The people gave back a bewildered roar. They did not understand, and Valerius sought in vain to lift his voice above their bedlam. The Shemites rode toward the temple steps, beating a way through the crowd with their spears.

Then a new, grisly element introduced itself into the frenzy. Out of the gloom of the temple behind Valerius wavered a slim white figure, laced with crimson. The people screamed; there in the arms of Valerius hung the woman they thought their queen; yet there in the temple door staggered another figure, like a reflection of the other. Their brains reeled. Valerius felt his blood congeal as he stared at the swaying witch-girl. His sword had transfixed her, sundered her heart. She should be dead; by all laws of nature she should be dead. Yet there she swayed, on her feet, clinging horribly to life.

"Thaug!" she screamed, reeling in the doorway. "*Thaug!*" As in answer to that frightful invocation there boomed a thunderous croaking from within the temple, the snapping of wood and metal.

"That is the queen!" roared the captain of the Shemites, lifting his bow. "Shoot down the man and other woman!"

But the roar of a roused hunting-pack rose from the people; they had guessed the truth at last, understood Valerius' frenzied appeals, knew that the girl who hung limply in his arms was their true queen. With a soul-shaking yell they surged on the Shemites, tearing and smiting with tooth and nail and naked hands, with the desperation of hard-pent fury loosed at last. Above them Salome swayed and tumbled down the marble stair, dead at last.

Arrows flickered about him as Valerius ran back between the pillars of the portico, shielding the body of the queen with his own. Shooting and slashing ruthlessly the mounted Shemites were holding their own with the maddened crowd. Valerius darted to the temple door—with one foot on the threshold he recoiled, crying out in horror and despair.

Out of the gloom at the other end of the great hall a vast dark form heaved up—came rushing toward him in gigantic frog-like hops. He saw the gleam of great unearthly eyes, the shimmer of fangs or talons. He fell back from the door, and then the whir of a shaft past his ear warned him that death was also behind him. He wheeled desperately. Four or five Shemites had cut their way through the throng and were spurring their

219

horses up the steps, their bows lifted to shoot him down. He sprang behind a pillar, on which the arrows splintered. Taramis had fainted. She hung like a dead woman in his arms.

Before the Shemites could loose again, the doorway was blocked by a gigantic shape. With affrighted yells the mercenaries wheeled and began beating a frantic way through the throng, which crushed back in sudden, galvanized horror, trampling one another in their stampede.

But the monster seemed to be watching Valerius and the girl. Squeezing its vast, unstable bulk through the door, it bounded toward him, as he ran down the steps. He felt it looming behind him, a giant shadowy thing, like a travesty of nature cut out of the heart of night, a black shapelessness in which only the staring eyes and gleaming fangs were distinct.

There came a sudden thunder of hoofs; a rout of Shemites, bloody and battered, streamed across the square from the south, plowing blindly through the packed throng. Behind them swept a horde of horsemen yelling in a familiar tongue, waving red swords—the exiles, returned! With them rode fifty black-bearded desert-riders, and at their head a giant figure in black mail.

"Conan!" shrieked Valerius. "*Conan!*"

The giant yelled a command. Without checking their headlong pace, the desert men lifted their bows, drew and loosed. A cloud of arrows sang across the square, over the seething heads of the multitudes, and sank feather-deep in the black monster. It halted, wavered, reared, a black blot against the marble pillars. Again the sharp cloud sang, and yet again, and the horror collapsed and rolled down the steps, as dead as the witch who had summoned it out of the night of ages.

220

Conan drew rein beside the portico, leaped off.
Valerius had laid the queen on the marble, sinking
beside her in utter exhaustion. The people surged
about, crowding in. The Cimmerian cursed them back,
lifted her dark head, pillowed it against his mailed
shoulder.

"By Crom, what is this? The real Taramis! But who
is that yonder?"

"The demon who wore her shape," panted Valerius.

Conan swore heartily. Ripping a cloak from the
shoulders of a soldier, he wrapped it about the naked
queen. Her long dark lashes quivered on her cheeks;
her eyes opened, stared up unbelievingly into the
Cimmerian's scarred face.

"Conan!" Her soft fingers caught at him. "Do I
dream? *She* told me you were dead—"

"Scarcely!" He grinned hardly. "You do not dream.
You are queen of Khauran again. I broke Constantius,
out there by the river. Most of his dogs never lived to
reach the walls, for I gave orders that no prisoners be
taken—except Constantius. The city guard closed the
gate in our faces, but we burst it in with rams swung
from our saddles. I left all my wolves outside, except
this fifty. I didn't trust them in here, and these
Khaurani lads were enough for the gate guards."

"It has been a nightmare!" she whimpered. "Oh, my
poor people! You must help me try to repay them for
all they have suffered, Conan, henceforth councilor as
well as captain!"

Conan laughed, but shook his head. Rising, he set
the queen upon her feet, and beckoned to a number of
his Khaurani horsemen who had not continued the
pursuit of the fleeing Shemites. They sprang from their
horses, eager to do the bidding of their new-found
queen.

221

"No, lass, that's over with. I'm chief of the Zuagirs now, and must lead them to plunder the Turanians, as I promised. This lad, Valerius, will make you a better captain than I. I wasn't made to dwell among marble walls, anyway. But I must leave you now, and complete what I've begun. Shemites still live in Khauran."

As Valerius started to follow Taramis across the square toward the palace, through a lane opened by the wildly cheering multitude, he felt a soft hand slipped timidly into his sinewy fingers and turned to receive the slender body of Ivga in his arms. He crushed her to him and drank her kisses with the gratitude of a weary fighter who has attained rest at last through tribulation and storm.

But not all men seek rest and peace; some are born with the spirit of the storm in their blood, restless harbingers of violence and bloodshed, knowing no other path....

The sun was rising. The ancient caravan road was thronged with white-robed horsemen, in a wavering line that stretched from the walls of Khauran to a spot far out in the plain. Conan the Cimmerian sat at the head of that column, near the jagged end of a wooden beam that stuck up out of the ground. Near that stump rose a heavy cross, and on that cross a man hung by spikes through his hands and feet.

"Seven months ago, Constantius," said Conan, "it was I who hung there, and you who sat here."

Constantius did not reply; he licked his gray lips and his eyes were glassy with pain and fear. Muscles writhed like cords along his lean body.

"You are more fit to inflict torture than to endure it," said Conan tranquilly. "I hung there on a cross as you are hanging, and I lived, thanks to circumstances and a stamina peculiar to barbarians. But you civilized men are soft; your lives are not nailed to your spines as are ours. Your fortitude consists mainly in inflicting torment, not in enduring it. You will be dead before sundown. And so, Falcon of the desert, I leave you to the companionship of another bird of the desert."

He gestured toward the vultures whose shadows swept across the sands as they wheeled overhead. From the lips of Constantius came an inhuman cry of despair and horror.

Conan lifted his reins and rode toward the river that shone like silver in the morning sun. Behind him the white-clad riders struck into a trot; the gaze of each, as he passed a certain spot, turned impersonally and with the desert man's lack of compassion, toward the cross and the gaunt figure that hung there, black against the sunrise. Their horses' hoofs beat out a knell in the dust. Lower and lower swept the wings of the hungry vultures.

Jewels of Gwahlur

1. Paths of Intrigue

THE CLIFFS ROSE sheer from the jungle, towering ramparts of stone that glinted jade-blue and dull crimson in the rising sun, and curved away and away to east and west above the waving emerald ocean of fronds and leaves. It looked insurmountable, that giant palisade with its sheer curtains of solid rock in which bits of quartz winked dazzlingly in the sunlight. But the man who was working his tedious way upward was already half-way to the top.

He came of a race of hillmen, accustomed to scaling forbidding crags, and he was a man of unusual strength and agility. His only garment was a pair of short red silk breeks, and his sandals were slung to his back, out of his way, as were his sword and dagger.

The man was powerfully built, supple as a panther. His skin was bronzed by the sun, his square-cut black mane confined by a silver band about his temples. His iron muscles, quick eyes and sure feet served him well here, for it was a climb to test these qualities to the utmost. A hundred and fifty feet below him waved the jungle. An equal distance above him the rim of the cliffs was etched against the morning sky.

He labored like one driven by the necessity of haste; yet he was forced to move at a snail's pace, clinging like a fly on a wall. His groping hands and feet found niches and knobs, precarious holds at best, and sometimes he virtually hung by his finger nails. Yet upward he went,

225

clawing, squirming, fighting for every foot. At times he paused to rest his aching muscles, and shaking the sweat out of his eyes, twisted his head to stare searchingly out over the jungle, combing the green expanse for any trace of human life or motion.

Now the summit was not far above him, and he observed, only a few feet above his head, a break in the sheer stone of the cliff. An instant later he had reached it—a small cavern, just below the edge of the rim. As his head rose above the lip of its floor, he grunted. He clung there, his elbows hooked over the lip. The cave was so tiny that it was little more than a niche cut in the stone, but it held an occupant. A shriveled brown mummy, cross-legged, arms folded on the withered breast upon which the shrunken head was sunk, sat in the little cavern. The limbs were bound in place with rawhide thongs which had become mere rotted wisps. If the form had ever been clothed, the ravages of time had long ago reduced the garments to dust. But thrust between the crossed arms and the shrunken breast there was a roll of parchment, yellowed with age to the color of old ivory.

The climber stretched forth a long arm and wrenched away this cylinder. Without investigation he thrust it into his girdle and hauled himself up until he was standing in the opening of the niche. A spring upward and he caught the rim of the cliffs and pulled himself up and over almost with the same motion.

There he halted, panting, and stared downward.

It was like looking into the interior of a vast bowl, rimmed by a circular stone wall. The floor of the bowl was covered with trees and denser vegetation, though nowhere did the growth duplicate the jungle denseness of the outer forest. The cliffs marched around it without a break and of uniform height. It was a freak of

226

nature, not to be paralleled, perhaps, in the whole world: a vast natural amphitheater, a circular bit of forested plain, three or four miles in diameter, cut off from the rest of the world, and confined within the ring of those palisaded cliffs.

But the man on the cliffs did not devote his thoughts to marveling at the topographical phenomenon. With tense eagerness he searched the tree-tops below him, and exhaled a gusty sigh when he caught the glint of marble domes amidst the twinkling green. It was no myth, then; below him lay the fabulous and deserted palace of Alkmeenon.

Conan the Cimmerian, late of the Barachan Isles, of the Black Coast, and of many other climes where life ran wild, had come to the kingdom of Keshan following the lure of a fabled treasure that outshone the hoard of the Turanian kings.

Keshan was a barbaric kingdom lying in the eastern hinterlands of Kush where the broad grasslands merge with the forests that roll up from the south. The people were a mixed race, a dusky nobility ruling a population that was largely pure negro. The rulers—princes and high priests—claimed descent from a white race which, in a mythical age, had ruled a kingdom whose capital city was Alkmeenon. Conflicting legends sought to explain the reason for that race's eventual downfall, and the abandonment of the city by the survivors. Equally nebulous were the tales of the Teeth of Gwahlur, the treasure of Alkmeenon. But these misty legends had been enough to bring Conan to Keshan, over vast distances of plain, river-laced jungle, and mountains.

He had found Keshan, which in itself was considered mythical by many northern and western nations, and he had heard enough to confirm the rumors of the treasure that men called the Teeth of Gwahlur. But its hiding-place he could not learn, and he was confronted with the necessity of explaining his presence in Keshan. Unattached strangers were not welcome there.

But he was not nonplussed. With cool assurance he made his offer to the stately, plumed, suspicious grandees of the barbarically magnificent court. He was a professional fighting-man. In search of employment (he said) he had come to Keshan. For a price he would train the armies of Keshan and lead them against Punt, their hereditary enemy, whose recent successes in the field had aroused the fury of Keshan's irascible king.

This proposition was not so audacious as it might seem. Conan's fame had preceded him, even into distant Keshan; his exploits as a chief of the black corsairs, those wolves of the southern coasts, had made his name known, admired and feared throughout the black kingdoms. He did not refuse tests devised by the dusky lords. Skirmishes along the borders were incessant, affording the Cimmerian plenty of opportunities to demonstrate his ability at hand-to-hand fighting. His reckless ferocity impressed the lords of Keshan, already aware of his reputation as a leader of men, and the prospects seemed favorable. All Conan secretly desired was employment to give him legitimate excuse for remaining in Keshan long enough to locate the hiding-place of the Teeth of Gwahlur. Then there came an interruption. Thutmekri came to Keshan at the head of an embassy from Zembabwei.

Thutmekri was a Stygian, an adventurer and a rogue whose wits had recommended him to the twin kings of the great hybrid trading kingdom which lay many days' march to the east. He and the Cimmerian knew each other of old, and without love. Thutmekri likewise had a proposition to make to the king of Keshan, and it also concerned the conquest of Punt—which kingdom, incidentally, lying east of Keshan, had recently expelled the Zembabwan traders and burned their fortresses.

His offer outweighed even the prestige of Conan. He pledged himself to invade Punt from the east with a host of black spearmen, Shemitish archers, and mercenary swordsmen, and to aid the king of Keshan to annex the hostile kingdom. The benevolent kings of Zembabwei desired only a monopoly of the trade of Keshan and her tributaries—and, as a pledge of good faith, some of the Teeth of Gwahlur. These would be put to no base usage, Thutmekri hastened to explain to the suspicious chieftains; they would be placed in the temple of Zembabwei beside the squat gold idols of Dagon and Derketo, sacred guests in the holy shrine of the kingdom, to seal the covenant between Keshan and Zembabwei. This statement brought a savage grin to Conan's hard lips.

The Cimmerian made no attempt to match wits and intrigue with Thutmekri and his Shemitish partner, Zargheba. He knew that if Thutmekri won his point, he would insist on the instant banishment of his rival. There was but one thing for Conan to do: find the jewels before the king of Keshan made up his mind, and flee with them. But by this time he was certain that they were not hidden in Keshia, the royal city, which was a swarm of thatched huts crowding about a mud wall that enclosed a palace of stone and mud and bamboo.

While he fumed with nervous impatience, the high priest Gorulga announced that before any decision could be reached, the will of the gods must be ascertained concerning the proposed alliance with

229

Zembabwei and the pledge of objects long held holy and inviolate. The oracle of Alkmeenon must be consulted.

This was an awesome thing, and it caused tongues to wag excitedly in palace and bee-hive hut. Not for a century had the priests visited the silent city. The oracle, men said, was the Princess Yelaya, the last ruler of Alkmeenon, who had died in the full bloom of her youth and beauty, and whose body had miraculously remained unblemished throughout the ages. Of old, priests had made their way into the haunted city, and she had taught them wisdom. The last priest to seek the oracle had been a wicked man, who had sought to steal for himself the curiously cut jewels that men called the Teeth of Gwahlur. But some doom had come upon him in the deserted palace, from which his acolytes, fleeing, had told tales of horror that had for a hundred years frightened the priests from the city and the oracle.

But Gorulga, the present high priest, as one confident in his knowledge of his own integrity, announced that he would go with a handful of followers to revive the ancient custom. And in the excitement tongues buzzed indiscreetly, and Conan caught the clue for which he had sought for weeks—the overheard whisper of a lesser priest that sent the Cimmerian stealing out of Keshia the night before the dawn when the priests were to start.

Riding hard as he dared for a night and a day and a night, he came in the early dawn to the cliffs of Alkmeenon, which stood in the southwestern corner of the kingdom, amidst uninhabited jungle which was taboo to common men. None but the priests dared approach the haunted vale within a distance of many miles. And not even a priest had entered Alkmeenon for a hundred years.

No man had ever climbed these cliffs, legends said, and none but the priests knew the secret entrance into the valley. Conan did not waste time looking for it. Steeps that balked these black people, horsemen and dwellers of plain and level forest, were not impossible for a man born in the rugged hills of Cimmeria.

Now on the summit of the cliffs he looked down into the circular valley and wondered what plague, war or superstition had driven the members of that ancient white race forth from their stronghold to mingle with and be absorbed by the black tribes that hemmed them in.

This valley had been their citadel. There the palace stood, and there only the royal family and their court dwelt. The real city stood outside the cliffs. Those waving masses of green jungle vegetation hid its ruins. But the domes that glistened in the leaves below him were the unbroken pinnacles of the royal palace of Alkmeenon which had defied the corroding ages.

Swinging a leg over the rim he went down swiftly. The inner side of the cliffs was more broken, not quite so sheer. In less than half the time it had taken him to ascend the outer side, he dropped to the swarded valley floor.

With one hand on his sword, he looked alertly about him. There was no reason to suppose men lied when they said that Alkmeenon was empty and deserted, haunted only by the ghosts of the dead past. But it was Conan's nature to be suspicious and wary. The silence was primordial; not even a leaf quivered on a branch. When he bent to peer under the trees, he saw nothing but the marching rows of trunks, receding and receding into the blue gloom of the deep woods.

Nevertheless he went warily, sword in hand, his restless eyes combing the shadows from side to side, his

231

springy tread making no sound on the sward. All about him he saw signs of an ancient civilization; marble fountains, voiceless and crumbling, stood in circles of slender trees whose patterns were too symmetrical to have been a chance of nature. Forest-growth and underbrush had invaded the evenly planned groves, but their outlines were still visible. Broad pavements ran away under the trees, broken, and with grass growing through the wide cracks. He glimpsed walls with ornamental copings, lattices of carven stone that might once have served as the walls of pleasure pavilions.

Ahead of him, through the trees, the domes gleamed and the bulk of the structure supporting them became more apparent as he advanced. Presently, pushing through a screen of vine-tangled branches, he came into a comparatively open space where the trees straggled, unencumbered by undergrowth, and saw before him the wide, pillared portico of the palace.

As he mounted the broad marble steps, he noted that the building was in far better state of preservation than the lesser structures he had glimpsed. The thick walls and massive pillars seemed too powerful to crumble before the assault of time and the elements. The same enchanted quiet brooded over all. The cat-like pad of his sandaled feet seemed startlingly loud in the stillness.

Somewhere in this palace lay the effigy or image which had in times past served as oracle for the priests of Keshan. And somewhere in the palace, unless that indiscreet priest had babbled a lie, was hidden the treasure of the forgotten kings of Alkmeenon.

Conan passed into a broad, lofty hall, lined with tall columns, between which arches gaped, their doors long rotted away. He traversed this in a twilight dimness, and at the other end passed through great double-

232

valved bronze doors which stood partly open, as they might have stood for centuries. He emerged into a vast domed chamber which must have served as audience hall for the kings of Alkmeenon.

It was octagonal in shape, and the great dome up to which the lofty ceiling curved obviously was cunningly pierced, for the chamber was much better lighted than the hall which led to it. At the farther side of the great room there rose a dais with broad lapis-lazuli steps leading up to it, and on that dais there stood a massive chair with ornate arms and a high back which once doubtless supported a cloth-of-gold canopy. Conan grunted explosively and his eyes lit. The golden throne of Alkmeenon, named in immemorial legendry! He weighed it with a practised eye. It represented a fortune in itself, if he were but able to bear it away. Its richness fired his imagination concerning the treasure itself, and made him burn with eagerness. His fingers itched to plunge among the gems he had heard described by story-tellers in the market squares of Keshia, who repeated tales handed down from mouth to mouth through the centuries—jewels not to be duplicated in the world, rubies, emeralds, diamonds, bloodstones, opals, sapphires, the loot of the ancient world.

He had expected to find the oracle-effigy seated on the throne, but since it was not, it was probably placed in some other part of the palace, if, indeed, such a thing really existed. But since he had turned his face toward Keshan, so many myths had proved to be realities that he did not doubt that he would find some kind of image or god.

Behind the throne there was a narrow arched doorway which doubtless had been masked by hangings in the days of Alkmeenon's life. He glanced through it and saw that it let into an alcove, empty, and

233

with a narrow corridor leading off from it at right angles. Turning away from it, he spied another arch to the left of the dais, and it, unlike the others, was furnished with a door. Nor was it any common door. The portal was of the same rich metal as the throne, and carved with many curious arabesques.

At his touch it swung open so readily that its hinges might recently have been oiled. Inside he halted, staring.

He was in a square chamber of no great dimensions, whose marble walls rose to an ornate ceiling, inlaid with gold. Gold friezes ran about the base and the top of the walls, and there was no door other than the one through which he had entered. But he noted these details mechanically. His whole attention was centered on the shape which lay on an ivory dais before him.

He had expected an image, probably carved with the skill of a forgotten art. But no art could mimic the perfection of the figure that lay before him.

It was no effigy of stone or metal or ivory. It was the actual body of a woman, and by what dark art the ancients had preserved that form unblemished for so many ages Conan could not even guess. The very garments she wore were intact—and Conan scowled at that, a vague uneasiness stirring at the back of his mind. The arts that preserved the body should not have affected the garments. Yet there they were—gold breast-plates set with concentric circles of small gems, gilded sandals, and a short silken skirt upheld by a jeweled girdle. Neither cloth nor metal showed any signs of decay.

Yelaya was coldly beautiful, even in death. Her body was like alabaster, slender yet voluptuous; a great crimson jewel gleamed against the darkly piled foam of her hair.

Conan stood frowning down at her, and then tapped the dais with his sword. Possibilities of a hollow containing the treasure occurred to him, but the dais rang solid. He turned and paced the chamber in some indecision. Where should he search first, in the limited time at his disposal? The priest he had overheard babbling to a courtesan had said the treasure was hidden in the palace. But that included a space of considerable vastness. He wondered if he should hide himself until the priests had come and gone, and then renew the search. But there was a strong chance that they might take the jewels with them when they returned to Keshia. For he was convinced that Thutmekri had corrupted Gorulga.

Conan could predict Thutmekri's plans, from his knowledge of the man. He knew that it had been Thutmekri who had proposed the conquest of Punt to the kings of Zembabwei, which conquest was but one move toward their real goal—the capture of the Teeth of Gwahlur. Those wary kings would demand proof that the treasure really existed before they made any move. The jewels Thutmekri asked as a pledge would furnish that proof.

With positive evidence of the treasure's reality, the kings of Zembabwei would move. Punt would be invaded simultaneously from the east and the west, but the Zembabwans would see to it that the Keshani did most of the fighting, and then, when both Punt and Keshan were exhausted from the struggle, the Zembabwans would crush both races, loot Keshan and take the treasure by force, if they had to destroy every building and torture every living human in the kingdom.

But there was always another possibility; if Thutmekri could get his hands on the hoard, it would be characteristic of the man to cheat his employers, steal the jewels for himself and decamp, leaving the Zembabwan emissaries holding the sack.

Conan believed that this consulting of the oracle was but a ruse to persuade the king of Keshan to accede to Thutmekri's wishes—for he never for a moment doubted that Gorulga was as subtle and devious as all the rest mixed up in this grand swindle. Conan had not approached the high priest himself, because in the game of bribery he would have no chance against Thutmekri, and to attempt it would be to play directly into the Stygian's hands. Gorulga could denounce the Cimmerian to the people, establish a reputation for integrity, and rid Thutmekri of his rival at one stroke. He wondered how Thutmekri had corrupted the high priest, and just what could be offered as a bribe to a man who had the greatest treasure in the world under his fingers.

At any rate he was sure that the oracle would be made to say that the gods willed it that Keshan should follow Thutmekri's wishes, and he was sure, too, that it would drop a few pointed remarks concerning himself. After that Keshia would be too hot for the Cimmerian, nor had Conan had any intention of returning when he rode away in the night.

The oracle chamber held no clue for him. He went forth into the great throne-room and laid his hands on the throne. It was heavy, but he could tilt it up. The floor beneath, a thick marble dais, was solid. Again he sought the alcove. His mind clung to a secret crypt near the oracle. Painstakingly he began to tap along the walls, and presently his taps rang hollow at a spot opposite the mouth of the narrow corridor. Looking more closely he saw that the crack between the marble panel at that point and the next was wider than usual.

He inserted a dagger-point and pried.

Silently the panel swung open, revealing a niche in the wall, but nothing else. He swore feelingly. The aperture was empty, and it did not look as if it had ever served as a crypt for treasure. Leaning into the niche he saw a system of tiny holes in the wall, about on a level with a man's mouth. He peered through, and grunted understandingly. That was the wall that formed the partition between the alcove and the oracle chamber. Those holes had not been visible in the chamber. Conan grinned. This explained the mystery of the oracle, but it was a bit cruder than he had expected. Gorulga would plant either himself or some trusted minion in that niche, to talk through the holes, and the credulous acolytes, black men all, would accept it as the veritable voice of Yelaya.

Remembering something, the Cimmerian drew forth the roll of parchment he had taken from the mummy and unrolled it carefully, as it seemed ready to fall to pieces with age. He scowled over the dim characters with which it was covered. In his roaming about the world the giant adventurer had picked up a wide smattering of knowledge, particularly including the speaking and reading of many alien tongues. Many a sheltered scholar would have been astonished at the Cimmerian's linguistic abilities, for he had experienced many adventures where knowledge of a strange language had meant the difference between life and death.

These characters were puzzling, at once familiar and unintelligible, and presently he discovered the reason. They were the characters of archaic Pelishtim, which possessed many points of difference from the modern script, with which he was familiar, and which, three centuries ago, had been modified by conquest by a

237

nomad tribe. This older, purer script baffled him. He made out a recurrent phrase, however, which he recognized as a proper name: Bît-Yakin. He gathered that it was the name of the writer.

Scowling, his lips unconsciously moving as he struggled with the task, he blundered through the manuscript, finding much of it untranslatable and most of the rest of it obscure.

He gathered that the writer, the mysterious Bît-Yakin, had come from afar with his servants, and entered the valley of Alkmeenon. Much that followed was meaningless, interspersed as it was with unfamiliar phrases and characters. Such as he could translate seemed to indicate the passing of a very long period of time. The name of Yelaya was repeated frequently, and toward the last part of the manuscript it became apparent that Bît-Yakin knew that death was upon him. With a slight start Conan realized that the mummy in the cavern must be the remains of the writer of the manuscript, the mysterious Pelishtim, Bît-Yakin. The man had died, as he had prophesied, and his servants, obviously, had placed him in that open crypt, high up on the cliffs, according to his instructions before his death.

It was strange that Bît-Yakin was not mentioned in any of the legends of Alkmeenon. Obviously he had come to the valley after it had been deserted by the original inhabitants—the manuscript indicated as much—but it seemed peculiar that the priests who came in the old days to consult the oracle had not seen the man or his servants. Conan felt sure that the mummy and this parchment were more than a hundred years old. Bît-Yakin had dwelt in the valley when the priests came of old to bow before dead Yelaya. Yet concerning him the legends were silent, telling only of a deserted city, haunted only by the dead.

Why had the man dwelt in this desolate spot, and to what unknown destination had his servants departed after disposing of their master's corpse?

Conan shrugged his shoulders and thrust the parchment back into his girdle—he started violently, the skin on the backs of his hands tingling. Startlingly, shockingly in the slumberous stillness, there had boomed the deep strident clangor of a great gong!

He wheeled, crouching like a great cat, sword in hand, glaring down the narrow corridor from which the sound had seemed to come. Had the priests of Keshia arrived? This was improbable, he knew; they would not have had time to reach the valley. But that gong was indisputable evidence of human presence.

Conan was basically a direct-actionist. Such subtlety as he possessed had been acquired through contact with the more devious races. When taken off guard by some unexpected occurrence, he reverted instinctively to type. So now, instead of hiding or slipping away in the opposite direction as the average man might have done, he ran straight down the corridor in the direction of the sound. His sandals made no more sound than the pads of a panther would have made; his eyes were slits, his lips unconsciously asnarl. Panic had momentarily touched his soul at the shock of that unexpected reverberation, and the red rage of the primitive that is wakened by threat of peril, always lurked close to the surface of the Cimmerian.

He emerged presently from the winding corridor into a small open court. Something glinting in the sun caught his eye. It was the gong, a great gold disk, hanging from a gold arm extending from the crumbling wall. A brass mallet lay near, but there was no sound or

239

sight of humanity. The surrounding arches gaped emptily. Conan crouched inside the doorway for what seemed a long time. There was no sound or movement throughout the great palace. His patience exhausted at last, he glided around the curve of the court, peering into the arches, ready to leap either way like a flash of light, or to strike right or left as a cobra strikes.

He reached the gong, stared into the arch nearest it. He saw only a dim chamber, littered with the debris of decay. Beneath the gong the polished marble flags showed no footprint, but there was a scent in the air —a faintly fetid odor he could not classify; his nostrils dilated like those of a wild beast as he sought in vain to identify it.

He turned toward the arch—with appalling suddenness the seemingly solid flags splintered and gave way under his feet. Even as he fell he spread wide his arms and caught the edges of the aperture that gaped beneath him. The edges crumbled off under his clutching fingers. Down into utter darkness he shot, into black icy water that gripped him and whirled him away with breathless speed.

2. A Goddess Awakens

THE CIMMERIAN AT first made no attempt to fight the current that was sweeping him through lightless night. He kept himself afloat, gripping between his teeth the sword, which he had not relinquished, even in his fall, and did not even seek to guess to what doom he was being borne. But suddenly a beam of light lanced the darkness ahead of him. He saw the surging, seething black surface of the water, in turmoil as if disturbed by some monster of the deep, and he saw the sheer stone walls of the channel curved up to a vault overhead. On each side ran a narrow ledge, just below the arching roof, but they were far out of his reach. At one point this roof had been broken, probably fallen in, and the light was streaming through the aperture. Beyond that shaft of light was utter blackness, and panic assailed the Cimmerian as he saw he would be swept on past that spot of light, and into the unknown blackness again.

Then he saw something else: bronze ladders extended from the ledges to the water's surface at regular intervals, and there was one just ahead of him. Instantly he struck out for it, fighting the current that would have held him to the middle of the stream. It dragged at him as with tangible, animate slimy hands, but he buffeted the rushing surge with the strength of desperation and drew closer and closer inshore, fighting furiously for every inch. Now he was even with the ladder and with a fierce, gasping plunge he gripped the bottom rung and hung on, breathless.

241

A few seconds later he struggled up out of the seething water, trusting his weight dubiously to the corroded rungs. They sagged and bent, but they held, and he clambered up onto the narrow ledge which ran along the wall scarcely a man's length below the curving roof. The tall Cimmerian was forced to bend his head as he stood up. A heavy bronze door showed in the stone at a point even with the head of the ladder, but it did not give to Conan's efforts. He transferred his sword from his teeth to its scabbard, spitting blood—for the edge had cut his lips in that fierce fight with the river—and turned his attention to the broken roof.

He could reach his arms up through the crevice and grip the edge, and careful testing told him it would bear his weight. An instant later he had drawn himself up through the hole, and found himself in a wide chamber, in a state of extreme disrepair. Most of the roof had fallen in, as well as a great section of the floor, which was laid over the vault of a subterranean river. Broken arches opened into other chambers and corridors, and Conan believed he was still in the great palace. He wondered uneasily how many chambers in that palace had underground water directly under them, and when the ancient flags or tiles might give way again and precipitate him back into the current from which he had just crawled.

And he wondered just how much of an accident that fall had been. Had those rotten flags simply chanced to give way beneath his weight, or was there a more sinister explanation? One thing at least was obvious: he was not the only living thing in that palace. That gong had not sounded of its own accord, whether the noise had been meant to lure him to his death, or not. The silence of the palace became suddenly sinister, fraught

242

with crawling menace.

Could it be someone on the same mission as himself? A sudden thought occurred to him, at the memory of the mysterious Bît-Yakin. Was it not possible that this man had found the Teeth of Gwahlur in his long residence in Alkmeenon—that his servants had taken them with them when they departed? The possibility that he might be following a will-of-the-wisp infuriated the Cimmerian.

Choosing a corridor which he believed led back toward the part of the palace he had first entered, he hurried along it, stepping gingerly as he thought of that black river that seethed and foamed somewhere below his feet.

His speculations recurrently revolved about the oracle chamber and its cryptic occupant. Somewhere in that vicinity must be the clue to the mystery of the treasure, if indeed it still remained in its immemorial hiding-place.

The great palace lay silent as ever, disturbed only by the swift passing of his sandaled feet. The chambers and halls he traversed were crumbling into ruin, but as he advanced the ravages of decay became less apparent. He wondered briefly for what purpose the ladders had been suspended from the ledges over the subterranean river, but dismissed the matter with a shrug. He was little interested in speculating over unremunerative problems of antiquity.

He was not sure just where the oracle chamber lay, from where he was, but presently he emerged into a corridor which led back into the great throneroom under one of the arches. He had reached a decision; it was useless for him to wander aimlessly about the palace, seeking the hoard. He would conceal himself somewhere here, wait until the Keshani priests came, and then, after they had gone through the farce of consulting the oracle, he would follow them to the hiding-place of the gems, to which he was certain they would go. Perhaps they would take only a few of the jewels with them. He would content himself with the rest.

Drawn by a morbid fascination, he re-entered the oracle chamber and stared down again at the motionless figure of the princess who was worshipped as a goddess, entranced by her frigid beauty. What cryptic secret was locked in that marvelously molded form?

He started violently. The breath sucked through his teeth, the short hairs prickled at the back of his scalp. The body still lay as he had first seen it, silent, motionless, in breast-plates of jeweled gold, gilded sandals and silken skirt. But now there was a subtle difference. The lissom limbs were not rigid, a peach-bloom touched the cheeks, the lips were red—

With a panicky curse Conan ripped out his sword. *"Crom! She's alive!"*

At his words the long dark lashes lifted; the eyes opened and gazed up at him inscrutably, dark, lustrous, mystical. He glared in frozen speechlessness.

She sat up with a supple ease, still holding his ensorcelled stare.

He licked his dry lips and found voice.

"You—are—are you Yelaya?" he stammered.

"I am Yelaya!" The voice was rich and musical, and he stared with new wonder. "Do not fear. I will not harm you if you do my bidding."

"How can a dead woman come to life after all these centuries?" he demanded, as if skeptical of what his

244

senses told him. A curious gleam was beginning to smolder in his eyes.

She lifted her arms in a mystical gesture.

"I am a goddess. A thousand years ago there descended upon me the curse of the greater gods, the gods of darkness beyond the borders of light. The mortal in me died; the goddess in me could never die. Here I have lain for so many centuries, to awaken each night at sunset and hold my court as of yore, with specters drawn from the shadows of the past. Man, if you would not view that which will blast your soul for ever, get hence quickly! I command you! Go!" The voice became imperious, and her slender arm lifted and pointed.

Conan, his eyes burning slits, slowly sheathed his sword, but he did not obey her order. He stepped closer, as if impelled by a powerful fascination— without the slightest warning he grabbed her up in a bear-like grasp. She screamed a very ungoddess-like scream, and there was a sound of ripping silk, as with one ruthless wrench he tore off her skirt.

"Goddess! Ha!" His bark was full of angry contempt. He ignored the frantic writhings of his captive. "I thought it was strange that a princess of Alkmeenon would speak with a Corinthian accent! As soon as I'd gathered my wits I knew I'd seen you somewhere. You're Muriela, Zargheba's Corinthian dancing-girl. This crescent-shaped birthmark on your hip proves it. I saw it once when Zargheba was whipping you. Goddess! Bah!" He smacked the betraying hip contemptuously and resoundingly with his open hand, and the girl yelped piteously.

All her imperiousness had gone out of her. She was no longer a mystical figure of antiquity, but a terrified

245

and humiliated dancing-girl, such as can be bought at almost any Shemitish market-place. She lifted up her voice and wept unashamedly. Her captor glared down at her with angry triumph.

"Goddess! Ha! So you were one of the veiled women Zargheba brought to Keshia with him. Did you think you could fool me, you little idiot? A year ago I saw you in Akbitana with that swine, Zargheba, and I don't forget faces—or women's figures. I think I'll—"

Squirming about in his grasp she threw her slender arms about his massive neck in an abandon of terror; tears coursed down her cheeks, and her sobs quivered with a note of hysteria.

"Oh, please don't hurt me! Don't! I had to do it! Zargheba brought me here to act as the oracle!"

"Why, you sacrilegious little hussy!" rumbled Conan. "Do you not fear the gods? Crom! is there no honesty anywhere?"

"Oh, please!" she begged, quivering with abject fright. "I couldn't disobey Zargheba. Oh, what shall I do? I shall be cursed by these heathen gods!"

"What do you think the priests will do to you if they find out you're an impostor?" he demanded.

At the thought her legs refused to support her, and she collapsed in a shuddering heap, clasping Conan's knees and mingling incoherent pleas for mercy and protection with piteous protestations of her innocence of any malign intention. It was a vivid change from her pose as the ancient princess, but not surprising. The fear that had nerved her then was now her undoing.

"Where is Zargheba?" he demanded. "Stop yammering, damn it, and answer me."

"Outside the palace," she whimpered, "watching for the priests."

246

"How many men with him?"

"None. We came alone."

"Ha!" It was much like the satisfied grunt of a hunting lion. "You must have left Keshia a few hours after I did. Did you climb the cliffs?"

She shook her head, too choked with tears to speak coherently. With an impatient imprecation he seized her slim shoulders and shook her until she gasped for breath.

"Will you quit that blubbering and answer me? How did you get into the valley?"

"Zargheba knew the secret way," she gasped. "The priest Gwarunga told him, and Thutmekri. On the south side of the valley there is a broad pool lying at the foot of the cliffs. There is a cave-mouth under the surface of the water that is not visible to the casual glance. We ducked under the water and entered it. The cave slopes up out of the water swiftly and leads through the cliffs. The opening on the side of the valley is masked by heavy thickets."

"I climbed the cliffs on the east side," he muttered. "Well, what then?"

"We came to the palace and Zargheba hid me among the trees while he went to look for the chamber of the oracle. I do not think he fully trusted Gwarunga. While he was gone I thought I heard a gong sound, but I was not sure. Presently Zargheba came and took me into the palace and brought me to this chamber, where the goddess Yelaya lay upon the dais. He stripped the body and clothed me in the garments and ornaments. Then he went forth to hide the body and watch for the priests. I have been afraid. When you entered I wanted to leap up and beg you to take me away from this place, but I feared Zargheba. When you discovered I was

247

alive, I thought I could frighten you away."

"What were you to say as the oracle?" he asked.

"I was to bid the priests to take the Teeth of Gwahlur and give some of them to Thutmekri as a pledge, as he desired, and place the rest in the palace at Keshia. I was to tell them that an awful doom threatened Keshan if they did not agree to Thutmekri's proposals. And oh, yes, I was to tell them that you were to be skinned alive immediately."

"Thutmekri wanted the treasure where he—or the Zembabwans—could lay hand on it easily," muttered Conan, disregarding the remark concerning himself. "I'll carve his liver yet—Gorgula is a party to this swindle, of course?"

"No. He believes in his gods, and is incorruptible. He knows nothing about this. He will obey the oracle. It was all Thutmekri's plan. Knowing the Keshani would consult the oracle, he had Zargheba bring me with the embassy from Zembabwei, closely veiled and secluded."

"Well, I'm damned!" muttered Conan. "A priest who honestly believes in his oracle, and can not be bribed. Crom! I wonder if it was Zargheba who banged that gong. Did he know I was here? Could he have known about that rotten flagging? Where is he now, girl?"

"Hiding in a thicket of lotus trees, near the ancient avenue that leads from the south wall of the cliffs to the palace," she answered. Then she renewed her importunities. "Oh, Conan, have pity on me! I am afraid of this evil, ancient place. I know I have heard stealthy footfalls padding about me—oh, Conan, take me away with you! Zargheba will kill me when I have served his purpose here—I know it! The priests, too, will kill me if

248

they discover my deceit.

"He is a devil—he bought me from a slave-trader who stole me out of a caravan bound through southern Koth, and has made me the tool of his intrigues ever since. Take me away from him! You can not be as cruel as he. Don't leave me to be slain here! Please! Please!"

She was on her knees, clutching at Conan hysterically, her beautiful tear-stained face upturned to him, her dark silken hair flowing in disorder over her white shoulders. Conan picked her up and set her on his knee.

"Listen to me. I'll protect you from Zargheba. The priests shall not know of your perfidy. But you've got to do as I tell you."

She faltered promises of explicit obedience, clasping his corded neck as if seeking security from the contact.

"Good. When the priests come, you'll act the part of Yeleya, as Zargheba planned—it'll be dark, and in the torchlight they'll never know the difference. But you'll say this to them: 'It is the will of the gods that the Stygian and his Shemitish dogs be driven from Keshan. They are thieves and traitors who plot to rob the gods. Let the Teeth of Gwahlur be placed in the care of the general Conan. Let him lead the armies of Keshan. He is beloved of the gods.'"

She shivered, with an expression of desperation, but acquiesced.

"But Zargheba?" she cried. "He'll kill me!"

"Don't worry about Zargheba," he grunted. "I'll take care of that dog. You do as I say. Here, put up your hair again. It's fallen all over your shoulders. And the gem's fallen out of it."

He replaced the great glowing gem himself, nodding approval.

"It's worth a roomful of slaves, itself alone. Here,

put your skirt back on. It's torn down the side, but the priests will never notice it. Wipe your face. A goddess doesn't cry like a whipped schoolgirl. By Crom, you *do* look like Yelaya, face, hair, figure and all! If you act the goddess with the priests as well as you did with me, you'll fool them easily."

"I'll try," she shivered.

"Good; I'm going to find Zargheba."

At that she became panicky again.

"No! Don't leave me alone! This place is haunted!"

"There's nothing here to harm you," he assured her impatiently. "Nothing but Zargheba, and I'm going to look after him. I'll be back shortly, I'll be watching from close by in case anything goes wrong during the ceremony; but if you play your part properly, nothing will go wrong."

And turning, he hastened out of the oracle chamber; behind him Muriela squeaked wretchedly at his going.

Twilight had fallen. The great rooms and halls were shadowy and indistinct; copper friezes glinted dully through the dusk. Conan strode like a silent phantom through the great halls, with a sensation of being stared at from the shadowed recesses by invisible ghosts of the past. No wonder the girl was nervous amid such surroundings.

He glided down the marble steps like a slinking panther, sword in hand. Silence reigned over the valley, and above the rim of the cliffs stars were blinking out. If the priests of Keshia had entered the valley there was not a sound, not a movement in the greenery to betray them. He made out the ancient broken-paved avenue, wandering away to the south, lost amid clustering masses of fronds and thick-leaved bushes. He followed it warily, hugging the edge of the paving where the shrubs massed their shadows thickly, until he saw ahead of him, dimly in the dusk, the clump of lotus-trees, the strange growth peculiar to the black lands of Kush. There, according to the girl, Zargheba should be lurking. Conan became stealth personified. A velvet-footed shadow, he melted into the thickets.

He approached the lotus grove by a circuitous movement, and scarcely the rustle of a leaf proclaimed his passing. At the edge of the trees he halted suddenly, crouched like a suspicious panther among the deep shrubs. Ahead of him, among the dense leaves, showed a pallid oval, dim in the uncertain light. It might have been one of the great white blossoms which shone thickly among the branches. But Conan knew that it was a man's face. And it was turned toward him. He shrank quickly deeper into the shadows. Had Zargheba seen him? The man was looking directly toward him. Seconds passed. That dim face had not moved. Conan could make out the dark tuft below that was the short black beard.

And suddenly Conan was aware of something unnatural. Zargheba, he knew, was not a tall man. Standing erect, his head would scarcely top the Cimmerian's shoulder; yet that face was on a level with Conan's own. Was the man standing on something? Conan bent and peered toward the ground below the spot where the face showed, but his vision was blocked by undergrowth and the thick boles of the trees. But he saw something else, and he stiffened. Through a slot in the underbrush he glimpsed the stem of the tree under which, apparently, Zargheba was standing. The face was directly in line with that tree. He should have seen below that face, not the tree-trunk, but Zargheba's body—but there was no body there.

Suddenly tenser than a tiger who stalks his prey, Conan glided deeper into the thicket, and a moment later drew aside a leafy branch and glared at the face that had not moved. Nor would it ever move again, of its own volition. He looked on Zargheba's severed head, suspended from the branch of the tree by its own long black hair.

3. The Return of the Oracle

CONAN WHEELED SUPPLELY, sweeping the shadows with a fiercely questing stare. There was no sign of the murdered man's body; only yonder, the tall lush grass was trampled and broken down and the sward was dabbled darkly and wetly. Conan stood scarcely breathing as he strained his ears into the silence. The trees and bushes with their great pallid blossoms stood dark, still and sinister, etched against the deepening dusk.

Primitive fears whispered at the back of Conan's mind. Was this the work of the priests of Keshan? If so, where were they? Was it Zargheba, after all, who had struck the gong? Again there rose the memory of Bît-Yakin and his mysterious servants. Bît-Yakin was dead, shriveled to a hulk of wrinkled leather and bound in his hollowed crypt to greet the rising sun for ever. But the servants of Bît-Yakin were unaccounted for. *There was no proof they had ever left the valley.*

Conan thought of the girl, Muriela, alone and unguarded in that great shadowy palace. He wheeled and ran back down the shadowed avenue, and he ran as a suspicious panther runs, poised even in full stride to whirl right or left and strike death blows.

The palace loomed through the trees, and he saw something else—the glow of fire reflecting redly from the polished marble. He melted into the bushes that lined the broken street, glided through the dense growth and reached the edge of the open space before the portico. Voices reached him; torches bobbed and their flare shone on glossy ebon shoulders. The priests of Keshan had come.

253

They had not advanced up the wide, overgrown avenue as Zargheba had expected them to do. Obviously there was more than one secret way into the valley of Alkmeenon.

They were filing up the broad marble steps, holding their torches high. He saw Gorulga at the head of the parade, a profile chiseled out of copper, etched in the torch glare. The rest were acolytes, giant black men from whose skins the torches struck highlights. At the end of the procession there stalked a huge negro with an unusually wicked cast of countenance, at the sight of whom Conan scowled. That was Gwarunga, whom Muriela had named as the man who had revealed the secret of the pool-entrance to Zargheba. Conan wondered how deeply the man was in the intrigues of the Stygian.

He hurried toward the portico, circling the open space to keep in the fringing shadows. They left no one to guard the entrance. The torches streamed steadily down the long dark hall. Before they reached the double-valved door at the other end, Conan had mounted the outer steps and was in the hall behind them. Slinking swiftly along the column-lined wall, he reached the great door as they crossed the huge throne-room, their torches driving back the shadows. They did not look back. In single file, their ostrich plumes nodding, their leopardskin tunics contrasting curiously with the marble and arabesqued metal of the ancient palace, they moved across the wide room and halted momentarily at the golden door to the left of the throne-dais.

Gorulga's voice boomed eerily and hollowly in the great empty space, framed in sonorous phrases unintelligible to the lurking listener; then the high priest thrust open the golden door and entered, bowing repeatedly from his waist, and behind him the torches sank and rose, showering flakes of flame, as the worshippers imitated their master. The gold door closed behind them, shutting out sound and sight, and Conan darted across the throne-chamber and into the alcove behind the throne. He made less sound than a wind blowing across the chamber.

Tiny beams of light streamed through the apertures in the wall, as he pried open the secret panel. Gliding into the niche, he peered through. Muriela sat upright on the dais, her arms folded, her head leaning back against the wall, within a few inches of his eyes. The delicate perfume of her foamy hair was in his nostrils. He could not see her face, of course, but her attitude was as if she gazed tranquilly into some far gulf of space, over and beyond the shaven heads of the black giants who knelt before her. Conan grinned with appreciation. "The little slut's an actress," he told himself. He knew she was shriveling with terror, but she showed no sign. In the uncertain flare of the torches she looked exactly like the goddess he had seen lying on that same dais, if one could imagine that goddess imbued with vibrant life.

Gorulga was booming forth some kind of a chant in an accent unfamiliar to Conan, and which was probably some invocation in the ancient tongue of Alkmeenon, handed down from generation to genera-tion of high priests. It seemed interminable. Conan grew restless. The longer the thing lasted, the more terrific would be the strain on Muriela. If she snapped—he hitched his sword and dagger forward. He could not see the little trollop tortured and slain by black men.

But the chant—deep, low-pitched and indescribably ominous—came to a conclusion at last, and a shouted

255

acclaim from the acolytes marked its period. Lifting his head and raising his arms toward the silent form on the dais, Gorulga cried in the deep, rich resonance that was the natural attribute of the Keshani priest: "Oh, great goddess, dweller with the great one of darkness, let thy heart be melted, thy lips opened for the ears of thy slave whose head is in the dust beneath thy feet! Speak, great goddess of the holy valley! Thou knowest the paths before us; the darkness that vexes us is as the light of the midday sun to thee. Shed the radiance of thy wisdom on the paths of thy servants! Tell us, oh mouthpiece of the gods: what is their will concerning Thutmekri the Stygian?"

The high-piled burnished mass of hair that caught the torchlight in dull bronze gleams quivered slightly. A gusty sigh rose from the blacks, half in awe, half in fear. Muriela's voice came plainly to Conan's ears in the breathless silence, and it seemed cold, detached, impersonal, though he winced at the Corinthian accent.

"It is the will of the gods that the Stygian and his Shemitish dogs be driven from Keshan!" She was repeating his exact words. "They are thieves and traitors who plot to rob the gods. Let the Teeth of Gwahlur be placed in the care of the general Conan. Let him lead the armies of Keshan. He is beloved of the gods!"

There was a quiver in her voice as she ended, and Conan began to sweat, believing she was on the point of an hysterical collapse. But the blacks did not notice, any more than they identified the Corinthian accent, of which they knew nothing. They smote their palms softly together and a murmur of wonder and awe rose from them. Gorulga's eyes glittered fanatically in the torchlight.

256

"Yelaya has spoken!" he cried in an exalted voice. "It is the will of the gods! Long ago, in the days of our ancestors, they were made taboo and hidden at the command of the gods, who wrenched them from the awful jaws of Gwahlur the king of darkness, in the birth of the world. At the command of the gods the Teeth of Gwahlur were hidden; at their command they shall be brought forth again. Oh star-born goddess, give us your leave to go to the secret hiding-place of the Teeth to secure them for him whom the gods love!"

"You have my leave to go!" answered the false goddess, with an imperious gesture of dismissal that set Conan grinning again, and the priests backed out, ostrich plumes and torches rising and falling with the rhythm of their genuflexions.

The gold door closed and with a moan, the goddess fell back limply on the dais. "Conan!" she whimpered faintly. "Conan!"

"Shhh!" he hissed through the apertures, and turning, glided from the niche and closed the panel. A glimpse past the jamb of the carven door showed him the torches receding across the great throne-room, but he was at the same time aware of a radiance that did not emanate from the torches. He was startled, but the solution presented itself instantly. An early moon had risen and its light slanted through the pierced dome which by some curious workmanship intensified the light. The shining dome of Alkmeenon was no fable, then. Perhaps its interior was of the curious whitely flaming crystal found only in the hills of the black countries. The light flooded the throne-room and seeped into the chambers immediately adjoining.

But as Conan made toward the door that led into the throne-room, he was brought around suddenly by a noise that seemed to emanate from the passage that led off from the alcove. He crouched at the mouth, staring into it, remembering the clangor of the gong that had echoed from it to lure him into a snare. The light from the dome filtered only a little way into that narrow corridor, and showed him only empty space. Yet he could have sworn that he had heard the furtive pad of a foot somewhere down it.

When he hesitated, he was electrified by a woman's strangled cry from behind him. Bounding through the door behind the throne, he saw an unexpected spectacle, in the crystal light.

The torches of the priests had vanished from the great hall outside—but one priest was still in the palace: Gwarunga. His wicked features were convulsed with fury, and he grasped the terrified Muriela by the throat, choking her efforts to scream and plead, shaking her brutally.

"Traitress!" Between his thick red lips his voice hissed like a cobra. "What game are you playing? Did not Zargheba tell you what to say? Aye, Thutmekri told me! Are you betraying your master, or is he betraying his friends through you? Slut! I'll twist off your false head—but first I'll—"

A widening of his captive's lovely eyes as she stared over his shoulder warned the huge black. He released her and wheeled, just as Conan's sword lashed down. The impact of the stroke knocked him headlong backward to the marble floor, where he lay twitching, blood oozing from a ragged gash in his scalp.

Conan started toward him to finish the job—for he knew that the black's sudden movement had caused the blade to strike flat—but Muriela threw her arms convulsively about him.

"I've done as you ordered!" she gasped hysterically. "Take me away! Oh, please take me away!"

"We can't go yet," he grunted. "I want to follow the priests and see where they get the jewels. There may be more loot hidden there. But you can go with me. Where's that gem you wore in your hair?"

"It must have fallen out on the dais," she stammered, feeling for it. "I was so frightened—when the priests left I ran out to find you, and this big brute had stayed behind, and he grabbed me—"

"Well, go get it while I dispose of this carcass," he commanded. "Go on! That gem is worth a fortune itself."

She hesitated, as if loath to return to that cryptic chamber; then, as he grasped Gwarunga's girdle and dragged him into the alcove, she turned and entered the oracle room.

Conan dumped the senseless black on the floor, and lifted his sword. The Cimmerian had lived too long in the wild places of the world to have any illusions about mercy. The only safe enemy was a headless enemy. But before he could strike, a startling scream checked the lifted blade. It came from the oracle chamber.

"Conan! Conan! *She's come back!*" The shriek ended in a gurgle and a scraping shuffle.

With an oath Conan dashed out of the alcove, across the throne dais and into the oracle chamber, almost before the sound had ceased. There he halted, glaring bewilderedly. To all appearances Muriela lay placidly on the dais, eyes closed as if in slumber.

"What in thunder are you doing?" he demanded acidly. "Is this any time to be playing jokes—"

His voice trailed away. His gaze ran along the ivory thigh molded in the close-fitting silk skirt. That skirt should gape from girdle to hem. He knew, because it had been his own hand that tore it, as he ruthlessly stripped the garment from the dancer's writhing body.

259

But the skirt showed no rent. A single stride brought him to the dais and he laid his hand on the ivory body— snatched it away as if it had encountered hot iron instead of the cold immobility of death.

"Crom!" he muttered, his eyes suddenly slits of balefire. "It's not Muriela! It's Yelaya!"

He understood now that frantic scream that had burst from Muriela's lips when she entered the chamber. The goddess had returned. The body had been stripped by Zargheba to furnish the accouterments for the pretender. Yet now it was clad in silk and jewels as Conan had first seen it. A peculiar prickling made itself manifest among the short hairs at the base of Conan's scalp.

"Muriela!" he shouted suddenly. "*Muriela!* Where the devil are you?"

The walls threw back his voice mockingly. There was no entrance that he could see except the golden door, and none could have entered or departed through that without his knowledge. This much was indisputable: Yelaya had been replaced on the dais within the few minutes that had elapsed since Muriela had first left the chamber to be seized by Gwarunga; his ears were still tingling with the echoes of Muriela's scream, yet the Corinthian girl had vanished as if into thin air. There was but one explanation, if he rejected the darker speculation that suggested the supernatural—somewhere in the chamber there was a secret door. And even as the thought crossed his mind, he saw it.

In what had seemed a curtain of solid marble, a thin perpendicular crack showed and in the crack hung a wisp of silk. In an instant he was bending over it. That shred was from Muriela's torn skirt. The implication was unmistakable. It had been caught in the closing

260

door and torn off as she was borne through the opening by whatever grim beings were her captors. The bit of clothing had prevented the door from fitting perfectly into its frame.

Thrusting his dagger-point into the crack, Conan exerted leverage with a corded forearm. The blade bent, but it was of unbreakable Akbitanan steel. The marble door opened. Conan's sword was lifted as he peered into the aperture beyond, but he saw no shape of menace. Light filtering into the oracle chamber revealed a short flight of steps cut out of marble. Pulling the door back to its fullest extent, he drove his dagger into a crack in the floor, propping it open. Then he went down the steps without hesitation. He saw nothing, heard nothing. A dozen steps down, the stair ended in a narrow corridor which ran straight away into gloom.

He halted suddenly, posed like a statue at the foot of the stair, staring at the paintings which frescoed the walls, half visible in the dim light which filtered down from above. The art was unmistakably Pelishtim; he had seen frescoes of identical characteristics on the walls of Asgalun. But the scenes depicted had no connection with anything Pelishtim, except for one human figure, frequently recurrent: a lean, white-bearded old man whose racial characteristics were unmistakable. They seemed to represent various sections of the palace above. Several scenes showed a chamber he recognized as the oracle chamber with the figure of Yelaya stretched upon the ivory dais and huge black men kneeling before it. And there behind the wall, in the niche, lurked the ancient Pelishtim. And there were other figures, too—figures that moved through the deserted palace, did the bidding of the Pelishtim, and dragged unnamable things out of the subterranean river. In the few seconds Conan stood frozen, hitherto unintelligible phrases in the parchment manuscript blazed in his brain with chilling clarity. The loose bits of the pattern clicked into place. The mystery of Bît-Yakin was a mystery no longer, nor the riddle of Bît-Yakin's servants.

Conan turned and peered into the darkness, an icy finger crawling along his spine. Then he went along the corridor, cat-footed, and without hesitation, moving deeper and deeper into the darkness as he drew farther away from the stair. The air hung heavy with the odor he had scented in the court of the gong.

Now in utter blackness he heard a sound ahead of him—the shuffle of bare feet, or the swish of loose garments against stone, he could not tell which. But an instant later his outstretched hand encountered a barrier which he identified as a massive door of carven metal. He pushed against it fruitlessly, and his sword-point sought vainly for a crack. It fitted into the sill and jambs as if molded there. He exerted all his strength, his feet straining against the floor, the veins knotting his temples. It was useless; a charge of elephants would scarcely have shaken that titanic portal.

As he leaned there he caught a sound on the other side that his ears instantly identified—it was the creak of rusty iron, like a lever scraping in its slot. Instinctively action followed recognition so spontaneously that sound, impulse and action were practically simultaneous. And as his prodigious bound carried him backward, there was the rush of a great bulk from above, and a thunderous crash filled the tunnel with deafening vibrations. Bits of flying splinters struck him—a huge block of stone, he knew from the sound, dropped on the spot he had just quitted. An instant's slower thought or action and it would have crushed him like an ant.

Conan fell back. Somewhere on the other side of that metal door Muriela was a captive, if she still lived. But he could not pass that door, and if he remained in the tunnel another block might fall, and he might not be so lucky. It would do the girl no good for him to be crushed into a purple pulp. He could not continue his search in that direction. He must get above ground and look for some other avenue of approach.

He turned and hurried toward the stair, sighing as he emerged into comparative radiance. And as he set foot on the first step, the light was blotted out, and above him the marble door rushed shut with a resounding reverberation.

Something like panic seized the Cimmerian then, trapped in that black tunnel, and he wheeled on the stair, lifting his sword and glaring murderously into the darkness behind him, expecting a rush of ghoulish assailants. But there was no sound or movement down the tunnel. Did the men beyond the door—if they *were* men—believe that he had been disposed of by the fall of the stone from the roof, which had undoubtedly been released by some sort of machinery?

Then why had the door been shut above him? Abandoning speculation, Conan groped his way up the steps, his skin crawling in anticipation of a knife in his back at every stride, yearning to drown his semi-panic in a barbarous burst of blood-letting.

He thrust against the door at the top, and cursed soulfully to find that it did not give to his efforts. Then as he lifted his sword with his right hand to hew at the marble, his groping left encountered a metal bolt that evidently slipped into place at the closing of the door.

In an instant he had drawn this bolt, and then the door gave to his shove. He bounded into the chamber like a slit-eyed, snarling incarnation of fury, ferociously desirous to come to grips with whatever enemy was hounding him.

The dagger was gone from the floor. The chamber was empty, and so was the dais. Yelaya had again vanished.

"By Crom!" muttered the Cimmerian. "Is she alive, after all?"

He strode out into the throne-room baffled, and then, struck by a sudden thought, stepped behind the throne and peered into the alcove. There was blood on the smooth marble where he had cast down the senseless body of Gwarunga—that was all. The black man had vanished as completely as Yelaya.

4. The Teeth of Gwahlur

BAFFLED WRATH CONFUSED the brain of Conan the Cimmerian. He knew no more how to go about searching for Muriela than he had known how to go about searching for the Teeth of Gwahlur. Only one thought occurred to him—to follow the priests. Perhaps at the hiding-place of the treasure some clue would be revealed to him. It was a slim chance, but better than wandering about aimlessly.

As he hurried through the great shadowy hall that led to the portico he half expected the lurking shades to come to life behind him with rending fangs and talons. But only the beat of his own rapid heart accompanied him into the moonlight that dappled the shimmering marble.

At the foot of the wide steps he cast about in the bright moonlight for some sign to show him the direction he must go. And he found it—petals scattered on the sward told where an arm or garment had brushed against a blossom-laden branch. Grass had been pressed down under heavy feet. Conan, who had tracked wolves in his native hills, found no insurmountable difficulty in following the trail of the Keshani priests.

It led away from the palace, through masses of exotic-scented shrubbery where great pale blossoms spread their shimmering petals, through verdant, tangled bushes that showered blooms at the touch, until he came at last to a great mass of rock that jutted like a titan's castle out from the cliffs at a point closest to the palace, which, however, was almost hidden from view by vine-interlaced trees. Evidently that babbling

265

priest in Keshia had been mistaken when he said the Teeth were hidden in the palace. This trail had led him away from the place where Muriela had disappeared, but a belief was growing in Conan that each part of the valley was connected with that palace by subterranean passages.

Crouching in the deep velvet-black shadows of the bushes, he scrutinized the great jut of rock which stood out in bold relief in the moonlight. It was covered with strange, grotesque carvings, depicting men and animals, and half-bestial creatures that might have been gods or devils. The style of art differed so strikingly from that of the rest of the valley, that Conan wondered if it did not represent a different era and race, and was itself a relic of an age lost and forgotten at whatever immeasurably distant date the people of Alkmeenon had found and entered the haunted valley.

A great door stood open in the sheer curtain of the cliff, and a gigantic dragon head was carved about it so that the open door was like the dragon's gaping mouth. The door itself was of carven bronze and looked to weigh several tons. There was no lock that he could see, but a series of bolts showing along the edge of the massive portal, as it stood open, told him that there was some system of locking and unlocking—a system doubtless known only to the priests of Keshan.

The trail showed that Gorulga and his henchmen had gone through that door. But Conan hesitated. To wait until they emerged would probably mean to see the door locked in his face, and he might not be able to solve the mystery of its unlocking. On the other hand, if he followed them in, they might emerge and lock him in the cavern.

Throwing caution to the winds, he glided through the great portal. Somewhere in the cavern were the priests, the Teeth of Gwahlur, and perhaps a clue to the fate of Muriela. Personal risks had never yet deterred him from any purpose.

Moonlight illumined, for a few yards, the wide tunnel in which he found himself. Somewhere ahead of him he saw a faint glow and heard the echo of a weird chanting. The priests were not so far ahead of him as he had thought. The tunnel debouched into a wide room before the moonlight played out, an empty cavern of no great dimensions, but with a lofty, vaulted roof, glowing with a phosphorescent encrustation, which, as Conan knew, was a common phenomenon in that part of the world. It made a ghostly half-light, in which he was able to see a bestial image squatting on a shrine, and the black mouths of six or seven tunnels leading off from the chamber. Down the widest of these—the one directly behind the squat image which looked toward the outer opening—he caught the gleam of torches, wavering whereas the phosphorescent glow was fixed, and heard the chanting increased in volume.

Down it he went recklessly, and was presently peering into a larger cavern than the one he had just left. There was no phosphorus here, but the light of the torches fell on a larger altar and a more obscene and repulsive god squatting toad-like upon it. Before this repugnant deity Gorulga and his ten acolytes knelt and beat their heads upon the ground, while chanting monotonously. Conan realized why their progress had been so slow. Evidently approaching the secret crypt of the Teeth was a complicated and elaborate ritual.

He was fidgeting in nervous impatience before the chanting and bowing were over, but presently they rose and passed into the tunnel which opened behind the idol. Their torches bobbed away into the nighted vault, and he followed swiftly. Not much danger of being

267

discovered. He glided along the shadows like a creature of the night, and the black priests were completely engrossed in their ceremonial mummery. Apparently they had not even noticed the absence of Gwarunga.

Emerging into a cavern of huge proportions, about whose upward curving walls gallery-like ledges marched in tiers, they began their worship anew before an altar which was larger, and a god which was more disgusting, than any encountered thus far.

Conan crouched in the black mouth of the tunnel, staring at the walls reflecting the lurid glow of the torches. He saw a carven stone stair winding up from tier to tier of the galleries; the roof was lost in darkness.

He started violently and the chanting broke off as the kneeling blacks flung up their heads. An inhuman voice boomed out high above them. They froze on their knees, their faces turned upward and a ghastly blue hue in the sudden glare of a weird light that burst blindingly up near the lofty roof, and then burned with a throbbing glow. That glare lighted a gallery and a cry went up from the high priest, echoed shudderingly by his acolytes. In the flash there had been briefly disclosed to them a slim white figure standing upright in a sheen of silk and a glint of jewel-crusted gold. Then the blaze smoldered to a throbbing, pulsing luminosity in which nothing was distinct, and that slim shape was but a shimmering blur of ivory.

"Yelaya!" screamed Gorulga, his brown features ashen. "Why have you followed us? What is your pleasure?"

That weird unhuman voice rolled down from the roof, re-echoing under that arching vault that magnified and altered it beyond recognition.

"Wo to the unbelievers! Wo to the false children of Keshia! Doom to them which deny their deity!"

268

A cry of horror went up from the priests. Gorulga looked like a shocked vulture in the glare of the torches.

"I do not understand!" he stammered. "We are faithful. In the chamber of the oracle you told us—"

"Do not heed what you heard in the chamber of the oracle!" rolled that terrible voice, multiplied until it was as though a myriad voices thundered and muttered the same warning. "Beware of false prophets and false gods! A demon in my guise spoke to you in the palace, giving false prophecy. Now harken and obey, for only I am the true goddess, and I give you one chance to save yourselves from doom!

"Take the Teeth of Gwahlur from the crypt where they were placed so long ago. Alkmeenon is no longer holy, because it has been desecrated by blasphemers. Give the Teeth of Gwahlur into the hands of Thutmekri, the Stygian, to place in the sanctuary of Dagon and Derketo. Only this can save Keshan from the doom the demons of the night have plotted. Take the Teeth of Gwahlur and go; return instantly to Keshia; there give the jewels to Thutmekri, and seize the foreign devil Conan and flay him alive in the great square."

There was no hesitation in obeying. Chattering with fear the priests scrambled up and ran for the door that opened behind the bestial god. Gorulga led the flight. They jammed briefly in the doorway, yelping as wildly waving torches touched squirming black bodies; they plunged through, and the patter of their speeding feet dwindled down the tunnel.

Conan did not follow. He was consumed with a furious desire to learn the truth of this fantastic affair. Was that indeed Yelaya, as the cold sweat on the backs of his hands told him, or was it that little hussy

269

Muriela, turned traitress after all? If it was—

Before the last torch had vanished down the black tunnel he was bounding vengefully up the stone stair. The blue glow was dying down, but he could still make out that the ivory figure stood motionless on the gallery. His blood ran cold as he approached it, but he did not hesitate. He came on with his sword lifted, and towered like a threat of death over the inscrutable shape.

"Yelaya!" he snarled. "Dead as she's been for a thousand years! *Ha!*"

From the dark mouth of a tunnel behind him a dark form lunged. But the sudden, deadly rush of unshod feet had reached the Cimmerian's quick ears. He whirled like a cat and dodged the blow aimed murderously at his back. As the gleaming steel in the dark hand hissed past him, he struck back with the fury of a roused python, and the long straight blade impaled his assailant and stood out a foot and a half between his shoulders.

"So!" Conan tore his sword free as the victim sagged to the floor, gasping and gurgling. The man writhed briefly and stiffened. In the dying light Conan saw a black body and ebon countenance, hideous in the blue glare. He had killed Gwarunga.

Conan turned from the corpse to the goddess. Thongs about her knees and breast held her upright against a stone pillar, and her thick hair, fastened to the column, held her head up. At a few yards' distance these bonds were not visible in the uncertain light.

"He must have come to after I descended into the tunnel," muttered Conan. "He must have suspected I was down there. So he pulled out the dagger"—Conan stooped and wrenched the identical weapon from the stiffening fingers, glanced at it and replaced it in his

270

own girdle—"and shut the door. Then he took Yelaya to befool his brother idiots. That was he shouting a while ago. You couldn't recognize his voice, under this echoing roof. And that bursting blue flame—I thought it looked familiar. It's a trick of the Stygian priests. Thutmekri must have given some of it to Gwarunga."

The man could easily have reached this cavern ahead of his companions. Evidently familiar with the plan of the caverns by hearsay or by maps handed down in the priestcraft, he had entered the cave after the others, carrying the goddess, followed a circuitous route through the tunnels and chambers, and ensconced himself and his burden on the balcony while Gorulga and the other acolytes were engaged in their endless rituals.

The blue glare had faded, but now Conan was aware of another glow, emanating from the mouth of one of the corridors that opened on the ledge. Somewhere down that corridor there was another field of phosphorus, for he recognized the faint steady radiance. The corridor led in the direction the priests had taken, and he decided to follow it, rather than descend into the darkness of the great cavern below. Doubtless it connected with another gallery in some other chamber, which might be the destination of the priests. He hurried down it, the illumination growing stronger as he advanced, until he could make out the floor and the walls of the tunnel. Ahead of him and below he could hear the priests chanting again.

Abruptly a doorway in the left-hand wall was limned in the phosphorous glow, and to his ears came the sound of soft, hysterical sobbing. He wheeled, and glared through the door.

He was looking again into a chamber hewn out of solid rock, not a natural cavern like the others. The domed roof shone with the phosphorous light, and the walls were almost covered with arabesques of beaten gold.

Near the farther wall on a granite throne, staring for ever toward the arched doorway, sat the monstrous and obscene Pteor, the god of the Pelishtim, wrought in brass, with his exaggerated attributes reflecting the grossness of his cult. And in his lap sprawled a limp white figure.

"Well, I'll be damned!" muttered Conan. He glanced suspiciously about the chamber, seeing no other entrance or evidence of occupation, and then advanced noiselessly and looked down at the girl whose slim shoulders shook with sobs of abject misery, her face sunk in her arms. From thick bands of gold on the idol's arms slim gold chains ran to smaller bands on her wrists. He laid a hand on her naked shoulder and she started convulsively, shrieked, and twisted her tear-stained face toward him.

"Conan!" She made a spasmodic effort to go into the usual clinch, but the chains hindered her. He cut through the soft gold as close to her wrists as he could, grunting: "You'll have to wear these bracelets until I can find a chisel or a file. Let go of me, damn it! You actresses are too damned emotional. What happened to you, anyway?"

"When I went back into the oracle chamber," she whimpered, "I saw the goddess lying on the dais as I'd first seen her. I called out to you and started to run to the door—then something grabbed me from behind. It clapped a hand over my mouth and carried me through a panel in the wall, and down some steps and along a dark hall. I didn't see what it was that had hold of me until we passed through a big metal door and came into a tunnel whose roof was alight, like this chamber.

272

"Oh, I nearly fainted when I saw! They are not humans! They are gray, hairy devils that walk like men and speak a gibberish no human could understand. They stood there and seemed to be waiting, and once I thought I heard somebody trying the door. Then one of the *things* pulled a metal lever in the wall, and something crashed on the other side of the door.

"Then they carried me on and on through winding tunnels and up stone stairways into this chamber, where they chained me on the knees of this abominable idol, and then they went away. Oh, Conan, what are they?"

"Servants of Bît-Yakin," he grunted. "I found a manuscript that told me a number of things, and then stumbled upon some frescoes that told me the rest. Bît-Yakin was a Pelishtim who wandered into the valley with his servants after the people of Alkmeenon had deserted it. He found the body of Princess Yelaya, and discovered that the priests returned from time to time to make offerings to her, for even then she was worshipped as a goddess.

"He made an oracle of her, and he was the voice of the oracle, speaking from a niche he cut in the wall behind the ivory dais. The priests never suspected, never saw him or his servants, for they always hid themselves when the men came. Bît-Yakin lived and died here without ever being discovered by the priests. Crom knows how long he dwelt here, but it must have been for centuries. The wise men of the Pelishtim know how to increase the span of their lives for hundreds of years. I've seen some of them myself. Why he lived here alone, and why he played the part of oracle no ordinary human can guess, but I believe the oracle part was to keep the city inviolate and sacred, so he could remain undisturbed. He ate the food the priests brought as an

offering to Yelaya, and his servants ate other things—
I've always known there was a subterranean river
flowing away from the lake where the people of the
Puntish highlands throw their dead. That river runs
under this palace. They have ladders hung over the
water where they can hang and fish for the corpses that
come floating through. Bît-Yakin recorded everything
on parchment and painted walls.

"But he died at last, and his servants mummified him
according to instructions he gave them before his
death, and stuck him in a cave in the cliffs. The rest is
easy to guess. His servants, who were even more nearly
immortal than he, kept on dwelling here, but the next
time a high priest came to consult the oracle, not
having a master to restrain them, they tore him to
pieces. So since then—until Gorulga—nobody came to
talk to the oracle.

"It's obvious they've been renewing the garments
and ornaments of the goddess, as they'd seen Bît-Yakin
do. Doubtless there's a sealed chamber somewhere
where the silks are kept from decay. They clothed the
goddess and brought her back to the oracle room after
Zargheba had stolen her. And, oh, by the way, they
took off Zargheba's head and hung it up in a thicket."

She shivered, yet at the same time breathed a sigh of
relief.

"He'll never whip me again."

"Not this side of hell," agreed Conan. "But come on.
Gwarunga ruined my chances with his stolen goddess.
I'm going to follow the priests and take my chance of
stealing the loot from them after they get it. And you
stay close to me. I can't spend all my time looking for
you."

"But the servants of Bît-Yakin!" she whispered
fearfully.

"We'll have to take our chance," he grunted. "I don't know what's in their minds, but so far they haven't shown any disposition to come out and fight in the open. Come on."

Taking her wrist he led her out of the chamber and down the corridor. As they advanced they heard the chanting of the priests, and mingling with the sound the low sullen rushing of waters. The light grew stronger above them as they emerged on a high-pitched gallery of a great cavern and looked down on a scene weird and fantastic.

Above them gleamed the phosphorescent roof; a hundred feet below them stretched the smooth floor of the cavern. On the far side this floor was cut by a deep, narrow stream brimming its rocky channel. Rushing out of impenetrable gloom, it swirled across the cavern and was lost again in darkness. The visible surface reflected the radiance above; the dark seething waters glinted as if flecked with living jewels, frosty blue, lurid red, shimmering green, an ever-changing iridescence.

Conan and his companion stood upon one of the gallery-like ledges that banded the curve of the lofty wall, and from this ledge a natural bridge of stone soared in a breath-taking arch over the vast gulf of the cavern to join a much smaller ledge on the opposite side, across the river. Ten feet below it another, broader arch spanned the cave. At either end a carven stair joined the extremities of these flying arches.

Conan's gaze, following the curve of the arch that swept away from the ledge on which they stood, caught a glint of light that was not the lurid phosphorus of the cavern. On that small ledge opposite them there was an opening in the cave wall through which stars were glinting.

But his full attention was drawn to the scene beneath

them. The priests had reached their destination. There in a sweeping angle of the cavern wall stood a stone altar, but there was no idol upon it. Whether there was one behind it, Conan could not ascertain, because some trick of the light, or the sweep of the wall, left the space behind the altar in total darkness.

The priests had stuck their torches into holes in the stone floor, forming a semi-circle of fire in front of the altar at a distance of several yards. Then the priests themselves formed a semicircle inside the crescent of torches, and Gorulga, after lifting his arms aloft in invocation, bent to the altar and laid hands on it. It lifted and tilted backward on its hinder edge, like the lid of a chest, revealing a small crypt.

Extending a long arm into the recess, Gorulga brought up a small brass chest. Lowering the altar back into place, he set the chest on it, and threw back the lid. To the eager watchers on the high gallery it seemed as if the action had released a blaze of living fire which throbbed and quivered about the opened chest. Conan's heart leaped and his hand caught at his hilt. The Teeth of Gwahlur at last! The treasure that would make its possessor the richest man in the world! His breath came fast between his clenched teeth.

Then he was suddenly aware that a new element had entered into the light of the torches and of the phosphorescent roof, rendering both void. Darkness stole around the altar, except for that glowing spot of evil radiance cast by the Teeth of Gwahlur, and that grew and grew. The blacks froze into basaltic statues, their shadows streaming grotesquely and gigantically out behind them.

The altar was laved in the glow now, and the astounded features of Gorulga stood out in sharp relief. Then the mysterious space behind the altar swam into the widening illumination. And slowly with the crawling light, figures became visible, like shapes growing out of the night and silence.

At first they seemed like gray stone statues, those motionless shapes, hairy, man-like, yet hideously human; but their eyes were alive, cold sparks of gray icy fire. And as the weird glow lit their bestial countenances, Gorulga screamed and fell backward, throwing up his long arms in a gesture of frenzied horror.

But a longer arm shot across the altar and a misshapen hand locked on his throat. Screaming and fighting, the high priest was dragged back across the altar; a hammer-like fist smashed down, and Gorulga's cries were stilled. Limp and broken he sagged across the altar, his brains oozing from his crushed skull. And then the servants of Bît-Yakin surged like a bursting flood from hell on the black priests who stood like horror-blasted images.

Then there was slaughter, grim and appalling.

Conan saw black bodies tossed like chaff in the inhuman hands of the slayers, against whose horrible strength and agility the daggers and swords of the priests were ineffective. He saw men lifted bodily and their heads cracked open against the stone altar. He saw a flaming torch, grasped in a monstrous hand, thrust inexorably down the gullet of an agonized wretch who writhed in vain against the arms that pinioned him. He saw a man torn in two pieces, as one might tear a chicken, and the bloody fragments hurled clear across the cavern. The massacre was as short and devastating as the rush of a hurricane. In a burst of red abysmal ferocity it was over, except for one wretch who fled screaming back the way the priests had come, pursued by a swarm of blood-dabbled shapes of horror which reached out their red-smeared hands for him.

Fugitive and pursuers vanished down the black tunnel, and the screams of the human came back dwindling and confused by the distance.

Muriela was on her knees clutching Conan's legs; her face pressed against his knee and her eyes tightly shut. She was a quaking, quivering mold of abject terror. But Conan was galvanized. A quick glance across at the aperture where the stars shone, a glance down at the chest that still blazed open on the blood-smeared altar, and he saw and seized the desperate gamble.

"I'm going after that chest!" he grated. "Stay here!"

"Oh Mitra, no!" In an agony of fright she fell to the floor and caught at his sandals. "Don't! Don't! Don't leave me!"

"Lie still and keep your mouth shut!" he snapped, disengaging himself from her frantic clasp.

He disregarded the tortuous stair. He dropped from ledge to ledge with reckless haste. There was no sign of the monsters as his feet hit the floor. A few of the torches still flared in their sockets, the phosphorescent glow throbbed and quivered, and the river flowed with an almost articulate muttering, scintillant with undreamed radiances. The glow that had heralded the appearance of the servants had vanished with them. Only the light of the jewels in the brass chest shimmered and quivered.

He snatched the chest, noting its contents in one lustful glance—strange, curiously shapen stones that burned with an icy, nonterrestrial fire. He slammed the lid, thrust the chest under his arm, and ran back up the steps. He had no desire to encounter the hellish servants of Bît-Yakin. His glimpse of them in action had dispelled any illusion concerning their fighting ability. Why they had waited so long before striking at the invaders he was unable to say. What human could guess the motives or thoughts of these monstrosities? That they were possessed of craft and intelligence equal to humanity had been demonstrated. And there on the cavern floor lay crimson proof of their bestial ferocity.

The Corinthian girl still cowered on the gallery where he had left her. He caught her wrist and yanked her to her feet, grunting: "I guess it's time to go!"

Too bemused with terror to be fully aware of what was going on, the girl suffered herself to be led across the dizzy span. It was not until they were poised over the rushing water that she looked down, voiced a startled yelp and would have fallen but for Conan's massive arm about her. Growling an objurgation in her ear, he snatched her up under his free arm and swept her, in a flutter of limply waving arms and legs, across the arch and into the aperture that opened at the other end. Without bothering to set her on her feet, he hurried through the short tunnel into which this aperture opened. An instant later they emerged upon a narrow ledge on the outer side of the cliffs that circled the valley. Less than a hundred feet below them the jungle waved in the starlight.

Looking down, Conan vented a gusty sigh of relief. He believed that he could negotiate the descent, even though burdened with the jewels and the girl; although he doubted if even he, unburdened, could have ascended at that spot. He set the chest, still smeared with Gorulga's blood and clotted with his brains, on the ledge, and was about to remove his girdle in order to tie the box to his back, when he was galvanized by a sound behind him, a sound sinister and unmistakable.

"Stay here!" he snapped at the bewildered Corinthian girl. "Don't move!" And drawing his sword, he glided into the tunnel, glaring back into the cavern.

Half-way across the upper span he saw a gray deformed shape. One of the servants of Bît-Yakin was on his trail. There was no doubt that the brute had seen them and was following them. Conan did not hesitate. It might be easier to defend the mouth of the tunnel—but this fight must be finished quickly, before the other servants could return.

He ran out on the span, straight toward the oncoming monster. It was no ape, neither was it a man. It was some shambling horror spawned in the mysterious, nameless jungles of the south, where strange life teemed in the reeking rot without the dominance of man, and drums thundered in temples that had never known the tread of a human foot. How the ancient Pelishtim had gained lordship over them—and with it external exile from humanity—was a foul riddle about which Conan did not care to speculate, even if he had had opportunity.

Man and monster; they met at the highest arch of the span, where, a hundred feet below, rushed the furious black water. As the monstrous shape with its leprous gray body and the features of a carven, unhuman idol loomed over him, Conan struck as a wounded tiger strikes, with every ounce of thew and fury behind the blow. That stroke would have sheared a human body asunder; but the bones of the servant of Bît-Yakin were like tempered steel. Yet even tempered steel could not wholly have withstood that furious stroke. Ribs and shoulder-bone parted and blood spouted from the great gash.

There was no time for a second stroke. Before the Cimmerian could lift his blade again or spring clear, the sweep of a giant arm knocked him from the span as a fly is flicked from a wall. As he piunged downward the rush of the river was like a knell in his ears, but his twisting body fell half-way across the lower arch. He wavered there precariously for one blood-chilling instant, then his clutching fingers hooked over the farther edge, and he scrambled to safety, his sword still in his other hand.

As he sprang up, he saw the monster, spurting blood hideously, rush toward the cliff-end of the bridge, obviously intending to descend the stair that connected the arches and renew the feud. At the very ledge the brute paused in mid-flight—and Conan saw it too— Muriela, with the jewel chest under her arm, stood staring wildly in the mouth of the tunnel.

With a triumphant bellow the monster scooped her up under one arm, snatched the jewel chest with the other hand as she dropped it, and turning, lumbered back across the bridge. Conan cursed with passion and ran for the other side also. He doubted if he could climb the stair to the higher arch in time to catch the brute before it could plunge into the labyrinths of tunnels on the other side.

But the monster was slowing, like clockwork running down. Blood gushed from that terrible gash in his breast, and he lurched drunkenly from side to side. Suddenly he stumbled, reeled and toppled sidewise— pitched headlong from the arch and hurtled downward. Girl and jewel chest fell from his nerveless hands and Muriela's scream rang terribly above the snarl of the water below.

Conan was almost under the spot from which the creature had fallen. The monster struck the lower arch glancingly and shot off, but the writhing figure of the girl struck and clung, and the chest hit the edge of the span near her. One falling object struck on one side of

281

Conan and one on the other. Either was within arm's length; for the fraction of a split second the chest teetered on the edge of the bridge, and Muriela clung by one arm, her face turned desperately toward Conan, her eyes dilated with the fear of death and her lips parted in a haunting cry of despair.

Conan did not hesitate, nor did he even glance toward the chest that held the wealth of an epoch. With a quickness that would have shamed the spring of a hungry jaguar, he swooped, grasped the girl's arm just as her fingers slipped from the smooth stone, and snatched her up on the span with one explosive heave. The chest toppled on over and struck the water ninety feet below, where the body of the servant of Bît-Yakin had already vanished. A splash, a jetting flash of foam marked where the Teeth of Gwahlur disappeared for ever from the sight of man.

Conan scarcely wasted a downward glance. He darted across the span and ran up the cliff stair like a cat, carrying the limp girl as if she had been an infant. A hideous ululation caused him to glance over his shoulder as he reached the higher arch, to see the other servants streaming back into the cavern below, blood dripping from their bared fangs. They raced up the stair that wound up from tier to tier, roaring vengefully; but he slung the girl unceremoniously over his shoulder, dashed through the tunnel and went down the cliffs like an ape himself, dropping and springing from hold to hold with breakneck reckless-ness. When the fierce countenances looked over the ledge of the aperture, it was to see the Cimmerian and the girl disappearing into the forest that surrounded the cliffs.

"Well," said Conan, setting the girl on her feet within the sheltering screen of branches, "we can take our time now. I don't think those brutes will follow us outside the valley. Anyway, I've got a horse tied at a water-hole close by, if the lions haven't eaten him. Crom's devils! What are you crying about *now?*"

She covered her tear-stained face with her hands, and her slim shoulders shook with sobs.

"I lost the jewels for you," she wailed miserably. "It was my fault. If I'd obeyed you and stayed out on the ledge, that brute would never have seen me. You should have caught the gems and let me drown!"

"Yes, I suppose I should," he agreed. "But forget it. Never worry about what's past. And stop crying, will you? That's better. Come on."

"You mean you're going to keep me? Take me with you?" she asked hopefully.

"What else do you suppose I'd do with you?" He ran an approving glance over her figure and grinned at the torn skirt which revealed a generous expanse of tempting ivory-tinted curves. "I can use an actress like you. There's no use going back to Keshia. There's nothing in Keshan now that I want. We'll go to Punt. The people of Punt worship an ivory woman, and they wash gold out of the rivers in wicker baskets. I'll tell them that Keshan is intriguing with Thutmekri to enslave them—which is true—and that the gods have sent me to protect them—for a houseful of gold. If I can manage to smuggle you into their temple to exchange places with their ivory goddess, we'll skin them out of their jaw teeth before we get through with them!"

Afterword

"THE DEVIL IN IRON" appeared in the August 1934 issue of *Weird Tales*—the tenth Conan story to be published there. It was the lead story of the issue, and copped the cover—a rather minor Margaret Brundage effort—and a fine Hugh Rankin interior illustration. Conan and Howard were at the height of their popularity by now with the *Weird Tales* readers, and the story was voted best of the issue, closely pressed by C.L. Moore's "Dust of Gods" (that same issue included Mary Elizabeth Counselman's famed short story, "The Three Marked Pennies"). *Weird Tales* featured a lengthy letters column, designated "The Eyrie"—as well as a monthly readers' poll for the favorite story of the issue. "The Eyrie" was a forum of reader comment and opinion, likes and dislikes, and made for interesting reading—the more so since frequently letters appeared from readers who were then, or soon would be, well-known writers in the field themselves.

As a rule, Conan earned the highest praise of those who wrote letters to "The Eyrie"—but not always. "The Devil in Iron" drew the following attack in the November letters column: "Conan is rapidly becoming a stereotyped hero. . . . . I am awfully tired of poor old Conan the Cluck, who for the past fifteen issues has every month slain a new wizard, tackled a new monster, come to a violent and sudden end that was averted (incredibly enough!) in just the nick of time, and won a new girl-friend, each of whose penchant for nudism won her a place of honor, either on the cover or on the interior illustration. Such has been Conan's history, and from the realms of the Kushites to the lands of Aquilonia, from the shores of the Shemites to the palaces of Dyme-Novell-Bolonia, I cry: 'Enough of this brute and his iron-thewed sword-thrusts—may he be sent to Valhalla to cut out paper dolls.'" This tirade was signed by a young Robert Bloch, who called for reader support of his viewpoint. Editor Farnsworth Wright invited Conan fans to sharpen their axes, since Bloch's own first story would be appearing in the January issue. Although subsequent letters called for his flayed hide, Bloch seems to have survived the battle; readers liked his first story, and he went on to become one of *Weird Tales'* most popular writers, eventually unleashing *Psycho*.

"The Devil in Iron" is withal a good example of Howard in his stride, writing a formula Conan story— with the Hyborian Age milieu this time transplanted to a framework drawn from cossacks and the Persian Empire. The story provides some familiar Conan devices: a lost city (labyrinthine and partially en-closed), a reanimated sorcerer/demon, a fight with a serpent, and, of course, a beauty in peril. For all that, "The Devil in Iron" holds up as a good Conan yarn. The dead city, Dagon (another favorite name of Howard's), is effectively eerie, the resurrection of the city and its inhuman ruler is well handled, and Khosatral Khel is one of Conan's most frightening opponents.

The following issue of *Weird Tales* presented Conan

in the first of his four serial-length appearances—this one a three-part serial that ran in the September, October, and November 1934 issues. "The People of the Black Circle" again claimed the position of lead story, and again drew a Margaret Brundage cover— this time one of her best efforts—and three splendid Hugh Rankin interiors. Rankin, whose interior drawings were a hazy, stylized use of charcoals that seldom reproduced well, was the first decent artist to work for *Weird Tales*. Howard very much liked Rankin's work and collected the original drawings from his stories with an eye toward arranging them into a display panel.

Even more so than "The Devil in Iron," "The People of the Black Circle" impresses the reader as a Hyborian Age version of what Howard's friend and fellow fictioneer, E. Hoffmann Price, has termed "Northwestern frontier stuff." That's northwestern Asia, not North America. This exotic locale was a great favorite of writers for the adventure pulps, most notably with Talbot Mundy, Ganpat, Mark Channing, and other top authors of the day, whose writing heavily influenced Howard. Howard's adaptation of this subgenre to his Conan series comes as no surprise: Talbot Mundy was one of his favorite authors, and *Adventure* was the first magazine Howard regularly bought and read. Moreover, from the very start Howard had been trying to break into the higher-paying and more prestigious adventure pulps. Thus— from India to Vendhya, the Himalayas to the Himelians, the Khyber Pass to the Zhaibar Pass, from El Borak to Conan—is only a short jump. If at times the Hyborian Age evokes a sense of alternate-universe *déjà vu*, it should be remembered that Howard's premise with his mythical history was that many of the races, languages, and legends of our own past are actually survivals and memories of the lost Hyborian Age.

Fritz Leiber, himself a noted writer of epic fantasy, has praised "The People of the Black Circle" as "the best of the Conan stories and perhaps the pinnacle of Howard's writing. Tightly plotted, pithily poetic, gorgeously ornamented, manned by grand heroes and villains and also by characters torn between good and evil, and above all brimming with glamor and glory, it can be compared without over-praise to the plays of Christopher Marlowe and John Webster."

The story is certainly one of Howard's best. It is of short-novel length, but is no padded-out short story. "The People of the Black Circle" is intricately plotted, headlong paced, and offers the reader a fascinating array of intriguing secondary characters and sinister horrors. The character of Khemsa is one of Howard's most fascinating villains—one wonders what the outcome might have been of his and Conan's struggle on the ledge, had not the four black seers intervened. Khemsa harkens back to the doomed hero-villain of the gothic novel—tempted by a beautiful woman into defying his master, there is a tragic heroism to his death. Khemsa: dragging his crushed body from beneath the avalanche, holding life in his shattered husk long enough to turn his former enemy Conan into his instrument of vengeance—for very clearly in this tale Conan is overmatched by the sorcerous powers he is pitted against, and only Khemsa's posthumous intercession makes his ultimate victory possible. Khemsa's casual command to the mesmerized prison guard: "I have no more use for you. Kill yourself!" is a suave cruelty that pales beside the darker menace of the Master of Yimsha's: "I think I will take your heart, Kerim Shah!"

Unlike the stereotyped characters that plague too much of epic fantasy, black or white cardboard dolls, Howard has here presented Kerim Shah and Khemsa as villains of a distinctly grey cast. Further, the elements of sorcery are integral to the plot; this is not a simple action yarn with a monster tossed in for the *Weird Tales* market.

A final note: Yasmina refers to the dread *Book of Skelos* in Chapter Two; the *Weird Tales* printing (p. 279) renders this as *Skalos*. Howard does make recurrent reference to this black book (or books), as the *Book of Skelos*. In Chapter Seven, the dying Khemsa cries out to *Skelos* (*Weird Tales* p. 498), indicating that the previous spelling of *Skalos* is a typographical error, and not a variant spelling for this story. As such I have corrected Yasmina's reference to the *Book of Skelos*.

Conan was back again in the next issue of *Weird Tales*, once more as the lead story. The December 1934 Weird Tales offered "A Witch Shall Be Born" with another fine Margaret Brundage cover and Hugh Rankin interior illustration.

Brundage, for those who do not remember her work, monopolized the covers of *Weird Tales* in the mid-1930's. She worked in pastels, and her forte was nude or seminude girls, usually in distress, frequently with overtones of bondage and flagellation. The readers waged a long and outraged controversy in "The Eyrie," attacking her covers as trash or defending them as art. The modern fantasy fan may not be aware that fans of that period had, or at least professed, a strong puritanical streak. Wright, with an eye toward the far

289

more lurid weird-menace pulps (*Terror Tales, Horror Stories*, et al.) that were handily outselling the more staid *Weird Tales*, made only token efforts to cloak Brundage's portrayal of "generous expanses of alabaster flesh." It may have been that Brundage's efforts to depict something other than exotic nudity were none too striking. But there was Wright's observation that an issue with a Brundage nude made money, an issue with a less erotic cover lost money, on the stands—which says something about the readers' true souls. Presumably "A Witch Shall Be Born" was a money-maker, with a scantily clad Salome standing over a semiclad Taramis, smiling as she wields a cat-of-nine-tails. It was a kinky combination that had earned a cover for Howard a year before with "The Slithering Shadow." Howard knew his markets, too.

While preparing my notes for this edition, I took an afternoon break for a few beers with Manly Wade Wellman, a regular reader and author for *Weird Tales* throughout that pulp's existence. I asked Wellman what he thought of Howard's Conan stories, which he had followed at the time in *Weird Tales*. Wellman replied that he had enjoyed them, particularly those that rose above forgettable stock situations: "With one mighty lunge Conan leapt out of the bottomless pit, and with one tremendous stroke he clove the demon in half." But after forty years, Wellman allowed, there was *one* scene that *really* stuck in his memory: Conan had been crucified, and . . .

And *that* scene is one of the most famous in the Conan series—in Howard's entire writing, and in the entire fantasy genre. While many who have read "A Witch Shall Be Born" will have forgotten the title and forgotten the plot, no one forgets Conan's crucifixion.

Conan in agony, helpless, close to death—crushing the vulture's neck in his teeth—enduring the ordeal of the felling of the cross—impatiently ripping the nails out of his feet with his mangled hands—holding saddle on a frenzied mount... The episode dominates the story and the series. Better than any other scene, it underscores Conan's barbaric vitality and indomitable soul.

The scene overshadows the remainder of the story—and "A Witch Shall Be Born" *is* an excellent story. It is Conan at his best—defeated and condemned to a hideous death, fighting back through his barbaric strength and iron-willed determination, ultimately triumphant in the final battle, dooming his enemies to a just vengeance. Salome is wondrously decadent—a frightening recurrent reincarnation of the destroying female. Constantius is a fine henchman, equally corrupt, albeit on a less inhuman scale.

Further, while the story is of novelette length, Howard has managed to foreshorten a series of events which, conventionally presented, would have dragged "A Witch Shall Be Born" out to much greater length, and in doing so, diluted the major thrust of the tale: Conan's vengeance. Howard achieves this through a number of innovative devices, whose effect is to present the passage of time and the rush of battles through an intermediate observer. Conan's initial rebellion and defeat are recounted by Valerius, lying wounded from the battle. The seven-month reign of terror by Salome and Constantius is presented succinctly and convincingly through a letter from Astreas to his fellow savant Alcemides. Conan's final battle with Constantius, obscured by dust and distance from the apathetic watchers, is described in a chilling fashion through a crystal ball by the dying priest, Zang.

It is an impressive tour de force, one that proves Howard had progressed far in the mastery of narrative technique. Here Howard has disdained what E. Hoffmann Price calls "mass-mayhem and mechanical meat-cutting" of headlong battles and graphic scenes of oppression, opting for a more oblique presentation. While many epic fantasy tales are padded with such standard fare, "A Witch Shall Be Born" stands out because Howard eschewed the bludgeon and struck well with the point. It is a measure of Howard's confidence in his mastery of the narrative that he no longer felt it necessary to waste pages describing various anatomy that Conan can hack apart. After the crucifixion scene, we *know* Conan is tough.

Howard did not appear at all in the next issue of *Weird Tales*, and the issue following contained one of his modern-day horror tales. But Conan was back in the March 1935 *Weird Tales* with "Jewels of Gwahlur." The story is a minor Conan adventure, and Wright seemed aware of the fact. The Brundage cover was claimed by another yarn this time, and "Jewels of Gwahlur" was assigned a secondary position in the magazine. Indeed, "Jewels of Gwahlur" lacks the precision of the later Conan stories, and one wonders whether it might not have been an earlier sale that Wright was holding in stock for such a drought (nor did Howard appear in the April *Weird Tales*).

After a series of episodes that depicted Conan as an adventurer in the East, "Jewels of Gwahlur" again casts Conan in the role of thievish rogue. Howard's own title for the story was "Teeth of Gwahlur," after the cursed treasure that provides the basis for the plot. It is a formula Conan story, with all hands scheming for a fabulous and forbidden treasure, and again Howard offers a lost city with labyrinthine passageways crammed with lurking peril, and again we encounter a scantily clad lovely who requires repeated rescuing.

If overfamiliar, "Jewels of Gwahlur" moves at a rapid pace, with lots of intrigue and double-crossing. The servants of Bît-Yakin are a nicely menacing pack of fiends, and their massacre of the priests is as grisly a scene as one could wish. "Jewels of Gwahlur" is entertaining, but lacks the fire of Howard at his best.

It was not that Howard had exhausted Conan's potential. Some of his best writing was yet to come. But for Howard, the road ahead would shortly turn into the darkness.

Karl Edward Wagner
Chapel Hill, North Carolina
February 1977